TO PAINT

A

WHITE

HORSE

To Paint A White Horse
By
Lindsey J. Carden

KELDAS
CHRONICLES

Published by Keldas Chronicles 2020
**

This book is a work of fiction. Names,
characters, businesses, places and events,
either are a product of the author's imagination or
are used fictitiously. Any resemblance to actual
persons, living or dead, events, or locales is
entirely coincidental.

ISBN 9780956944269

.

Chapter 1

'Dig it deep, or the fox'll be at it!' That's what Simon Naylor had been told; the problem was he'd never dug a grave before.

He drove purposely through the darkness looking for a suitable place as his eyes peered into the night; the headlights of the 4 x 4 shining the way ahead onto tangled bracken and naturalised shrubs. The track ahead steepened sharply as Simon fumbled for the control button to slide the car window down, but he still couldn't see any better through the mist; it wouldn't make much difference anyway as he didn't really know where he was heading. Simon wished he'd taken more notice of this land while his father was alive, but he was gone and it was too late to ask questions.

Simon had inherited his father's country house, two vehicles and an elderly stepmother, Lucy. Granted, he'd always envied the BMW and always wanted the 4 x 4, especially as it was a green one, and so had his wife for that matter, but living in Leeds somehow didn't justify it. Simon cared enough about the environment to avoid them. But as he drove slowly up the steep hill, under the cliff-face in the dark of night, it would be his saving-grace.

What had possessed his father at the age of seventy-three to marry again and buy this property in Chardwell, Simon didn't know. Yet this house was stunning. Well-built Yorkshire stone walls, framed with tall sash windows that sat resplendent, draped in ivy; green all year round. A grey slated roof which shone as silver in the light of this beautiful valley. Simon punished himself and thought if he'd been a better son, he would have taken the trouble to ask; but he'd been too busy building his own empire. And now his stepmother, Lucy, was installed in the small and refurbished Garden Cottage with the promise of a comfortable life, and Simon, Melanie and their three daughters were living in the beautiful, ivy clad Georgian Grange, a house they knew nothing about.

Simon braked hard and the 4 x 4 awkwardly came to a halt; it wouldn't safely climb any higher. He took a torch from the seat beside him, and slid out, his boots slipping on the damp bracken on the hillside. With one hand holding his torch and the other touching the side of his vehicle for security, he groped about in the darkness. Finding the tailgate, he lifted it and as he stooped beneath, he banged his head; a usual occurrence for him, a man of six-foot three. He rubbed his forehead and knew this job would take courage. He pulled out his spade and used it as a support. Then staggering through the bracken, with his boots catching in the undergrowth, he peered at the ground, then tapped the spade onto the earth to find a piece that wasn't rock.

And, as he stared at the ground, he saw nothing, but if his eyes could penetrate through the rock and debris below he would see the beautiful shape of a massive white horse carved into the hillside. But Simon was oblivious as we all may be if we walked on secret burial remains, and there was no sacredness in this, no gentle stepping off the soil to honour the dead, he was totally unaware of the horse that had been lying as silently as it had, covered over for the last seventy years, longing to be exposed, moving slightly on shifting rock and gravel, yet still alive, almost crying out to be found.

With a weighty breath, he lifted a heavy lump wrapped in Hessian from the back of the 4 x 4 and rested it on the ground. Then he took the spade and began to dig, but with each attack, he jarred his wrists and shoulders.

Things hadn't gone so well since they'd moved to The Grange. For a start, Lucy had been difficult. Not that she was being the wicked stepmother and demanding money; Lucy wasn't like that, yet Simon guessed why his father had bought this house and land, it was to pacify Lucy, and what Lucy didn't get – she let you know about. Simon had already rectified a problem with the cottage, which she'd claimed was too cold, despite it being a warm spring. He'd repaired her garage roof that was leaking, and totally revamped the cottage interior, but now the garden was overgrown. And then his old, black dog had died. Midge was nearly sixteen, and had been rejuvenated with life at The Grange, chasing rabbits he'd never seen in Leeds. Simon thought the old dog had just worn himself out with all the excitement, much like his father, but the vet had done a post-mortem and they were stunned when he'd said that Midge had eaten poison. There was no poison anywhere as far as they knew, so it was assumed Midge had picked something up off the hillside, which a gamekeeper had illegally planted on the land to kill crows or rabbits.

As Simon dug, pangs of apprehension hit him as he moaned with each thrust of the spade; he had to get this job done tonight and bury the dog. He couldn't let Melanie see how upset he was over Midge. With grimy hands he wiped a tear away that was rolling down his cheek, and decided to bring the girls up tomorrow and let them see the grave, maybe bring some flowers. He planned to get a puppy when it was safe, as soon as they could find the poison and discover why it had been put there.

Simon brushed a few strands of his dark and greying hair away from his eyes and promised himself to get a haircut before he went back to work. If his boss could see him, he would laugh, as he'd said he would rue this life in the country. Simon had taken a month off work; he'd hung up his best Dunhill suits and they hadn't been out of the wardrobe since his father's funeral. He'd have to get back to work soon and hoped the daily commute back to Leeds wouldn't be too much of a trek. He'd done it repeatedly after his father's death; arranging the funeral, comforting Lucy; he knew the quickest route, by day and night.

Melanie had hugged him when he'd suggested they all move out to The Grange, and immediately she had started talking ponies. But his eldest girl, Jess, used every bit of teenage cunning to change Simon's mind, but she had to comply and she didn't like it. And Simon now had money issues. They could rent out their house in Leeds and that would offset his mortgage. The Grange was paid for, but could he sustain it? Yes, it was in good repair for his father had done everything inside the house to pacify Lucy, but outside was a mess and Simon was no gardener.

Suddenly, from out of the darkness a weak voice said: 'I wouldn't dig there, Mr Naylor!' Simon rested his hand on his rapidly beating heart and peered out into the night then, in the headlights of his car, saw an elderly man struggling up the steep slope. 'For pities sake, Sam....! What are you doing up here?' Simon wiped his eyes, and hoped the old man hadn't noticed he'd been crying.

'I'm sorry, Mr Naylor... But it wouldn't be wise to bury Midge there. I saw you're vehicle from my cottage window... Thought I ought to check up, like. Wouldn't want intruders.'

'Well, it's me, Sam...Okay!'

'I still think you should bury the dog somewhere else.'

'It's my land, Sam... I'll bury Midge where I like.' It felt good to say that.

'Well, it's just that there's a white horse buried under there, that's all. And, as I said, it wouldn't be wise.'

'Okay, Okay, where...? Where do you suggest?' Simon leant on his spade to balance himself upright. 'I'll have to bury him tonight – I've gotta get this job done.'

Sam wandered across to the fence and pointed through the darkness to what was probably a meadow. 'Look, bring him over here and I'll help you. The earth'll be softer.'

'No, Sam, please.' Simon muttered. 'I'd rather do this alone.'

And the old man nodded. 'As you wish.'

Balancing on the slope and using his spade as support, Simon waited as Sam Parkinson disappeared back into the darkness away from the headlights of the Landrover. He used the time to unzip his jacket, but a spring breeze blew up, and flapped his coat relentlessly around his body as he started to dig again. Simon thought one more spade depth would do it and continued as the breeze gusted even more, whistling in his ears, a deafening noise.

Throwing down the spade, he gently lifted Midge's body and scrambled into the pit. The sanctity he'd hoped for had fled with the wind, as the job had to be hurried. He jumped out and started to throw spadefuls of soil over the dog's stiffened remains, and then cringing as he cautiously stamped on each layer to firm the ground, sorry at his task. Simon then felt his coat catch on some brambles and he pulled at it awkwardly and cursed as the fabric ripped in his hand. Then he felt his coat pulling from his shoulders, as if someone was tugging at him. He lost his balance, fell backwards on the steep and rocky hill, and as he did so grabbed at the brambles and bushes with his bare hands.

Tumbling and rolling on the earth, Simon fell over, wincing with each scratch, the skin on his hands and face tearing on the brambles; in no control and falling clumsily and at pace. His mind reflecting as he fell, thinking how foolish it would be to die here and leave his wife and young children for the sake of an old dog, but wondering, who had pulled him over in the first place and why. He hoped beyond reason that he would soon stop and land softly, longing to be vertical again. But Simon landed heavily in what he assumed was a clump of nettles. He rolled onto his stomach, knelt up on his hands and knees and moaned as he shouted: 'Who's there? What the deuce are you doing? You could have killed me then! Why did you push me?' Simon glanced around, but he appeared to be alone. He lifted his head but his neck ached with pain as he looked up into the darkness and shouted: 'Sam, are you there...? Help...!' Simon fell back onto his side and held his ribs, moaning and muttering. He flexed his hands, arms and legs, and realised nothing was broken. Sitting up again he once more struggled to stand and shouted again.

'Sam.... Sam.' But Simon guessed it was useless; Sam would have been out of ear-shot minutes ago. Then, as he sat and wondered if he could walk, he heard the sound of deep and heavy breathing, like someone gasping for breath. The noise was peculiar; unworldly. A jagged light flashed up the bank, then footsteps now at a regular pace, crunching and sliding on the gravel path, but the footsteps were going uphill not down, as was the light. Simon remained painfully silent fearing the intruder more than the pain in his back. He fell back onto his side and waited.

Melanie stood at the bedroom window watching for the car headlights. It was the best perspective she had of the bank from the back of the house. Part of her wanted to laugh at Simon's midnight dash to bury his old dog, and part of her wanted to weep at the circumstances.

Jess had taken the dog out on the bank, letting him ferret about in the bracken, and now blamed herself for the dog being poisoned. She hadn't been watching him, but was using the excuse to exercise Midge so she could sit on the bench at the top of the bank, to send endless text messages; the only place she could get a decent signal. And now Jess was up in her bedroom, the ceiling thumping with the beat from her CD player, unaware that her father was burying the dog. The twins were fast asleep and that was a blessing. Melanie didn't know how they would react in the morning when they saw Midge's empty basket. She would have to break the news. Simon had done enough.

As Melanie caught her reflection in a large gold framed mirror hanging over a white marble fireplace, she tousled her hair and thought it needed more highlights. She'd done nothing since they moved but pack and unpack, and with the help from a woman in the village, dusting and cleaning, moving furniture, dry-cleaning, washing and re-hanging the curtains that draped the huge windows. Simon had been anxious to get the jobs done in a month so he could get back to work. Melanie knew the funds were low. Simon's father had left them some money, but with death duties and the like, there wouldn't be much left, except The Grange, the 4 x 4, the BMW and Lucy.

Melanie knew she had a good husband and he never kept her guessing and valued her opinion. He wanted to keep his happy marriage, happy. Jess, Ellie and Phoebe were enrolled in good local schools. The girls would have a much better life in the country and, if all went well for Simon, a directorship was in the offering. Yes, Melanie agreed to everything; it was a prospect for a better life. Their chance had come, sadly with a death, but it was there for the taking. They knew The Grange could have been sold for a packet.

The morning's pilgrimage to Midge's grave was done in misty drizzle. Ellie and Phoebe cried hysterically, like hyenas, one inciting the other. Jess had refused to come with them.

Dressed in PVC Macs and pink spotted wellingtons, the girls were now smothered in mud and chalk. Ellie laid down a bunch of pink tulips tied with a ribbon, and Phoebe brought daffodils. There were plenty of flowers in the wilderness of a garden, and Melanie was already bedraggled from clambering through the undergrowth to get them. Simon had promised a small plaque for Midge as soon as he could get to Skipton.

Simon's face bore the scratches this morning of last night's venture. He had minimised the extent of his fall to Melanie, and he certainly didn't tell her he thought he'd been pushed.

When both girls looked at Simon, he knew they wanted a prayer. He thought he would sound stupid – but he did it; what an irony to have to pray for an old dog when he'd never once prayed for his dead father. 'Thank you for the lovely life you shared with us. We will miss you.' Well, what more could be said; Simon didn't do prayers.

Lucy saw them all coming down the hill and was touched by the unity. She would catch Simon on the way in; surely he would be civil to her in front of the girls. Not that he was ever rude, but Lucy detected in his voice sometimes a dutiful yet begrudging manner. Lucy liked Simon, although she knew little about him. Simon had been a witness at their wedding and Lucy guessed what he was thinking then. He was unlike his father in every way; Harry Naylor was always a confident man and Simon seemed the opposite. Simon spoke in a nervous manner, stumbling over his words, sometimes, even a slight stammer, which made him appear uncertain about things. Lucy thought Simon sensitive and lacking authority, whereas Harry Naylor had a self-assured attitude, yet he was keen to please; Simon was always reticent, he had to make all this last. But for Harry, at seventy-three and with a carefree attitude to his cash, he found it much easier to spend; not much to lose, and taking the last few bites from his cherry.

'Have you thought anymore about the garden, Simon?' Lucy shouted from the open window that she was pretending to clean, where in fact she had just dashed to the cupboard for a duster.

'I'm sorry, Lucy....What?'

'The garden, Simon.'

'Yes, the garden.'

Melanie patted one of the girls on the back in a gesture to move them quickly indoors so she could remove herself from this conversation, but Simon was compelled to stop and knew he couldn't stall Lucy any longer.

'Lucy.... It's hard for me...' He wanted to tell her cash was short, but needed to keep his privacy. He wanted to say the garden was the last thing on his mind and to be satisfied with what you have: a pretty stone cottage and a better life now than before she met his father, for Simon knew Lucy had been living in a small flat above a fish and chip shop in Skipton. But instead, he said: 'I'll see what I can do.... But, remember, I'm a human resource manager. I'm not a gardener. I don't know a weed from a flower. I'll have to get someone in.'

Later that evening, Simon fell into his bed; Melanie was sitting propped up, reading her latest chic-lit. The bed bounced with Simon's weight and he sighed.

'Come on love ... chill out a bit. Shall I get you a drink?'

He didn't answer her question as if he hadn't heard, as the fears were growing in his head about his fall on the bank, and wondering if he'd made the right decision to move here in the first place. Then, in a low voice and speaking into empty space he said: 'I didn't expect this bother with Lucy.'

Melanie put the marker in her book and leant her head on his shoulder. 'It's not a bother, Simon. You're tired. You're probably still upset over Midge, and over your Dad.' Melanie was glad she remembered to mention him. Yes, they had grieved for his father, but the responsibility being the only child had wearied Simon and they had buried their grief with Harry Naylor, and far too quickly.

'Tomorrow we'll get some numbers together, maybe check the net. Yellow pages ... maybe ask Sam. He'll know someone who could do the garden.'

'What about the money?'

'I'll just get estimates. I haven't a clue how much it'll cost. At least it will give me time to think, and it might keep Lucy quiet if she sees someone around the place measuring up.'

Despite the comfort of the yellow glow from his bedside lamp, Simon switched it off and remained propped up on his pillow. This time of night was wonderful; pure darkness in Chardwell, a thing Simon had never known in Leeds. He comforted himself as he imagined the log fires and soft lighting in winter and anticipated the shade and coolness in summer: swifts screeching and chasing each other across the garden during the day and owls hooting at night. Simon always pulled the curtains back before he got into bed with no one to over-look them. He loved to watch the daybreak creep into his bedroom and on a clear night look out at the stars and the moon if it was a good one; sprigs of ivy tap-tapped against the window panes in a swift breeze. Melanie lay with her hand resting on his neck and was soon breathing heavily; Simon was glad she was asleep. He shut his eyes and thought of Midge chasing about the paddock, stalking rabbits and scratching in rat holes. He couldn't help but smile. Poor Midge. Yes, the bank was a good place for the grave. Then more worries came as he wondered whether he should keep the women away from the bank; had he just imagined he was pushed over, maybe so. But then the poison was real and Midge's death was the consequence. He thought again about the garden, the lawns to cut with his father's ride-on mower, which would be good therapy for him; he could cope with that. But the vegetable plot would have to go, unless Melanie had some sudden inclination to become a kitchen gardener and grow some organic stuff. Maybe even Jess would help, or maybe not. The girls would like growing flowers, but Simon knew he would be useless and not have a clue. He would ask Sam tomorrow.

Thank goodness for Sam, a reliable neighbour, balanced and level headed. Simon found some in the village to be affected. Chardwell people were far enough away from civilisation to be insular yet near enough for some to be, surprisingly, worldly. He even thought that attitudes changed depending which end of the sprawling village you lived. The geography of Chardwell meant terraces of solid stone cottages streamed through the valley, spotted intermittently with modern bungalows, even a small council estate. But The Grange was partway up the hill, under the bank; stately pillars protected a large oak door and lavender bushes and old roses prepared themselves for the summer as they surrounded this beautiful house. The straggly remnants of daffodils fell onto the gravel driveway. This was the last house in the village, and that could label Simon and his family either elevated or estranged from Chardwell society. So Sam was his closest ally. He'd already advised on the best plumbers and decorators for Lucy's cottage, surely he would know a good landscape gardener.

Simon opened his eyes, looked out into the darkness and suddenly recalled Sam's words: "There's a white horse buried under there."

Chapter 2

The phone rang seven times and the 1571 lady spoke up. Simon left a dis-jointed message to someone; he'd already left messages at three other garden contractors and was now running out of patience and time.

Jonathan Miller heard the phone ringing as he struggled with his key in the lock. He threw the plastic carrier bag down on the floor that held his running shoes and his Superman costume - too late.

Jonathan rubbed his moistened forehead with his hand, brushing back the short strands of fair hair that remained on his receding brow. He'd slept all night in the back of a taxi, driven by his mate, Barney. It was Monday morning and Jonathan should be at work, but the drive back from London had been dismal: there had been a four-hour delay on the M1.

'Katie... Katie... Are you home? Moses ... Moses...! Puss.... Puss.' It was funny that the cat hadn't come to meet him. He shouted upstairs. No reply. He returned to the porch and picked up several letters and, not looking at any, threw them on the kitchen worktop with a pile of other unopened letters. And then Jonathan saw something and he shuddered and muttered: 'Oh no.... What are you doing to me, Katie....? Not again.'

The letter propped up against the kettle, done in a manner that he couldn't possibly miss, was all too familiar. Three times now she'd gone. Jonathan groaned. He wanted to put it with the pile of other unopened letters that he knew were bills and final demands because, like them all, he knew exactly what this one would say. Thoughts ran through his head: *Jon... Gone to my mother's. Taken Moses.... Be back at the weekend.* That was the most hopeful thought. Then: *Jon.... Can't stand our way of life any longer. Gone to my mother's. Don't call.* That was the worst scenario. But, as he bravely opened the envelope, careful not to tear it, in case it was the last letter he ever got from her, he read:

Dear Jon.... I love you so much, you know that. But that was one marathon too many, you know that too. I've taken Moses. We've gone to my mother's. If you can sort out this mess of a life, I'll come back. But sometimes - Oh it's the only way I can get through to that lovely receding head of yours.

Love Katie.

Ps. Don't worry. I won't tell your mother.

Jonathan wanted to weep but he couldn't, he'd done it all before, besides, he was too tired to cry and the marathon had weakened him more than it should. The argument they'd had before he left had put him in poor spirits and he'd run 26 miles in anguish, and consequently there was a stranger handing him a medal at the finishing line and a manly hug from a good friend, Barney. The friend was welcome but Jonathan needed the tender embrace of his wife. Katie was right: it was one race too many. He was thirty-nine and his legs and back ached today like nothing on earth, his ankles and hands were swollen with fluid. But with the promise of £1,600, donated this time for: "Barney's Taxis" - trips for kids with anything and everything kids could get, and more.

Jonathan could have said no, he now wished he had. But how could he. He loved Katie and he also loved Barney's kids, he also feared his mother, his accomplice, the sweet lady in the blue Crimplene dress. She always said: "Oh, just do one more marathon, Jon.... Barney would be grateful, and just think of those children." Katie had said: "Don't do it, Jonathan….What about me.... Charity ... Home ... all that stuff. We can't afford for you to keep travelling here there and everywhere to races. Hiring helicopters and paying for parachute jumps." Jonathan should have listened to his wife but he thought she would understand; after all, she'd met him at the London Marathon. He was running dressed as Homer Simpson that day. She was a fairy princess in a pink, silk dress with fluffy straps. She'd hit the wall, so had Jonathan but he wouldn't admit it. Katie hadn't seen his face under his mask, but he made her laugh between his gasps for air. He helped her through it - the twenty-mile mark. Jonathan was fit. He'd said he'd earn £1,200 that day and he wasn't bragging; that would go to Cancer Research. She was running for a private fund, sending some family who had a boy with a heart condition to Disneyland, Florida.

Jonathan had told her he was a gardener, but Katie didn't know whether to believe him or not, she'd never seen a gardener that looked like Homer Simpson, and when he took off his costume after the race she was relieved the pot belly was false and Jonathan Miller was cute.

Jonathan pressed the 1571 number.

'This is Simon Naylor, from The Grange ... Chardwell. I'm looking for a gardener. Sam

Parkinson has recommended you.… If you've got time, could you come and give us a quote. I just need a tidy up - I think. Maybe a bit of stonework to repair and a new path. Brick blocks or York Stone perhaps, anyway, I'd appreciate it if you could call back. Number is ...'

Jonathan went upstairs kicking his Superman costume in contempt as he passed, stamping hard on each stair. He stood and saw his dishevelled bedroom and empty bed just as he had left it, and wondered how he could ever get along without Katie.

When the phone rang again, Jonathan was just getting out of the shower. He leapt across the bedroom; shampoo and soap suds dripped from his fair hair onto the carpet. Maybe it was Katie. 'Oh, hello Mum....'

'Jon.… How did you get on? What was your time?'

'Oh ... two- fifty-five. Quicker than last time. It was cooler.'

'I've told Barney you'll come to the school next week to present the cheque. I think we could have some kind of buffet - a few pies and pizzas for the kids. What do you think?'

Jonathan didn't like to say to his mother what he was thinking at that moment in time so he said: 'How are you today. Did the nurse come?'

'She did my legs again. The ulcer's not much better though.'

'Shame....'

'Are you coming later? I have a recipe for Katie. And I wondered if she would wash and set my hair.'

Jonathan paused. He slipped on a bathrobe from the bedroom door to make himself presentable to talk to his mother and knew he would have to make some excuse.

'No, Mum ... she can't come, she's had to work. Look, I'll call in later. Byee'

Jonathan didn't know how long he'd been sitting wet and cold on the stairs. Nothing mattered anymore. He should have felt hungry, famished in fact; he always ate like a horse after every run. He picked up his mobile phone, punched in several text messages to Katie but deleted them again. He didn't feel he had the courage to speak to her, he wanted to say sorry like he always did, he wanted to be upbeat and make promises about paying the bills, taking her on holiday, no more marathons, but he felt it was pointless. He wanted to say that wild horses wouldn't drag him away from this marriage. Then he heard Danny's car. He knew it was him: a turbo diesel something or other that was once someone's pride and joy and now had been tarted up beyond recognition. Cobalt blue.

Danny knocked and walked in.

Jonathan tightened the belt on his bathrobe and slowly edged downstairs.

'What time did you do?' Danny took off his beanie and walked straight into the kitchen. Jonathan knew he was looking for Katie, because if she were here she would make him a cooked breakfast.

Danny and Katie had a thing going – nothing wrong – it was just that she liked his youth and he envied her wisdom, and Danny hoped one day when he was older to have a wife with pretty brown hair like Katie, slim, and intelligent, a good cook.

'Two hours, fifty-five.... Quicker than last time.' Jonathan took an envelope from the kitchen drawer and threw it back across the room to the young man. 'Sorry it's late.'

'I've had no money all weekend!' Danny examined his pay packet.

'Look, I'm sorry, okay.... It won't happen again.'

Danny knew that wouldn't be the case because when Jonathan was away his wages were always late, unless Katie had been persuaded to call in with them. Danny glanced at the handwriting on the front and could see it was Katie's. He needn't check it, it would be right. Katie never got it wrong. The only mistakes would be Jonathan's. Then for the first time Danny noticed Jonathan's demeanour. 'Tired?'

'Words to that effect!' Jonathan just shrugged his shoulders and Danny knew it was time to go. He'd got half of what he wanted.

'Don't forget Mrs Johnston's grass today... and by the way, you look a nerd in that hat.' Jonathan had to say it as he watched Danny pull his latest woolly hat down almost over his eyes.

Katie was always telling Danny not to cover up his lovely dark brown hair, and he'd just grown it on the strength of her advice. She'd said it was too nice to shave off all the time; he trusted Katie's opinion. And now it cost him a packet to get it trimmed at that new boutique-salon in Skipton, but it was an easy style: just brush it in the wrong direction.

'Last week you said I looked a nerd without it.'

Jonathan managed a smile for the first time that day. 'I'll catch up with you later.'

*　　*　　*

Alice Miller was swatting a fly with her walking stick when she saw her son's car come up the road and crunch to a halt on her driveway. Her heart leapt. It always did when he came. She had been sitting in the window now for forty-five minutes and was getting agitated. She noticed Jonathan was alone and was sorry, because she wouldn't get her hair washed and set, yet glad, because she could indulge herself in her son while she had him. Alice quickly devised a plan in her head of how she could persuade him to take her to Skipton tomorrow.

Alice did like her daughter-in-law because Jonathan did – Katie was never seen as a threat – not in the eight years of their marriage. Alice thought her to be intelligent, quiet, polite, and good for Jonathan, and she knew she had the upper hand with Katie like she always had with her son; it was as well she lived alone. Alice had been a widow for thirty-seven years, since Jonathan was a baby. Jonathan never remembered his father and Alice had told him very little. All he knew was that his father was a postman and that he'd died suddenly. Jonathan assumed it was a motoring accident or a heart attack. When Jonathan, as a child, had tried to talk about his father, the subject matter was quickly changed and assumed to be unspeakable territory.

Alice had never re-married. She had felt too old when she married Jonathan's father in the first place, and was surprised when he proposed to her. And after his death, Alice didn't think she could cope with a courtship again, not with a young boy to bring up. So, Jonathan became her saviour.

She walked to the kitchen and held her body taut ready for his kiss. She would let him feel her disapproval for being late. Jonathan came in the back door, as he always did. The front door and hallway were to be kept spotless to impress visitors, as was most of this pebble-dashed, middle-class semi. The leaded windows were always pristine and shining. Jonathan had once broken an antique jug and bowl that was displayed precariously in the hallway as he'd barged in from school with his old satchel, and so it was always the back door since then. Jonathan was glad because he had a fear of his mother's house, he wondered where all this stuff came from; probably inherited from some old aunt or other, and everything appeared to be set out like a show house: ornaments and figurines displayed like trophies, silver polished and set on a fine mahogany dining table that was never used for dining, not even at Christmas or on special occasions; yet the best china was used often for afternoon tea with the ladies of the Chardwell Women's Institute, but Alice never invited any one for a meal, not even Jonathan's friends. As a child, if they did come they were to play in the garage or the garden and always eat on the yellow Formica table in the kitchen.

Jonathan wandered towards her, head down and didn't speak. Alice thought he looked thin, unwell even, but there was still a pleasing handsomeness to his face, just like his father. He so reminded her of him: funny, caring, giving, procrastinating, always cheerful. She was sorry Jonathan had no children. That was a pity. What was he playing at?

The kiss was given, quickly and coldly. 'About the presentation of the cheque,' Jonathan said as he backed away, still not looking at her, and he went outside to fill the coal bucket. The next job would be to chop sticks for the morning. He returned with the bucket. 'Can we just send it? Post it, you know.'

Alice was just hovering in the kitchen and purposely fell back into the dining chair. 'No, Jon. We can't just "*post it*".... You should be proud of what you've done ... Heavens ... I'm proud of you son. No.... We'll have a nice tea. Get some pizzas and chicken nuggets. The children would love to see you in your Superman costume. You could do that flying-in trick on the skate board, like last time.'

That was the limit. 'It won't do, Mother....' And he went back to the shed to chop the sticks.

Alice couldn't leave it. What was wrong with him? She clamoured from the chair again and followed. 'Jon ... Jonathan.'

As he chopped each stick he did it with venom, contempt, he knew she was behind him but he ignored her.

'Oh, Jon. Your father would have been so proud of you.' This was the usual line of persuasion - get to the heart. 'He loved children.' More sticks chopped. 'You know I can't do all that organising myself.... My legs have been bad all day....' And more sticks chopped.

He relented. 'We'll see....We'll see.' And Alice knew she'd won.

Then she asked where Katie was and Jonathan lied.

Katie was disappointed when Jonathan didn't call or text her, but not surprised. She knew he would be at his mother's by now and wouldn't want to use her phone; he would be embarrassed and wouldn't want to tell Alice and worry her about their problem marriage. Moses purred as he lay by her side on the bed and Katie wiped a tear away. She touched his black and white paws and he purred even more and rolled over on his back, his legs now curled in ecstasy up in the air. Katie wished she could be as relaxed. Moses was always settled at her mother's; well, she still had her own bedroom. Katie had stayed the two other times when she'd left Jonathan, and she stayed regularly if he was working away or running away.

Katie's mother hadn't interfered. She liked Jonathan. She thought she knew why her daughter had left. It would be the usual: Jonathan not thinking of Katie's feelings, not remembering her anniversary, not paying the council tax, running after his mother, or just being Jonathan.

Katie sent a text message. She guessed he would now be explaining to his mother some excuse as to why he was alone, being discreet, not wanting to upset her.

So she made it easier for him: Are you Okay...? What time did you do? Call me tonight. We need to talk – AGAIN.

CHAPTER 3

Jess was in her bedroom window watching Danny Wytherstone in the pickup truck when she discovered she was in love. She watched him use his mobile phone, texting some girl perhaps. He was really playing Rally 2 on his Nokia 5500. She thought the man he came with had a pleasant face and lovely fair hair; he was perhaps a bit younger than her father. Jess thought these two gardeners weren't like the designer crew that came yesterday, all dressed in green with tree emblems on their polo shirts and a smart van painted with the same symbol, full of job descriptions and phone numbers. This van was plain white - grubby white.

She could hear her father talking to the fair-haired man; he had a kindly voice. She wished her new-found lover would get out of the van so she could hear him speak. Jess thought some young men let themselves down when they spoke, with squeaky, half-broken voices, which had never altered since adolescence. But Jess wouldn't be disappointed in Danny's voice. And Danny's arrival suddenly made living happily at The Grange a possibility, if only she could see him again. She hoped her father would give them the job. She would see to that.

At the age of sixteen and studying A Levels, for Jess, the move away from Leeds had been dreadful. Why move to this flea-ridden house in the middle of nowhere? She'd thought of packing her bags and running away - why not - her father was always going on about how he'd left school at sixteen and started work in a printer's. Then he got his own flat in Leeds, because Jess's grandfather, Harry, was too busy buying and selling companies to bother with him. This wasn't quite true, it was only Simon's misguided perception of a childhood influenced by his mother who hated his father enough to divorce him, and expected her only son to do the same. So Simon told Jess he wanted better for her. But Jess hadn't listened. She'd left home once already. It was on a weekend, but the weather had turned nasty and the friend she'd stayed with had caught the flu, so Jess came home on the bus and had to explain herself to her mother; her father just winked. He knew what it was all about.

Slipping on a pink cropped T-shirt over her skinny body, Jess scrunched up her auburn hair into a knot. She didn't need make-up. Her beautiful eyebrows shaped her face. She was sorry her nose was a little pointed; yet her mother said it gave her character.

Jess decided to walk about the garden and hope the boy in the van noticed her. And he did.

Much like Jess, Lucy was noseying out the window of the Garden Cottage when she saw Jonathan Miller's van arrive and she hurriedly put on some shocking pink lipstick. Glancing in the mirror, and hoping she didn't look too ancient, she tousled her newly done hair, then looked across the lawn to Sam's cottage. She could see Sam at a distance already limping out of the cottage with his walking stick, at too great a pace for an elderly man who reckoned to be diabetic and crippled with arthritis. Lucy, even more hurriedly than an elderly lady should, took her jacket and pushed her small Chihuahua, Boris, to one side as she left the cottage, determined to get to Jonathan Miller before Sam did.

'I just want a good tidy up.' Simon said as they wandered in and out of each section of the garden.

Jonathan was excited. This one had potential. 'And is this the path you want replacing?' and he kicked some of the old flagstones with his boot.

'Yes, that's it. Also, could you rebuild that garden wall and re-do the patio by the Garden Cottage.'

Jonathan walked across to Lucy's cottage that once would have been the home of the farm manager or the gardener, or any other person that worked at The Grange during its glory days, when it was a working farm. Simon followed Jonathan, and Lucy followed Simon.

'These flags get slippery with moss. They're dangerous.' Lucy said.

'It's a dark corner, isn't it?' And Jonathan gazed at the sky. 'Won't get much sunlight. There's some lovely shrubs here though, we could cut some back and let a bit of daylight in.' Already the mild spring was bringing on the lush green sprouting tips of moss roses, orange blossom, and a purple wisteria which would eventually trail over the lintel of the cottage.

It wasn't long before Sam Parkinson arrived. He pushed his way forward to shake Jonathan's hand. 'This lad's a local celebrity you know.' Patting Jonathan on the back. 'What time did you do?'

'Yes, what time did you run, Jonathan?' Lucy wanted Simon to know she knew of Jonathan, too. 'How is your mother, dear?'

Uncomfortable with all the attention, Jonathan looked to the floor. 'Two fifty-five,' he muttered for the umpteenth time that week. 'And my mother's well, thank you, Mrs Naylor.'

Simon was bewildered.

'He's a runner.... You've done 'em all haven't you, Jon?' Sam persisted.

'Well, not quite.' Jonathan was anxious to turn the attention away from him and back to business and wishing Sam and Lucy would leave, he walked away to the back of the house hoping to distance himself from their interference. But as he walked along the track under the bank, he was still followed by Simon, Lucy and Sam. Jonathan glanced up at the bank. 'How far do you want me to go, Mr Naylor?' He was joking.

'Oh, stop here for heaven's sake. Nature will take care of the rest.' Simon didn't see the joke.

'I think nature's already taken care of this lot,' there was nothing but bracken, thistles and brambles scrambling over the wall. Jonathan nodded and walked back towards the house with his notebook. 'Right, I think I've got everything.' And he shook Simon's hand and left.

They all watched Jonathan drive away. Lucy left the men alone and Jess was still smiling at the young man in the front of the van. She was collecting the milk from a crate by the gateway; she didn't usually get the milk in.

Lucy had successfully achieved what she'd intended and had a smirk on her face. She would now dress in her best yellow trouser suit and go out for lunch, meet her friend in Skipton and tell her about the charming young man, Jonathan Miller, the marathon runner, the one who was always in the paper, that he was going to do her garden.

But Sam lingered and followed Simon as he wandered to the back of the house to look again at the garden wall. 'Did you find the poison, Mr Naylor?'

'No. No, I haven't had time. Jess has been scratching about up there. She felt a bit guilty. She needn't have. Call me Simon, by the way.'

'I wouldn't let her mess about up on the bank. It's not a safe place to be alone.'

'Tell me about it, Sam!'

'Oh, why's that?' And Sam held his gaze but Simon didn't reply so Sam continued. 'Any way, you'll never find any poison now, and even if you did, they'll plant some more.'

'They...? They...? Who...?'

And this time it was Sam's turn to ignore the question. 'You should let the lads clear this lot.' He turned and stared up at the huge banking and laughed.

'Oh yeh, do you think I'm made of money. Anyway, I don't want them to disturb your precious *"beast"* buried under the bank.'

'Ah, that's where you're wrong.' Sam poked his walking stick into the mass of bracken and weeds behind the wall. 'Did your father never tell you about the horse?'

'Dead horse stories weren't exactly our normal topics for conversations, Sam.'

'This is all gritstone, you see. Loose rock and shingle.' The older man reached over the wall and pulled at some turf to reveal a hidden layer of grey rocky stone covered in strands of wire netting. 'Yes, there's a white horse under all this rubbish. And it's over three hundred foot high - a lovely mare. She was covered over during the war - enemy planes and all. There's an airfield nearby; would have guided them straight to it, if you know what I'm saying. So they chucked netting and turf on her. You can still see the shape if you know what to look for. Did your father not tell you that either?' But Sam guessed the truth and it meant more embarrassment for Simon. 'It's like one of those puzzles, you know. Those made of dots in an obscure picture that everyone else can see but you, and then when you do see it, it never leaves you. On a clear moonlit night you'll see her.'

Jonathan started to mow the lawn at The Beeches Hotel, a mundane job but good money and regular work. Jobs like this were his bread and butter. He carefully negotiated every flowerbed and footpath. Danny was weeding a border under the trees, trying hard not to dig out the real plants. Jonathan was adding up in his mind how much to estimate for the contract at The Grange. It was good medicine for him, because over the last few days he'd done nothing but worry about his relationship with Katie. He'd wondered about her text message: "*we must talk,*" she'd said. Why? He thought they'd done all the talking, and what would it solve? What did she want from him? She was punishing him and it was hurting, but this not letting go; that wasn't playing fair. Jonathan didn't want to be free of her, but neither did he want tormenting. He knew he'd made dreadful mistakes and had apologised in the past a hundred times. But he just couldn't get it right. He doubted he ever would.

He'd eventually spoken to Katie over the phone but all they'd talked about were trivialities, his running the marathon, who he'd met, how much money he'd made for Barney's Kids, she had even asked after his mother's health, things that ironically were some of the reasons for her leaving. And so a garbled invitation to dinner was made; Jonathan had to do something; he couldn't give up and she'd agreed; it was a start. He would tell her about the job prospects at The Grange. Tell her about Simon Naylor who he knew little about. Maybe Katie would know more.

Jonathan recalled when Simon's father, Harry Naylor, moved in to The Grange, he'd hoped at the time to get the garden contract then, but he'd seen endless tradesmen there: decorators, plumbers, builders, and thought like most folk, Harry Naylor would leave the garden until last, but the poor man had died.

This would be a good job for Jonathan. He'd had his fair share of gut wrenching work in the early days, and vowed he wouldn't take on any more; things like digging out lost causes for people who'd been too busy or too idle to do their own garden, hoiking out couch grass and weeds, anything that would earn him a decent wage. He'd even once done a "Garden-o-Gramme." Pre-paid work as a gift for someone. He'd refused to dress up like a garden gnome as his client had suggested. She'd seen him running as a garden gnome in The Great North Run; in fact, Jonathan still held the record for being the fastest garden gnome and, if his mother had her wish, he would become the fastest, Superman, Elvis and Homer Simpson.

Then a few designing jobs came Jonathan's way and things started to pick up. His first design attempts were copies from other people's ideas, but he was improving. The business kept afloat – only just; it was as well Jonathan was a man of modest means, but a pity he was useless at management and forgetful at paying bills. He had a college degree, a H.N.D. He'd have been an electrical engineer – again - if his mother had had her way, but now she boasted to everyone about Jonathan's design skills. But Jonathan didn't fix things; he was just good at breaking them: lawnmowers, strimmers, promises and hearts; so that's where Danny came in. He liked tinkering around with the machinery and since Danny joined the business, the equipment had never run as smoothly. Jonathan took Danny on last summer because he couldn't cope with all the mowing, and things went so well that he increased his workload, hoping he could keep him. This was Danny's first job from leaving school; he was nearly eighteen.

If there was any hard landscaping to do, Jack Albright was roped in out of retirement. Danny did the labouring and Jack did the building and the complaining. Jack was a relative of Jonathan's, an uncle on his father's side. Jonathan didn't understand where Jack fit into the "Miller" genealogy. He never asked anymore; it was too complicated. His mother had told him several times but it didn't register, it was irrelevant information and not necessary for life. So, Jack Albright was just an uncle.

In his head Jonathan came up with a workable figure for The Grange, he wouldn't do a cheap job, but he would do a good job. He didn't want to take advantage but neither would he work for nothing, and a too low an estimate could give a false impression. He hoped there would be the prospect of a regular maintenance contract. He was glad Simon Naylor wanted the garden to be authentic. Jonathan could do the modern stuff, the concrete and the jungle gardens, clean lines and easy maintenance, but he preferred the old world cottage romantic types. His usual designs were based around lavender and box hedging with pink and white roses. He could even do an authentic ruin. Between them, they'd built a ruin for a man up the valley: a Gothic arch, and Jack Albright had done nothing but complain then, but the finished job was wonderful.

Sitting in the van at lunchtime, Danny noticed the meagre contents of Jonathan's pack-up. 'What's up? On Atkins or something?'

Jonathan was embarrassed and envious as he watched Danny bite into the crusty Cornish pasty he'd bought at the village bakery that morning.

Danny thought it wasn't like Katie to keep Jonathan starved, she was always trying to satisfy his huge appetite, borne out of running and work, and so his lunch box was usually full of healthy stuff. So Jonathan closed the lid on his sandwich box and said: 'How's the car running?'

It was unusual for him to ask after Danny's car, because Jonathan didn't know or care about one model from another. He would now talk about anything to distract the conversation away from his paltry lunch and the reason behind it.

Danny didn't notice that Jonathan had just changed the subject, and he took the chance to ramble about the stuttering engine, and how a mate could help him service it on the cheap, if only he could trust him with his precious car.

Simon tapped on Lucy's kitchen door and waited. He heard Boris, Lucy's ginger Chihuahua yapping and, as the yapping became louder; Boris flung his small and evil body at the back door. Simon glanced down at his best work shoes and the turn-ups on his clean trousers and realised he'd made a big mistake; should he bolt now?

Lucy was usually purposely slow and methodical in all she did, and she wouldn't hurry to the door for Simon. He smiled when she appeared. Her appearance amused him.

She was always immaculate, like a Barbie for pensioners. When she was courting his father, they'd christened her The Primrose Lady, because she often wore yellow. All shades of. It was Melanie that noticed and Jess that coined the phrase, and now they all struggled not to call her Primrose in her presence. Lucy's hair was coloured auburn, one of Clairol's best shades, once done over the kitchen sink to touch up the grey roots, but since her rise to wealth, was done regularly at the hairdressers. She was slim - skinny even; a secret smoker and drinker. Simon never knew her age, but guessed she could be seventy or more; he was close. When his father first said they were to marry, Simon laughed. But he wasn't laughing now.

Lucy did bring something good out of his father, something Simon had never seen. His own mother, now dead, had completed her divorce years ago. She had complained of a life of neglect, while Harry, much like Simon, was building his empire. What a pity that Simon's mother never got to reap the rewards as Lucy did. She'd never holidayed out of the country, but Harry had taken Lucy to Egypt, New Zealand, Thailand, even a cruise. Harry had spent money lavishly: the brand new Beamer, 6 Series.... the Landrover Discovery. They'd regularly eaten out and Harry's body weight had told that story. And he'd done everything and anything that a man of seventy-three could do.

Simon never begrudged anything of Lucy, he had been glad to see his father happy again and living a good retirement; a reward for all his hard work. The move to The Grange was the last frivolous act.

Lucy hadn't made it hard for Simon over the will. His father had been wise; the pre-nup had been well written. But Lucy did deserve a good home and didn't dislike the Garden Cottage now that it was refurbished.

So Simon broached the subject of the garden. 'I liked Jonathan Miller. I hope he gives a good quote.'

'As long as he does a decent job.' Lucy watched Simon standing awkwardly at the door. He appeared uneasy. Boris was still gurgling and foaming at the mouth.

'Do you want some tea?'

'No ... no.... I just wanted to let you know about the garden.'

'Good.... Well, thank you.' Lucy grinned.

Again, Simon remained standing at the door.

'Your father would be pleased with what you're doing, Simon.' She tried to reassure him.

He just nodded.

'He had grand plans for the garden,' Lucy continued.

'Did he? I didn't know.' More shame.

'Just wait a minute and I'll show you.' Lucy left Simon with Boris, both dog and man wanted to inflict as much pain as they could to each other. She went to a large oak sideboard in the lounge, slid open the bottom drawer and shouted back. 'I should have given you these before.' She returned to the kitchen door with a bulky, brown envelope and handed it to him.

Simon twisted the envelope in his hand then pulled out several documents.

'Your father drew these plans for the garden.' She said.

'Why didn't you tell me before, Lucy?'

'Well, I didn't want to interfere.' And he thought: *Why not? You did with everything else.*

She continued. 'Well, I didn't want you to think you had to do this, and follow your father's footsteps.'

Simon twisted his wrist and glanced at his watch, tapping the envelope on his mouth. 'Er ... can I look at these later. I just wanted to know if you were happy about the garden,' then he stopped and turned. 'Did Dad ever tell you about a chalk horse ... on the bank?'

Lucy saw a few petals fall from a cluster of pink roses in a vase on the windowsill and went across to tidy them, like she was stalling for time. Simon noticed.

Then in a low voice and turning her back to him she said, 'Harry wanted it restoring, but it was going to cost too much. He felt it was a travesty that it should be left to waste. He thought if he restored it, it would put Chardwell back on the map and be good for local tradesmen, hotels, pubs and the like. He also thought it would make him popular - be accepted. He liked that idea. You know how insular these village folk can be. It's all in there.' And she pointed to the envelope.

When Simon returned to the house, Melanie was in the kitchen arguing with Jess – again. The twins were careering up and down the hallway with teddy bears on horseback, running around and whinnying with childlike screechy voices.

'Tell her, Simon.... She can't go out again tonight.' Melanie was flushed.

'Dad.... I hardly ever go out these days. I never have the chance. It's just a party.'

Melanie continued: 'You've got school tomorrow, Jessica.'

'Whoa ... whoa, stop. You're all giving me a headache.' Thoughts of his office in Leeds and the traffic noise suddenly started to appeal to him. He threw down the envelope on the worktop. 'If your mother says you're not going out, you're not going!'

That night Simon couldn't sleep because the argument with Jess had hassled him. She had persisted and ended up slamming doors, being rude to Melanie, saying they were stifling her and they were dreary, out-dated parents who didn't understand. Yet Simon's conversation with Lucy had pleased him; at least he was getting something right with her. The twins had persuaded him to take them on a pilgrimage to Midge's grave. And

Melanie just loved him. He propped himself up on his pillow and through the un-drawn curtains saw nothing but the night sky. A good moon shone into his bedroom. Simon also knew another reason why he couldn't sleep because a full moon always affected him. He shut his eyes and opened them time and time again. Melanie was heavy breathing, and the sole of her foot was resting comfortably on his shin.

He stealthily slid out of bed to close the curtains and block out the moonlight, looking into the garden as he did so. The lawn appeared translucent blue with the moonlight. The statue on the lawn of a cherub holding a bow over the fountain stood out eerily. Then he focused on the trees and bushes at the back of the house that were creeping up the bank, and then he saw it. First the legs, then the head, then the body and tail – massive - the shape of a horse, just as Sam had said. Sam must have known the horse would be visible tonight. Simon thought of wakening Melanie, but she had a heavy day tomorrow with him starting back at work, besides, he wanted to keep this to himself - just tonight - it was special. Simon felt he'd been chosen. He felt a vibrancy run through him and knew it would be hours before he slept. He wandered downstairs to the kitchen, found Lucy's envelope and spread the documents out on the kitchen table.

CHAPTER 4

Jonathan was sitting on a small wooden bench in the boys' changing rooms at the Chardwell Primary School, and he was dressed as Superman.

This place brought back memories of his childhood: crying because he was in trouble, and laughing because they'd played some prank on one of their teachers. He smiled as he appeared to be a giant in amongst the miniature urinals, toilets and washbasins; was he once really so small? The room smelt, just as it did then, of carbolic soap, paper towels and hard Izal toilet paper. He had a few minutes to wait before Barney shouted for help and, like Superman, Jonathan always responded. He would make a spectacular entrance, gliding in on a skateboard, and the kids would love it.

Tonight he was nervous, not because of his job of entertaining the children and presenting a cheque for £1,600, but because he was meeting Katie later. He also had the problem of what to wear, just as he had on their first proper date after the London Marathon eight years earlier.

He remembered Katie running in her fairy costume, looking pretty, and her brown hair tied back and held in place with the pink fluffy hairband. When he'd taken her for drinks after the marathon, she just wore her tracksuit. Her face was pale and puffy after the race, and she had small pockets of fluid under her eyes, which he also knew he had.

He'd said he would keep in touch, and he did and a date was set.

Then complacency set in, borne from low self esteem and Jonathan was late. He really believed Katie wouldn't show up again, but she had, despite the busy journey on the M62 from her home in Manchester. He was to meet her in Burnley - it was almost half-way. And back then in Burnley, she wore a stylish black dress and high-heels. He thought he'd made a mistake and she would be too sophisticated for him and wouldn't approve, but he was wrong. That day he'd worn a new pair of fawn jeans and a black linen shirt, which had cost him, and he thought the money would be wasted. But he didn't remember that. And today, hanging on the metal locker of the school cloakroom was a blue shirt and a newly pressed pair of chinos, chosen because they were the only clean things he had. The large clock ticking loudly on the wall said: 6:30pm.

As he pondered, reluctantly dressed as Superman, a wry grin came across his face that he should keep his costume on and make her laugh – maybe not.

Jonathan gazed longingly at the large cardboard cheque in his hand and was momentarily tempted to keep it, thinking it would pay the gas bill, the telephone bill, water rates and more, but the temptation didn't last. Not as long as the indigestion would last if he ate any of the undercooked quiches lovingly provided for Barney's Kids, by the Chardwell Women's Institute.

He heard Barney's call and it was time to make his entrance.

'Just have a small piece of Mrs Middleditch's pork pie, Jonathan,' his mother whispered. 'You don't want to be rude.' but Jonathan did want to be rude and restrained himself, 'No.… Mum. I've got to get Katie soon and I want to leave room for dinner.'

'Why on earth didn't you bring her with you?'

'Oh, I'm to pick her up in Skipton. She's been visiting her mother. She's been over there a day or so.' He hesitated and was relieved he could make this sound plausible and not have to lie.

'Well, call in on the way home, the both of you.'

'No.… Er … I'm tired. It'll be late and Katie will want to get straight home.' And this time he did lie, but hoped it would be the truth.

Alice Miller turned her back on her son and spoke to another women handing out egg and cress sandwiches, 'He's a good lad, is my Jon. He can't stay long because he's taking his wife out for a romantic dinner. . .. Don't you think that's lovely?' The woman agreed. Everyone reluctantly agreed with Alice. They all loved Jonathan Miller but had an unhealthy fear of his mother.

Superman made the excuse that he had to fly to another destination to rescue some other needy soul and, as he left the school hall, once more on his skateboard, the children cheered. The change of clothes and drive to Skipton was done hastily and, as Jonathan drove the winding lane he saw Simon Naylor coming home from his first day back at work; they both waved. But Jonathan's hurry was pointless, as Katie was also late. She'd done this on purpose. And now his blue shirt was crumpled from waiting in his car and Superman was back in the Tesco carrier bag.

When Katie finally arrived she looked beautiful and Jonathan wasn't disappointed. Her appearance excited him, and he thought it a good sign that she had made an effort. He thought her dress must have been new because most of her stuff was still hanging, undisturbed, in his wardrobe back home. He knew because the wardrobe had been inspected every night when he came home from work to see if she'd been back, but, as yet, nothing had been touched.

He wondered if Katie would complain about how much the meal would cost – that would have to go on the Visa, well, one more wouldn't make much difference. This one had to be special. But Katie didn't complain, in fact she would make this one hurt him. He guessed what she was doing. She ordered Sushi and he ordered soup. She ordered lobster and he ordered lasagne. And Katie knew what *he* was thinking.

Talking was hard at first, and that wasn't like him, he was usually lively. So, in fractured sentences, he asked after her mother and then work, but the words were slow in coming, his voice was constricted and his mouth was dry. Then he reached across the table and took her hand; he'd seen it done on telly but the cutlery, glasses and plates were all in the way. He fumbled and knocked her wine glass and quickly grabbed it before it spilt. 'I'm glad you've come,' he said, his heart beating rapidly.

She pulled her glass closer and sipped the wine, knowing it was safer in her hand. It also meant she could keep quiet until she could think of how to reply.

'I've been thinking,' he said, uncomfortable with the silence, but Katie quickly interrupted him, 'and so have I.'

It was Jonathan's turn to sip his wine and compose himself. He coughed as the wine hit the back of his throat. It filled in the gap. 'I know I've made promises before and failed.'

'Don't, Jon.... I don't want promises.'

'I know... I know... I'm sorry.... But if you don't want promises.... I don't know what you do want.'

'Well, how long will it take you to learn...? To let the penny drop? When will you stop this nonsense and sort yourself out.'

He didn't want to hear this. She wasn't supposed to be saying these things. She was supposed to be full of apologies and "let's get back together's" but he had to be realistic. 'So.... Okay then.... What have *you* been thinking? Tell me because I'm a man and I don't understand stuff like this ... I need help ... I need to know.' And Jonathan called her bluff, because she hadn't been thinking anything and had no idea what to say to him. She only knew that she was still angry with him. He had said no more charity running but had weakened; his mother and Barney had seen to that. She knew Jonathan was addicted to running: 12 miles - three times a week, then be exhausted and fall asleep on the sofa. Or he would be slow to catch up with his work or not being thorough in collecting monies from the bad payers who nearly bankrupted them. And then he had to pay Danny and Jack. The only thing she did know was that she still loved him and she wanted a proper life, running maybe, but together; hill walking, cycling, shopping on a Saturday, eating chocolates, drinking wine, having a baby.

His eyes drooped and he lowered his head, and was clearly tired. Katie didn't like to see him like this. She knew she was hurting him and it was hurting her, but she wouldn't give in, and so her reply was. 'Sort things out, Jon, and then maybe....'

Wild ideas ran through his head. What could he say because his mother had already lined up another worthy cause to run for, and this time it was in the New York Marathon and that would be expensive – flights - hotel bills- extra time off work. He didn't dare tell her. He was putting it to the back of his mind because he'd always wanted to do it. He was good enough. It would be his last, but he shouldn't let himself be tempted. So he just said: 'How's Moses? I've missed him.'

Katie squeezed his hand and wanted to cry but the restaurant wasn't the place.

When Katie got back to her mother's she fell on the bed and sobbed face down in her pillow so no one could hear her. She pulled at the roots of her hair and rubbed her eyes until they were sore. It didn't matter if she crumpled her new dress. She nearly had weakened in the car. He'd said how much he loved her and he would try anything to sort things out. He meant it; he always did mean it but it never lasted. It would have to this time. When he kissed her, gently, on the lips, she felt comfortable and safe with him; she could feel him trembling. He had stared into her eyes, his mouth partly open in expectation, waiting for a positive response, but Katie had disappointed him. And now her pride had persuaded her to remain alone, but she didn't want to be.

Katie didn't want a divorce, and that wasn't because she couldn't manage on her own; it was because she knew she couldn't manage without

Jonathan. Katie missed his sense of humour, his mischievous disposition, she also missed Danny; she missed her home, but she wouldn't give in. Her part time job wouldn't support her and she didn't want to stay indefinitely at her mother's house, even though her mother said she didn't mind, but Katie needed the independence. She was pleased Jonathan had put a quote in for the job at The Grange and she really hoped he would get the work. He was getting some good recommendations and maybe things would pick up, if only he could manage his business and social affairs properly. She had to think of Moses too.

She eased off the bed, unzipped her new satin dress and let it slip off her body onto the floor, then went to the bathroom and washed her face, splashing the cold water onto her cheeks to stimulate her thinking. She cleaned her teeth, wrapped herself in a white towelling bathrobe and went downstairs to talk to her mother.

Simon's drive home from Leeds went better than he had expected, with not too much traffic on the roads, and that was mainly because he was late. He'd been catching up all day and it would take him at least a month to get over the backlog of interviews and appointments. As Simon approached Chardwell valley, he kept glancing upwards as he drove towards the bank rising steeply at the back of his house; something he would become fixated with; but he couldn't discern any trace of the white horse. He stopped and pulled into a lay-by. What this massive horse must have looked like from the road here at the start of the valley, excited him, and a surge of adrenalin shot through him at the realisation that this was his land, with his house sitting pretty in front of it. Simon knew there were chalk carvings up and down the country, some grand affairs. How magnificent this horse would have looked, he did not know, but decided to do some research on the internet tonight, to see if he could find anything; there must be someone who knew it once existed. He loved the idea of restoration but the job would be huge; expensive in time and money and well beyond him. His father had all the documents, the original plans even. Simon didn't understand geology and he didn't know what type of rock this horse was built on. Sam Parkinson had told him but he couldn't remember. Simon slipped the BMW back into gear and pulled away, he was hungry, and he wanted to see his family. As he approached the village, he drove slowly through its winding street. He passed the tea shop, the pub, the fish and chip shop, the baker's, the butcher's, several guesthouses, the hotel, a newsagent and post office. He guessed, as his father had once told Lucy, that local tradesmen would love to see the horse restored. And he planned to talk to each one of them at the weekend.

Melanie had been invited to play badminton that evening with a local group. Simon was to baby-sit the twins. He ran the bath for the girls and, with Jess's help would soon have them in bed. Jess was hovering and getting in his way; she was asking questions she wouldn't normally ask. *Did work go okay, Dad? Some kid at school said Leeds United had signed a new player. It'll do Mum good to have a night out.* Every member of the household was now in the bathroom and Simon assumed Jess wanted to ask him something.

He drained the bathwater and coaxed the twins to their bedroom and Jess still followed him. By now she would normally have been in her bedroom spending the evening pretending to do her homework where in fact she would be texting and e-mailing friends; social media was banned from Simon's computer, and Jess wasn't allowed to touch it without permission, and she didn't know the password.

Simon went to his study to open his mail. Jess sat on the edge of an old leather sofa and watched him slit open each letter as she fiddled with the tassels on a red velvet cushion. He opened a bill for Midge's last visit from Benjamin Bilton, MRCVS. It said this was for Midge's last treatment, and was described as euthanasia. He raised his eyebrows at the cost. There was a credit card application, then another and another; a letter from his solicitor with some good news from his father's estate, explaining that more loose ends were tied up. Then there was a letter he couldn't identify.

Glancing upwards, and realising Jess was still watching him, Simon read the letter and raised his eyebrows again. It was from Jonathan Miller, H.N.D.H - Landscape Gardener and Designer - Garden Contractors. He was disappointed for it was more than he thought, but thankfully less than the other quote from the uniformed green-tree outfit, and Simon didn't want to pay for any more logos to be stitched on their t-shirts. He put Jonathan's letter to one side and booted up the computer. Jess stretched across as close as she could to the letter, she had guessed who it was from as she had seen the local postmark.

'Have you decided yet, Dad? About the garden?'

'Huh...?'

'Is that from Jonathan Miller, then...? Was it a good quote?' She pointed at the letter and wanted to pick it up, but daren't.

'None of them are good, Jessica.'

She came closer to him and showed an inordinate interest in the garden. 'Lucy will be mad with you, if you don't get on with it.'

He swivelled around in his chair to face her. 'Look Jess.... I'm busy....What do you want?'

'Oh, you're always busy these days, Dad.' And she stood to leave, ready to storm out of the room and another door would bear the brunt of her wrath. Simon gently held her arm; he didn't want to hire a joiner to repair all his doors and he didn't want a headache. 'Stop... wait. I'm sorry, you're right,' and she flopped back on the sofa. 'Right.... I'm all yours.... Talk to me.... Tell me all about your music, make-up, boys, anything.... I'm all ears.'

Jess scowled. She would no way talk to HIM about that stuff. 'Duh...!' she gestured. 'I just wanted to know about *THE GARDEN*. Have you chosen anyone yet?'

Simon picked up Jonathan's letter. 'Maybe.'

'I think you should choose him.... That man ... the marathon runner from the village, I liked him.'

'It's not a matter of liking ... but as you seem to be so interested in the garden all of a sudden I'll hire him, maybe you can help. It would keep the costs down.'

She smirked.

'Anything else?' He waited.

Jess pulled her cardigan sleeves down over her hands and kissed him, because he'd said exactly what she wanted him to say. And, as soon as she could she would text her friend and tell her the good news that Danny Wytherstone would be working at The Grange. Things were looking up.

CHAPTER 5

It was a Saturday morning, so Simon volunteered to go and collect the meat for the weekend from the village butcher's. Melanie was astounded and wondered what he was up to. He strongly resisted taking the twins with him; he must concentrate. But before he did his shopping he needed advice.

Walking up to the cottage next door, he pushed open Sam's rickety blue gate, striding cautiously through honey bees that were lazily feeding on purple strands of aubrietia and yellow alyssum that were cascading over the crazy-paved path. He knocked the old wooden door, but all was quiet. Simon walked to the back of the cottage but saw the driveway was empty where Sam's Nissan Micra was always parked. He returned to The Grange and jumped in the Land Rover.

Simon drove to the village and parked outside Bradshaw's the village butcher. A brass bell tinkled as he entered the shop. He waited his turn behind two elderly ladies who stopped talking to each other as he arrived. The shop smelt of cold meat and sawdust.

Then one woman, who he'd never met before, spoke to him as if she knew him; everybody in Chardwell thought they knew Simon Naylor. They would know more about Simon and his family than he knew himself.

Joshua Bradshaw wrapped up the piece of sirloin and two-pounds of homemade pork sausages. 'Is there anything else, Squire?' That wasn't pertaining to Simon's status it was just his customary greeting. 'Fresh home baked pork pies, maybe? And I have some lovely spring lamb. Go down a treat with some of that garden mint growing up at The Grange.'

Melanie had warned him of this ploy to sell you more. So Simon declined and just handed a twenty to him; heaven knows the price of the beef was enough. Then he turned to check they were alone. 'Do you know much about the old chalk horse on my bank, Josh?'

Joshua stuck his hands in the pocket of his red stripy apron that only just fitted his expanding waistline. 'Before my time,' he said and wandered through a metal fly curtain to a room at the back of the shop and disappeared.

Simon watched the curtain threads clinking together before they settled and he waited, thinking the butcher must have gone out the back to get him something. But Joshua never returned. Simon fumbled with the meat in the carrier bag and began to feel uneasy. Had the phone rang? He hadn't heard it. He pretended to read some For Sale notices on a corkboard on the shop wall: *Cleaners wanted...* Baby *rabbits for Sale... Jonathan Miller... HND... Landscape Gardener.* And so he left.

The meat was thrown unceremoniously onto the passenger seat of the Land Rover. He locked the car door and walked to the newsagent's. Simon bought The Times and some sweets for the girls and hovered around the shop. The girl behind the counter, the newsagent's daughter, was a friend of Jessica's.

'Is your mother home?' Simon asked after a few other formalities.

'Mum's out the back.'

Simon walked outside to a small yard at the back of the shop. 'Hello.... Hello ... Samantha. Are you there?'

Samantha Shakeshaft emerged with a yard brush; she had empty cans of cola, crisp packets and scraps of rubbish in her hand. 'Good morning, Simon,' her eyes twinkled, genuinely pleased to see him.

'Have you got a minute, Samantha?'

'Yes, why...? What's the matter?' She spoke in soft seductive tones as she approached and stood close to him; too close for comfort, as Simon remembered she was a needy widow.

He scanned around the yard for eavesdroppers. He would word his question differently to her, and tried to speak clinically: 'I've discovered there was a chalk horse at the back of my house. Intriguing isn't it. Do you know anything about it, Samantha?' Surely she would.

'That old thing.... A one trick pony.... Nothing but a bother.... Have you put your name down for the village cricket team yet?'

'Er ... no.... But I will do.' Simon was pleased by the suggestion and considered it a good ruse to get involved with Chardwell life, but disappointed in Samantha's dismissal of the horse.

'We need a good batsman. Someone with a bit of nouse. I'll have a chat with the captain if you like - put your name forward. I have some influence, if you know what I mean.'

Simon didn't know, but guessed by her tone of voice it was feminine persuasion.

'Yes, yes please.'

'I've got your number, Simon.' And Samantha Shakeshaft lowered her eyelids, then walked away and continued to sweep the yard.

Simon gritted his teeth, went to the Land Rover and threw the papers and sweets on the passenger seat along with the meat and sausages. He jumped in and drove at pace to the other end of the village to the Three Feathers. The landlord was at the front door, reaching up with a green plastic hosepipe, watering the red geraniums in some newly erected hanging baskets, ready for the summer. Simon was determined.

He drew up right in front and jumped out. 'Morning, Graham.'

'Morning, Simon.'

'Am I invisible?'

The landlord was bewildered.

'Oh, I'm sorry.' Simon wiped his brow. 'I seem to be getting vague answers this morning.'

The landlord, still confused, continued to water the plants. 'Maybe you're just asking the wrong questions.'

Simon stopped. He hadn't thought of that. 'Well, I'll ask you then, Graham…. That chalk horse on my bank. Do you know anything about it?'

'What chalk horse?'

Simon had intended to call at the guesthouses, the baker's and the hotel but would leave them for another day, he was now disheartened. As he drove back to The Grange, passing Sam's cottage, Sam was in the garden getting some shopping out of his car. Simon pulled up sharply, didn't switch off the engine and, leaving the car door wide open, exposed the meat the papers and the sweets to the elements.

'Sam.... Ah, Sam…. Thank goodness you're back.' He walked at pace up the driveway.

The old man didn't speak at first but acknowledged Simon's presence by touching the neb of his cap. 'You look in a hurry.'

'No... no, I'm not. I'm just rattled,' he confessed. 'I just wanted to tell you that I've seen her... I've seen the horse. First it was just a faint image, and then she was as clear as a bell.' Simon waited.

Sam smiled and Simon knew he could continue. 'Lucy gave me the papers, the map, blue prints, everything. I'm interested, Sam. Can you tell me more?'

And now Sam appeared cautious. 'Come inside.'

Simon ducked his head under the lintel of the old cottage and wiped his feet. Sam went to a small kitchen and Simon followed. 'I'm glad you've seen it ... your father saw her too.'

'Did he..?. I never knew... I never asked....'

'No, well, not a bad thing.'

Simon didn't understand that statement, but continued. 'Oh, right ... I've just been asking in the village but everyone seems to evade the question. I'm not stupid, Sam…. So what's wrong with them? What's wrong with the horse?'

'You asked in the village! Heavens why?'

'Wasn't it the obvious thing to do? Besides, I came to find you but you were out. Anyway, I had the time and I thought they would know. I thought they would be interested enough to tell me. I'm intrigued by all this. I want to do something about this horse.'

'Well, have you got the spirit? Have you got the capital? You're father had one and not the other.' And Simon knew which one.

'Did he talk to you about the horse, Sam?'

'Aye, he did. Did you see the costing?'

'No, nothing definite. All I have are the drawings and a few scratchy sums on paper.' Simon shook his head again.

'I looked on the internet last week and couldn't find a thing about a horse in Chardwell. But it's called Leucippotomy…. It's an art…. Gigantic horses built on the hillsides of England!'

'Well, I'll be…? Never heard of that. I daren't know a thing about the internet, but she was here, alright.' And he went to the cupboards to put the shopping away, packing everything neatly and reaching up and with his back to Simon he said: 'You shouldn't have asked in the village.'

'I thought it would be popular. I thought they'd be pleased I was interested.'

Jonathan put the last of his mother's shopping away. That was another Saturday morning's ritual finished. The next was to eat the customary slice of cake – scone – or whatever was left over from whatever his mother had been baking. Today it was pork pie, and Jonathan knew where it had come from, and he knew how old it was.

'Will Katie be able to get me some new nighties this week?' Alice had the sun in her eyes as she spoke. This house was always sunny. French windows exposed a beautiful garden. In summer it would be full of roses and sweet-peas and today the spring sunshine bounced off the polished silver and antique furniture.

'Yeh, I'm sure she will.' Jonathan was more embarrassed about the request for Katie than discussing his mother's nightwear. 'I'll ask her to call in and check what size you want and all.' Jonathan swallowed the pie by washing it down with more tea.

'You'll have to book early, Jon, for your hotel and flights to New York. They'll all get booked up quickly.'

'It might already be too late.' He somehow hoped it was, to relieve him of the temptation.

'Nonsense.... Get on with it, Jon.' She was always saying this to him.

'Have you any idea how much the flights will be?' He squinted, as the sun was now in his eyes, 'besides, I'm not that keen on going to the States at the moment.'

'Oh Jon.... Don't back out on me, no one around here's ever done the New York Marathon. You'll be in all the papers again. A local celebrity.'

'And do I care?'

'Now, Jonathan. That's not the attitude.'

He knew what this was really all about. Yes, his mother did care for Barney's Kids and all his charity work but she also loved the attention it drew to her. Jonathan wanted to steer this conversation away from running but guessed it would then swing back to Katie. He sat quietly for a while, and then he thought of something. 'I've got the contract to do the garden at The Grange.'

Alice's hands started to tremble around her teacup, splashing hot tea on her lap.

'Oops - be careful.' He reached across to steady her and wondered why she was visibly shaken.

She tried to stand from her chair, but Alice could never do anything quickly. The hot tea was burning her leg.

'Stay there. Stay there. I'll get a towel.' Jonathan lifted the cup and saucer filled with tea, careful not to spill any more on his mother's plush carpet, and went to the kitchen to find a tea towel.

Alice dabbed her skirt dry. 'Oh help me up, love. I'll have to change it. It was clean on this morning.'

Jonathan was pleased he was now excused. He took her arm and felt her arthritic bones clicking in his fingers, and he grimaced as he always did. 'Can you manage?'

'Yes, you get off now, love.'

Alice left him standing at the foot of the stairs, bewildered, because he knew that for the first time in his life, she had wanted him out of the house.

Jonathan spent the afternoon running. He'd do his twelve miles. Along the cinder path of the old railway line, cascading with brambles and fronds of rose-bay-willow herb that would soon burst open - three miles. Along the river bank - half a mile. Along the lane to Chardwell and through the winding village street, passing the butcher's the newsagent's and The Three Feathers - two miles. Then the lane to The Grange – two and a half miles. Up the steep footpath at the back of The Grange and along the bank top - one mile, and back down the disused railway lines - three miles. Running was good for Jonathan, it gave him time to think and plan. Sometimes with each step, he would beat out any aggression in him: angry with his mother for interfering with his life, angry with himself for letting her, and yet what else could he do. Alice was lonely and he gave her reason to live.

Jonathan had once over longed for the father he had lost and never known to love. He would never recall sitting on his knee as a baby, or his father's laughter or teasing, and the pinching of a chubby cheek or the pride of a man who loved his child. Why his mother had never married again, he had no idea. Alice had been an attractive woman and his father a handsome man, as the wedding photograph of them on his mother's mantelpiece suggested. It was, strangely enough, the only photograph he'd ever seen of his father.

As he ran, he thought of Katie and wondered what she would be doing. On Saturday morning she would normally be tidying up at home and then shop in Tesco's alone.

But the thoughts of her depressed him. So he planned in his head the strategy for his work at The Grange. He had already telephoned Uncle Jack Albright.

Jack had said: 'I'm supposed to be retired, Jon.'

'I know, I know. I'm sorry.... Just one more, please,' and he reluctantly agreed to help as Jonathan knew he would. Jack would do a good job with Danny labouring. And Jonathan decided to take some stone samples on Monday to show Simon Naylor what they could use for the path and the wall. He'd have to get some samples first; yes, he had to fit that in. Then he remembered his strimmer was still at the repairers, beyond any help Danny could give. Why hadn't they rung him to tell him it was ready? Maybe it was irreparable. Maybe he was supposed to ring them? Whatever, it meant more outlay. And he cursed when he considered he might have to buy a new one.

The railway track was easy on his legs. His soft running shoes scuffed gently and regularly with his pace. The lanes were hard on his ankles and hips. The steps up the bank at The Grange, he always struggled with and, as he ran up at a steady pace, crunching and sliding on the gravel path, he gasped, even his breathing he timed and counted to its normal working pace. And then on to the scree near the top, where the new season's bracken would be starting to push over the path and scratch his legs, leaving a red rash as it always did; he was probably allergic to it. He would stop at the top of the bank, just once, and have a look over at The Grange, see the houses and the garden from a different aspect. He was eager to start the work on Monday morning.

Jonathan lingered more than usual at the bank top, hands on hips, his eyes scanning the land at The Grange. He could see Lucy Naylor in the garden of her small cottage pegging out some washing. Shrubs and small trees overgrew the small space. Melanie Naylor was cleaning a child's red plastic bike. He hoped he could provide some beautiful flowers for her once he had re-vamped the garden. More spring bulbs and an herbaceous border. Maybe plant a red vine on the sunny side of the house; a Virginia Creeper or the like. He checked his watch and moved on.

As he took the lane at the top of the bank onto the railway line, he checked a right and then left and strode out onto the short trip to the next path.

Jonathan heard a vehicle coming at pace and he looked down where his feet were in relation to the grass verge and stonewall. The white van passed and Jonathan felt the draft so close he panicked and feeling the side of the van touch his arm, he dived onto the verge, falling into the wall, and banging his head against the rock. Never in his life had he been so close to death. Jonathan pulled his legs in clear from the lane and sat up on the grass, his hands tingling now with nettle stings, his heart racing. The lime green high-visibility vest he always wore had proved useless.

CHAPTER 6

Simon was pleased Jonathan was a good timekeeper, he had said 8 o'clock and 8 o'clock it was. He didn't know that a few weeks earlier Jonathan would have been late - hopelessly late, but he was trying hard - anything to put his life back on track and win over his wife.

Simon also liked Jonathan's disposition. He was a cheerful person and treated the young man, Danny Wytherstone, well. Simon also believed he was an honest and trustworthy man, someone who he could leave to do a good job. His only disappointment was that no stone samples had arrived as had been promised; they would eventually come when Jonathan remembered to call at the stonemason's yard and when he made time to do it. But there was still plenty to get on with.

Melanie had been instructed to keep the men plied with cold drinks, as it was a warm day and there was some heavy grafting to do, lifting the old path and demolishing the broken garden wall. The job for Simon, a white-collar worker, seemed formidable – for Jonathan, it was just another good day's work.

Jess was also pleased Jonathan Miller came on time. She would normally be showering and in no hurry to get to school, which was thankfully only a ten minute drive away. But now she could spend a half an hour before school watching Danny from every window of The Grange, depending on where he was working. She'd seen him jump out of the pick-up and haul out wheelbarrows and crowbars and all sorts of gardening paraphernalia. Then she'd watched him follow her father and Jonathan Miller around the garden.

Jess examined every inch of Danny's physique from a distance: he wasn't very tall but he probably had a lot more growing to do. He had a tanned, clean complexion from spending hours working out of doors, winter and summer; Jess was too far away to see the new outbreak of acne on both of Danny's cheeks. When he walked, he walked with all toes pointing inwards. She also noticed Danny's work clothes and liked the jeans that he was wearing; they were twisted and ripped, but never-the-less, clean. His Leeds United shirt gave him something in common with her father. She couldn't see much of Danny's hair today for he was wearing a baseball cap. Jess had asked around the school, discreetly, and it appeared he had a sister a year lower than her, and Jess was already scheming how she could make friends with the girl.

Danny was ripping up the old paving slabs and wheeling them around the side of the house to the skip when Jess finally went to school. She had waited for the right moment to pass as closely as she could to him. That was when he tipped his barrow of rubbish in the skip and walked back to the garden. She said "hi" and he just smiled, and that was enough for the both of them. She then noticed Danny's acne and he saw her pointed nose, but for neither of them, did it matter.

The spring sunshine beat down and they slogged all morning, not speaking much but working hard.

61

Melanie arrived with two bottles of mineral water and homemade cookies. After a brief conversation, she left the two men alone.

Jonathan blew out a gasp of air as he sat on the old garden wall and Danny followed suit, but without the gasp, and said: 'If you didn't do so much running you wouldn't be knackered all the time.' And then tipped the bottle of water to his mouth and gurgled as he drank.

'I'm not tired.' Jonathan complained.

'You're half asleep!'

Danny was right, Jonathan was tired but not from running, it was from worry and through lack of sleep: Katie - figures running through his head – stones – cement – skips. So Jonathan sat up from his slouched position to prove the younger man wrong. He sipped from his bottle and took one of the cookies, examining the chocolate chips and smiling, then speaking seriously and with a mouthful of crumbs said: 'I nearly got cleaned up last night.' He took another swig of water. 'Some bloke or other in a white van knocked me into the wall.'

Danny looked up at Jonathan; he'd already noticed the graze on his forehead. 'You don't think Katie has hired a hit -man, do you?' And he nodded.

'Aye, well. She might want to. Maybe she was in the van!'

'Bad as that is it?'

'Something like that, yes. Ah well. If we get this path and wall cleared by tomorrow night, Jack can come and measure up. Then on Wednesday we'll start on that shrubbery. Get rid of all this rubbish and have a bonfire. Then start afresh. I think Simon will see a big difference when he comes home tonight.'

'You should get someone to look at that.'

'What?'

'That bang on your head, man.'

'It's nowt.'

Danny now changed the subject because he thought it was more than *"nowt."* 'He's a decent bloke, isn't he?'

'Who?'

'Simon what's-his-name'

'Oh yes.'

'Pretty girl isn't she?'

'Where?'

'Man, you are tired. Or that bang on the head's done you no good.' And Danny, frustrated with Jonathan's lack of concentration, took his newspaper and started to read the football pages. He always read from back to front but with little mention of Leeds United he scanned the other pages. 'Look at this!' he tried to interest Jonathan, 'It says here that gardeners are top of the list of tradesmen that women find sexy. We've even beaten the builders!'

Jonathan smiled. 'Keep your trousers pulled up then, Dan. It must be the backsides they don't like.'

Encouraged by some humour at last in Jonathan, Danny continued to rag him. 'So why are you tired then? If it's not from the running, it must be Katie. Is she keeping you awake all night?'

Jonathan wished it were true.

'So have you buried her under the patio then?'

'Who?'

'KATIE'

'For pity's sake, Danny. Stop the questions. Try and think about the job.'

A raw nerve was touched and Danny knew it. If Jack Albright had been here he would have cruelly persisted with the banter. He could dig and dig into Jonathan's life, as they often did with Danny's, but Danny had to be cautious, Jonathan was his boss and Jack was a relative and on equal par, he could say what he liked and he always did. But the barracking wasn't always two - way, Danny and Jonathan wouldn't leave Jack Albright unscathed. Jack was a perfectionist. And Jonathan and Danny couldn't live up to his ideals. Jack would work tirelessly cutting stone, measuring boundaries and walls, sometimes slowing the work down. "*Measure twice, cut once,*" was his motto. When it came to the machinery Jonathan's was "*fiddle about with it once, kick it twice.*"

Jess was clock watching all day. She even rang Melanie at lunchtime, making some excuse about forgetting her history book, but then asked after the gardeners. She managed to get away from school in good time, and would normally have hung around the papershop with her friend Emily Shakeshaft, but she gave Emily some excuse and hurried home.

The truck was still in the yard. The skip was full of broken paving slabs, old bricks and stones, and Danny was filthy. Jess rushed indoors, quickly upstairs and changed. It didn't matter that the late afternoon had brought in a brisk north wind that whistled down the valley, she would still wear her low slung, linen jeans and a black cropped t-shirt that said on the front: "I'm the 8th wonder of the world".

Danny was throwing tools in the back of the pickup when Jess appeared. She liked him even better, filthy.

'Have you dug all that stone up yourself?' This was the first full sentence she spoke to him, as she went and hovered around the skip.

'Most of it.' Danny lied.

'How long will it take? - the garden. I mean.'

'Maybe three weeks, maybe four – I don't know.'

'My name's Jess.'

'Hi, Jess ... I'm Danny.'

'Oh, hi, Danny.' She sounded surprised.

Jonathan emerged equally as filthy, and ran a loaded wheelbarrow straight up a plank and tipped the contents into the skip, sending dust all over. Jess could see Danny had lied about the work, but it didn't matter.

'Hello, Mr Miller.'

Jonathan just smiled but Danny was standing transfixed, like he was set in cement.

'Fetch the tools from out the back, Dan. Then we're off.'

Danny managed to move.

When he returned Jonathan was alone and getting in the truck. Danny threw the tools in the back and jumped in. The engine was started.

Jonathan threw a crumpled newspaper and the half empty water bottles on the front of the dashboard. 'Don't screw this job up over that girl, Dan.'

'No chance.' Danny muttered.

Every chance. Jonathan thought.

*   *   *

That evening Jonathan should have been out training but it promised rain, it wasn't usually enough to stop him, yet anyone could see he was tired and his close brush with early death had made him nervous of running out on the bank top. Then Jonathan guessed if he wasn't to race again and keep Katie's wish, he wouldn't need to train any more – well not as much, yet he doubted he could stop, it had been part of his life for so long. He didn't call in to his mother's on his way home as he sometimes did, and decided to go later. He went straight home to shower and have the shave that was missed that morning. There were no hunger pangs, despite the heavy day, so he decided to get fish and chips later. That would be another thing he could have more of if he stopped running.

The empty house was cold comfort and another night in alone, unwelcome, so Jonathan was drawn to visit his mother earlier than planned.

As he pulled up to Alice's house there was a red Nissan Micra parked outside. He thought it was Sam Parkinson's, and right enough Sam was inside, sitting comfortably in the parlour and drinking tea. Jonathan thought it unusual to see him there, as Alice didn't usually have much time for Sam, as there was some unspoken history between the two of them.

'Your mother tells me you're going to run in New York this year, Jonathan.'

Alice stood up and that usually meant someone had to leave and Jonathan even considered it could be him, so he hesitated at the door. 'I don't know, Sam. Too expensive – too busy – too tired.'

'Sam was just leaving.' Alice interrupted. 'Just nip upstairs and get my blue cardigan please, Jonathan - be a love.'

And right enough, Sam was just leaving when Jonathan returned. So Jonathan went to kiss his mother who was now sitting by the French windows at an oak dining table. Alice took the blue lacy cardigan from his hand and slipped it over her shoulders. 'I've something to tell you, son.' Alice said. 'I know you're not getting any younger, Jon. I wouldn't normally do this.'

'Thank you for reminding me, but what wouldn't you normally, do?' he asked

She struggled to her feet, went to roll up the lid on an old walnut desk, and took out her chequebook and a fountain pen. She carefully and deliberately uncurled the chequebook from its leather folder and unscrewed the top off the gold-nibbed pen. 'The return tickets to New York and three nights in a hotel. How much do you think it will cost? I'll sponsor you this time. I did your first one and this may be my last.'

Jonathan softened, 'Don't talk silly,' but Alice continued, assertively. 'Barney said he'll book your flights and hotel rooms - taxis - everything - you don't have to lift a finger – just run. He'll do it over the internet tonight.'

She had done it again and Jonathan was burning inside because he'd fallen for her ruse. Now was the time to stand up to her.

'Look, Mum. I don't want to do this race. I don't want to go to New York. I can't keep leaving Katie. I must earn some money. I'm not fit. I've had fish and chips for tea - junk food. And you're giving me pork pies - I'm sick of pasta and salad.'

But Alice wasn't going to give in. 'Then I'll double it, and you take Katie with you. I'll leave it blank and you can fill in what you need later.' She signed the cheque and handed it to him. Then for the first time she looked him in the eye and noticed the graze on his forehead. 'What have you done to your head?'

'Some idiot nearly cleaned me up when I was training.'

'Were you on the road?'

'Yes, the lane at the top of the bank.'

The pen fell from Alice's hand onto the carpet, splashing black ink over the soft cream coloured fibres. 'Oh, Jon. Promise me you'll never go running up there again, please, son.' The tone in her voice, sober and tearful. He was touched.

Jonathan bent low and picked up the pen. 'I'll get something to get rid of that stain.'

'Never mind the stain. You hear me, Jonathan, you don't go running on the bank again.'

Simon wandered around the back of the house with Lucy in tow.

'They've worked hard, Simon. They're good lads.'

He could already see the difference. With some of the rubbish removed and the space it created made the garden look bigger, the skip was full and Simon could see for himself Jonathan and Danny had worked hard. It would be good to come home each night and see how much they'd done. He went indoors, threw his leather briefcase on the table and kissed his wife.

'What's for dinner?' he was surprised to see Jess helping. He was amazed to see Jess there.

'Do you like the garden, Dad?' Jess was sitting on the edge of the kitchen table peeling carrots. 'It's exciting isn't it? Did you know Jonathan was a marathon runner?'

'First name terms now, eh.... But yes. I did know.'

'Mum says he's going to re-plant the borders with some new stuff – roses – like an old English garden - romantic, you know.'

Simon wondered about the romance - for him and Melanie, yes, but not Jess, not yet.

'Danny Wytherstone's from the village too. His sister goes to my school.'

Simon knew what this was all about. So he teased her. 'I'm going for a walk up the bank before we eat. Will you come with me, Jess? We can survey the garden from above. Give me your ideas.'

She had to co-operate.

As they passed Midge's grave Simon stopped, hesitant, because this was just where he had fallen. He leant on a fence post and looked across Chardwell, way into the distance. 'Do you think we'll be happy here, Jess?'

'Oh, yes I think so.'

'Are you glad we're doing the garden?'

But she didn't want to take the bait.

'I never found any poison, Jess. Maybe we could get a puppy soon.'

She came in close to him and took his arm. 'Will it be safe, Dad?'

'I hope so, honey. There's no more I can do.'

Simon would make it safe; he had to. He had promised the twins pet rabbits in the meantime.

'You should have put some decent shoes on, Jess.' He smiled at her pink and white trainers, coated in mud and he took her hand.

They were both breathless, struggling up the scree to the head of the bank. There was a wooden seat on top, which, one day, Simon intended putting a plaque on in memory of his father. He knew he used to sit up here a lot with Sam, well, so Lucy had told him. There were already some faint inscriptions on the seat, long removed. Simon sat down and Jess followed. Grey clouds bubbled over the distant hills and were threatening; they mustn't linger. The noise of a curlew . . . kli-kli-kli . . . made them both look upwards. 'It sounds like a telephone ringing, Dad.'

'It does, yes…. Look at his beak, Jess. Can you see it?'

'Yeh, it's cool.'

'Do you know Jess there was once a chalk horse under this banking. She was three hundred foot high. Cut out of the rock - a white mare. You could see her for miles, according to Sam.'

'No…!'

'Yes, and maybe one day I'll do something about her. Your grandfather wanted it restoring before he died. It was his dream.'

'Can we do it…? Restore the horse?'

'If your grandfather were alive, then yes, but without him, I don't know.'

'You must miss him loads.'

She was right; Simon did miss his father, and dreadfully, and he wished he'd taken more time for him, but then Simon knew his father didn't want it. 'I do miss him, Jess. He was always sharp, was your grandfather. He could get things done. He was independent though. Lucy said he had big plans for this place. I don't know if I have his spirit, Jess.' As he recalled Sam's words. 'And I certainly don't have the money. If only there was some way - Lottery money - a restoration project- government grant – something – anything - to get it done, but I don't know where to start.'

Jess stood over the edge of the bank but saw nothing but rocks, weeds, and brambles.

'Can't see a thing, Dad.'

'I'll show you one night – the moon has to be right. I'll show you the plans.'

Jess was pleased he'd told her. She loved her father.

CHAPTER 7

The automatic doors of the Town Hall opened noisily and a draft of cool air blew in. Katie sat at the receptionist desk and, glancing up to see who had arrived, continued to speak to someone down the telephone mouthpiece which was wired around her face: 'We close at four thirty...' and then, holding her hand over the mouthpiece, spoke quietly, 'Good morning Sam.' Sam tipped the neb of his cap and Katie continued, 'but you can post the documents through the front door. There's a large letterbox. Thank you. Goodbye.' When Katie had finished speaking, Sam was standing close to her desk.

'Are you well, Sam?'

'I'm fine. I just needed to get another parking disc.'

Katie pulled out her work sheet and pencilled in a few notes. The phone rang again: 'Town Hall. Can I help you?' Katie said as she watched Sam wandering away; glad, because she didn't want an awkward conversation.

Katie had wondered how long she could keep up this pretence of her and Jonathan's separation, and how long she could keep away from Jonathan. Last night she had nearly weakened, after another lonely evening lying on the bed with Moses, and listening to him purring, it brought her no comfort. She had helped with the dishes and then when her mother went out to a writing class, Katie was alone again. She had guessed that Jonathan would have been out training. She even considered going for a run herself, but her trainers were back home. Katie had no worries of who she met in Skipton; she could keep herself isolated, as she knew few people in the town to ask awkward questions. Her mother had only moved here six months ago; ironically, to be nearer Katie and Jonathan.

She had flicked on the small television in her bedroom and watched the news – boring – every channel was the same, then Panorama came on and she guessed Jonathan would be watching that now, sitting alone in his running gear, with not even Moses to console him. He would shower next.

She'd picked up the phone, intending to ask him to come around. She desperately wanted to see him, for him to put his arms around her waist. But she had dropped the receiver without dialling his number and spent another evening crying.

When Sam returned with his parking disc, Katie prayed for another caller, but the prayer wasn't answered.

Sam spoke first: 'Jon's doing a good job up at The Grange, isn't he?'

'Er, yes.' Katie was ashamed she didn't know. She would definitely call him tonight and ask.

'I see he made the papers again this week.'

Katie was embarrassed because she didn't know Jonathan was in the newspaper again.

Sam continued. 'It's a good picture of him with Barney's Kids. He fills that Superman costume well.'

Katie agreed because it was true.

'Was that his best sponsorship yet?'

'Yes, yes I think it was.' The subject was now getting touchy. She would definitely ring Jonathan tonight, at least to show a sense of decency and ask after Barney's Kids.

'I hear he's running the New York Marathon in November.'

Sam didn't notice Katie bristle as he spoke and her face whiten, and her longing quickly changed to despair; she was incensed. No, she wouldn't ask Jon anything; there would be no telephone call.

Katie watched Sam leaving and she couldn't speak. She headed for the staff toilets and left her colleague alone at the desk, wondering.

The hurt in Katie was unbearable. How could he do this after all his promises? She locked the cubicle door, fell backwards, leant on the wall, and held her head in her hands. She tried not to cry, but her throat constricted. She lifted her head in defiance, trying hard to hold off the tears. Gulping in the air, she couldn't help but moan, and hoped no one else was near.

Every morning Jess had the same routine: up early, shower, wash her hair and wait for the truck to arrive and watch.

As the days progressed, Danny's appearance changed several times: from jeans to combats, then tracksuit bottoms and then back to jeans. She liked the jeans best. The longest conversations with him were in the evening after school; because she noticed as the days went on, they arrived at The Grange later and later. One evening her father was home early and Jonathan took Simon to the back of the yard to show him some stone samples that had finally materialised. They were a long time discussing the quality of the stone and its colour and Danny was left to tidy up then clear the tools away and wait. Jess took the opportunity to talk to him. There was little eye contact between the two of them, both staring at the ground and fidgeting with some garden implement, anything, to hide embarrassment. Danny told her about his work: a day and a half a week at college - night classes even – and today, the dentist later. She told Danny about her A levels and school. She hoped this job would last until half term, and a whole week off would give her ample time to chat up Danny.

Then one morning an older man joined them. He was tall and slim with a wiry, grey, moustache. Danny said he was a builder and his name was Jack Albright, an uncle of Jonathan's. For Jess, it became harder to talk because Jack was always with Danny. Yet this elderly man made things fun. He was always teasing, and not just Danny, but Jonathan as well. Jess liked him and so did Lucy and now Lucy's interest in the garden took on another dimension. Jess had the problem of how she could chat up Danny without Lucy interfering.

Jess had also met with Danny's sister as she'd intended. Amy Wytherstone was in the year below her, but not much younger in age. They'd made friends and not just because of Danny, Jess genuinely liked Amy and Amy liked Jess. Amy told her Danny had no girlfriends at the moment as he was too interested in his car, but that wasn't the truth because Danny was interested in girls, he was just too shy of doing anything about it. Jess would make it easy for him.

She didn't want to push matters and hang around his house; Danny lived in a three-bedroomed council house, in a small crescent in the far end of the village. And Jess wasn't a snob, although her father owned The Grange, she'd been brought up in Leeds, on an ordinary middleclass housing estate. She soon learned from Amy everything that was important to Danny; his car, his taste in music, how he loved his mum and hated his dad.

Later that day Katie sighed heavily when she saw Danny sauntering into the town hall with his hands in his jeans pockets looking bewildered. She'd never seen him near the place before, so why come today. He wandered in and hesitated as to which corridor to take, completely lost. He had his mother with him.

'I'm looking for rent rebates,' Mrs Wytherstone said. 'Oh, hello Katie,' and she rustled a carrier bag and set it down on the desk. Danny rolled his eyes.

Katie just smiled and pointed the way.

Danny thrust his car keys in his pocket and waited until his mother was out of sight down one of the corridors, then he approached Katie. 'So this is where you work, then?' His face flushed a little and he turned his head, coyishly, nervous of any eye contact.

'Only three days a week.' Katie was equally shy, but for different reasons. 'Have you not been to college this afternoon, Dan?'

'Yes, but I had to leave early - Dental appointment. Then Mum wanted a lift here. Will you tell Jon I passed my exam.'

Katie now flushed as to how she could do that.

'By the way, you paid my wages wrong last week.'

'Oh, that figures.' She picked up a pen and handed it to Danny. 'Sign in here please, Dan, for you and your mum.'

Danny scrawled an illegible name. 'I assume Jon did the wages then?'

Katie twisted the signing-in sheet back towards her and didn't reply.

'Well, will you tell Jon I can come in early tomorrow morning to help unload that delivery of stone. But he'll have to pick me up. My car's going in the garage tonight.'

Katie squewed her mouth awkwardly to one side. Now she would have to ring him.

Jonathan sat in the kitchen, with his hands grimy and sweaty, clinging to the mobile phone. He'd just walked in the door, tired and bemused, he wondered what else he'd done wrong. The tone in Katie's voice was cold. She sounded like she hated him and, at that point in time, she probably did.

'I'm coming for some stuff tomorrow while you're at work. Just thought I'd warn you.'

Did he hear her right! 'Why? Why? Oh please, Katie.' He moaned. 'I thought we were sorting things out.'

'I've told you why. You know why. It won't do, Jonathan.' She was standing in the ladies cloakroom again, her voice echoing amongst the metal cubicles and she was choking on her words.

'What's changed? What have I done now?'

'Oh, you men are stupid at times,' and she hung up.

Jonathan was devastated and believed this was now the beginning of the end. How could she do this to him?

Fighting back anger from disappointment and thumping his fist on the table, Jonathan pushed his chair away, went to the dining room and searched through an old teak sideboard, half empty of contents. At the back of one of the sliding cupboards, he found a bottle of wine that he'd been saving for her return. He poured a glass, with his hands shaking, sat at the table like a drunk with one hand holding the bottle in case anyone tried to take it away from him; he would drink this, and more, all night – he didn't care how it would affect him. It would go straight to his head because Jonathan wasn't much of a drinker and he didn't even like wine.

The following morning when Danny didn't turn up for work, Jonathan wondered if he should pack it all in, and go and run around the world like Forrest Gump. Jack Albright did nothing but moan about the boy with expressions like: "*Young ones today - National Service - spoilt children,*" and "*No discipline.*" Jonathan had heard it all before, yet he was disappointed. This was the first time Danny had ever let him down.

Jonathan unloaded the stone single-handed, as the driver claimed he had a bad back and Jack just shouted directions. At 8:30, Jonathan's mobile rang.

'Are you coming to get me, or what?' Danny said, his voice fragmented with a poor signal.

'Where the deuce are you?'

'Home. Where do you think!'

'What on earth are you doing at home?'

'You're supposed to be picking me up. I told Katie. You know my car's off the road.'

Jonathan muttered some indiscernible words and went to start up the truck.

It was a silent journey for both men as they drove back to The Grange. Danny was no fool. He knew something was wrong and it disturbed him. He loved Katie and he respected Jonathan. When he'd first gone to work for Jonathan, Danny would do nothing but talk about him to his family, to the point of idolisation. Danny's father had never lived up to much and although Jonathan wasn't perfect, he still admired him because of all the donations he'd earned; even just the running was something to brag to his friends about, for Jonathan to have the stamina and the fitness to do it, and do it well. Jonathan had told him of the training he did, the weights he worked, and the diet he lived on: high protein - lots of meat and pasta, "Keep off the junk food and you'll not get spots," he would say. His mother had told him this a hundred times but Danny never listened to her, but he did listen to Jonathan; he was a good guy and Danny's admiration and respect for him made it so that he didn't want to see Jonathan hurt. Danny would keep his conclusions to himself. But as soon as they were all together, Jack started the moaning and the teasing. It was tea break and Danny was reading Jonathan's newspaper. At one time Danny would have laughed it off, but today he didn't.

'Been out all night Danny on one of your "cruises" or have you had your head smashed up with some illegal substance.'

'You don't know what's up with me, Jack.' And Danny scowled.

'Leave him alone, Jack.' Jonathan wasn't in the mood for foolery and defended the young man, knowing it was his fault.

'What's up with you? You're like a bear with a sore head today.'

'Maybe.' Jonathan poured some tea from his flask.

So Jack started on Jonathan. 'I've told you before. Running's killing you man.'

'Maybe so.' Jonathan didn't care anymore what might be killing him. Yes, just run and run her out of his system.

'You're no good like this.' Jack persisted.

'Shut up, Jack.' Danny protected his boss and threw down his paper. 'Leave him be.'

Jonathan wondered what Danny was thinking and it worried him, yet he was glad to have an ally.

CHAPTER 8

This beef is rubbish. I'm going vegetarian.'

They'd heard this before from Jess.

'What have you done to it, Mum?'

'I've done nothing different!'

'Well I thought you had a good butcher.'

'We do have a good butcher.'

'Jess…. Eat your meal and don't be rude.' Simon intervened

'I'm not. I'm being honest. It's rubbish.'

'She is being honest, Simon.' Lucy spoke calmly to ease the tension. 'The beef isn't good.'

'What's for pudding, Mum.' Jess asked, hoping it was homemade trifle with a good measure of sherry.

Sunday lunch at The Grange was to be special. Simon wanted it to be a major part of his new life in the country and this house had almost demanded it. The oak panelled dining room was trimmed lavishly with red and gold China tableware and silver cutlery. Pure white, linen napkins rolled in silver rings and fresh flowers in the middle of the table. Today they were iris and gypsophila. The huge table would seat sixteen. Jess had to be home, no matter what excuses she made and Lucy was always included. But, this week, as Simon carved the joint of beef, he could see that it wasn't as good as usual; he was no chef and the taste confirmed his fears. The twins were chasing the beef around their plates, not able to get their young teeth into the fibres, so they pushed it to one side and smothered their Yorkshire puddings with more gravy to mask the fact that they were eating very little.

Melanie cleared the plates and the beef was thrown, unceremoniously, into the bin; the twins were asked to stack the dishwasher and Jess, as usual, was given the job of clearing the rest of the table and washing the heavily soiled pots and pans. Then she was free.

Melanie made coffee and Simon went to sit with Lucy in the conservatory. Sometimes - most times - he would fall asleep and leave the women to talk; it comforted him to doze, listening to their soft, yet, monotonous voices, but today Simon couldn't relax. Firstly, because he'd caught Boris cocking his leg up on one of the potted palms. Simon managed to take a swing at him without Lucy noticing. And secondly, Simon was wondering about Josh Bradshaw's beef.

He looked up at Lucy for reassurance but her appearance mesmerised him, and he wondered if he'd had too much wine with his meal. She was dressed for dinner in her best daffodil coloured dress, something she always did when Simon's father was alive. Her hair must have been newly coloured as it seemed darker than usual, and the thought suddenly struck Simon that, all along, she may be wearing a wig; he tried not to gaze too much, but he had something important to ask her.

'When Dad started with the plans to restore the white horse, did he get any opposition?'

Lucy blew air through her paper-thin lips. 'Opposition! I'll say... you'd have thought they all would want it restoring, yet your father drew nothing but blanks. But you know what he like: determined - stubborn - call it what you like.'

'Did he come to any conclusions as to how he could do it?'

'Well, I don't really know, Simon. The horse wasn't old enough to be taken on by the charities like English Heritage and others, he tried that, and, of course, he didn't want to sell the land to anyone else. So he canvassed all the local tradesmen; he thought someone would support him and set up a fund, but no, they didn't want to dig into their pockets. He even considered getting the local paper involved but never got that far,' then her voice faltered.

Simon lowered his head and regretted questioning her; he should have let more time pass. 'I'm sorry Lucy. I just wondered.'

The curls on her brown hair bobbled as she shuddered, 'You've every right to ask, Simon....' Boris jumped up on her lap and licked her face. She pulled a lacy handkerchief from her handbag.

Simon was amazed from a man's point of view why she needed to bring a handbag at all when she only walked from across the garden, but that was Lucy.

'No, in fact,' she blew her nose, 'I wish he'd never pursued it ...or he might still be alive.'

Melanie didn't want to interrupt, but sensing discomfort between them, whispered: '*Simon.*' But Lucy started to say heartfelt things, things she thought she would never tell, but she was growing to love and trust her new-found step-family.

She pointed, her hand shaking, with her bony index finger clad in gold rings that were too big and no longer fit.

Simon glanced at the red leather armchair by the conservatory door. 'I found him in the chair, over there.' She let herself be distracted by a blackbird swooping down into the garden and complaining, then turning her attention across to the hillside, she continued: 'your father was blue – purple, all colours. I knew he was dead, but I couldn't leave him. I tried to resuscitate him while I waited for the ambulance. I know it was useless but I had to do something. The doctor said it was his heart, but no one checked. There was no need for a post-mortem as he'd only just seen the doctor. Harry had been unwell all week. He'd been speaking to Josh Bradshaw, the butcher. I heard them through the door, arguing, raising their voices. I wanted to interrupt and calm your father down, and then Josh left in a hurry. I thought I'd better let your father cool down before I went into him. I wish I'd gone sooner, maybe he would still have been alive.'

Simon sat forward in his chair. Melanie went across the room to Lucy to comfort her. She sat on the sofa beside her and put her arm across her shoulder.

'Did you tell the doctor, Lucy, about the argument?' Simon said.

'No, no of course not. I didn't want to rake up anything, but Josh was the last person to see him alive - to speak to him even. When I found your father his eyes were open. It was funny, I don't know how this happens but his arm was raised upwards, his elbow was resting on the arm of the chair, like he was waving. I couldn't leave him like that; it looked funny for a dead man, so I gently pulled it down. I didn't dare touch his eyes.'

Simon didn't want to face the scene that was flashing through his head. 'Tell me again why no one checked, Lucy.'

'Your father had seen the doctor only a few days earlier. You know he had a dickey heart?' That was one thing Simon did know. 'He'd been on pills for years, so nothing needed to be done.'

'Or nothing *was* done!'

'Well, you know what it said on his death certificate.'

Simon sat in the study with all his father's documents across his desk. He read and re-read, taking in all of the details, wondering if he'd missed anything. Lucy's implications troubled him. He wondered why she'd never told him before about Josh Bradshaw, even about the doctor's indifference, yet he didn't know the law and he couldn't be suspicious of everyone, despite thinking the contrary.

He carefully opened out the sketch of the horse, done on the original paper, and found a recent photocopy that he guessed his father had made. The old document was spotted with brown foxing, but was still clear to read, it had all the original measurements. It was a beautiful drawing done on lined paper, and it confirmed Sam's statement that the horse was over 300' high. There were also some old photographs showing erosion, probably taken after heavy flooding, some photographs of men working on the horse, some black and white, perhaps taken before the second world war, then some photographs, coloured ones, probably in the sixties or seventies of men on the bank attempting but failing to restore it. He found receipts and statements for 26 tons of lime and chalk chippings. He read all of them. It took four men, four days to stop erosion. Local men drafted in. There were documents from the war, even the official letter from the government requesting, no – commanding, that the horse be covered over with turf and netting. Then, when the army came and covered her over, there was uproar in the village but no one could risk their national security.

Simon changed into his old jeans and grabbed his jacket. He found his camera and checked the battery was charged, then managed to leave the house without the twins spotting him. He went to the garden shed and fumbled around in the murky corners for tools. He found a spade and a rake, a large reel of measuring tape, all covered in strands of cobwebs. There were some secateurs and old wooden posts and a mallet and he threw them all in the back of the Land Rover. He drove the vehicle slowly over the gravel chippings to the front of the house and was surprised to see Jess was there. She was talking to some young girl from the door of a cobalt blue car, and the car's engine was running noisily. Simon pulled up. He didn't recognise Danny Wytherstone sat in the driving seat. He didn't know the other girl.

'Hi, Dad ... this is Amy.' Jess seemed a little anxious.

Amy Wytherstone hung her head out of the car window. 'Hi, Mr Naylor.'

'And of course you know Danny.' Jess stuck her hands deep into the pocket of her jeans.

Simon hung out of the window of the Land Rover to see who was in the car. 'Oh, hello Danny. Not had enough of this place for one week, then?'

Danny just smiled.

'You going out, Dad.' Jess was pleased Simon was being friendly so she reciprocated. She could see he had changed into some old corduroy jeans and a rugby shirt and guessed he was in no hurry.

'Er, look, I need a hand. Do you youngsters fancy a bit of fun.'

Jess wasn't sure what a "bit of fun" from her father's perspective consisted of, but anything would be fun if it included Danny.

'I'm going to find the horse.'

'You're seriously losing it, Dad.'

'Okay. Don't bother then. I'll go on my own.' And he slid up the electric window pretending to leave.

Jess stepped forward. 'No, Dad, wait....'

Danny kept the engine running, keen to show he was just Amy's taxi driver and said, 'Well…. I'll leave you to it.'

'No. You can come as well, Danny, if you've got time. I need a strong pair of hands.'

'I'm not so good with horses, Mr Naylor.'

Jess laughed. 'My dad's deluded, Danny. It's not a real horse. It's a stone carving or something. Come on Amy we must see this.'

The young people bundled in the Land Rover and Simon proceeded to drive at the back of the house and high up the bank, as far as the vehicle would let him.

'We walk from here.' Simon opened the tailgate, slid out the tools, and gave each of them something to carry.

Simon reached the summit first with Danny close behind him, gasping for air and wondering what he had let himself in for.

Simon stopped and pulled out another photocopy. 'Any good with plans, Dan?'

Danny held one corner of the blue print, glad that the horse wasn't real, 'this is awesome.'

'This is the horse were looking for. It's here. I've seen her once at night when the moon was on her. It reflects the shape off some of the chalk.'

But Danny was troubled. He'd taken a risk coming to The Grange as it was, and he knew Jonathan would be annoyed with him if he found out, but Amy had insisted she just wanted a lift and it was a chance to see Jess again but in different circumstances. And Simon Naylor did genuinely seem pleased to see him.

'Right…. Here goes.' Simon slithered down the bank onto the weeds and undergrowth.

'Dad . . . be careful.' Jess screamed

'Don't follow me!'

But Danny ignored him and slithered down the bank after Simon as the girls watched from the top.

Simon threw Danny a reel of tape from his pocket and tried to pace across the bank, tripping over brambles, walking awkwardly on the gradient.

'Everything's in old money - yards and stuff. But she should start about here, seven paces from the seat.' And so he started: shovelling through the undergrowth trying to expose the chalk. Tangled branches of brambles and thistles tore at his trousers and scratched his legs. He found some threads of netting. 'Here, Danny … here.' And they started to pull at the old and rusted wire. 'This is it. She's under here.' And as they continued, balancing on the steep slope, tapping in marker posts, the girls joined them, pulling away armfuls of weeds and rubbish to mark the boundaries of the horse. They cleared a whole section and then stood on a grassy mound. 'This is the eye, I think,' but as Simon climbed on to the dry grassy mound the turf slithered off the stone and he fell on his back. Jess screamed again as Simon slipped a good few metres on his back with Danny hanging on to his jacket. 'Are you alright, Mr Naylor.'

Simon was winded, and he muttered, 'I'm fine.' The experience had unnerved him again, yet he was glad he was the only one to slip.

'Come up now, Dad.' Jess shouted. 'Does Mum know you're up here? She'll kill you.'

Simon's pride was hurt as Danny pulled him back up to the top of the bank. His shirt was torn, his hands scuffed and scratched and his face bloodied. But he wouldn't give in.

Simon Naylor had a determination; the more things were denied him, and the harder he worked to get them. He didn't know it but he was like his father. In his job, he'd succeeded by quietly and purposely getting on with things, minding his own business and working hard. In love, he'd succeeded too. He'd spotted Melanie at a friend's wedding and decided then he would do anything to get a date with her. He'd no money at the time to tempt her with and didn't think he was particularly blessed with good looks, but he had a character that Melanie immediately liked. He wasn't a bragging sort of person and neither did he ooze confidence, but the confidence was no doubt there. Simon pushed himself without thinking, sometimes he did succeed but when he failed, he would still make the best of a bad situation. His father always said: "he who hesitates is lost," and so he tried to push, in a quiet and unassuming manner. He thought it a good tactic: *don't let your enemy know your strengths; let them believe you're weak*. That was the ploy. He had used this in business and he would use this strategy over the horse. All in the village may have seen Simon as an indecisive fool, but he was neither. He would keep up this charade and win this horse back.

CHAPTER 9

Monday morning, and Simon was hurting. His legs and arms were bruised and his elbows were bloodied and torn. He'd wrenched his back and everything else that could still move. Melanie had bathed his wounds the night before, and had laughed at his childish exploits to climb on the horse in the first place. If only she knew how near he had been to a tragedy, if not for Danny being close by to save him. Jess didn't tell her mother she thought her dad was going to die as he fell so far and, in Jess's eyes, Danny's status had risen to higher echelons, bordering on heroism. But Simon was troubled with more than the pain in his bones, as Lucy's assertions about his father's death had unsettled him and a pattern was starting to emerge that he found distasteful, suspicious, repugnant and, if true, evil. Something was amiss regarding his father's death and this horse, and he truly believed now that on his first attempt to walk on the banking to bury old Midge, he had been pushed. He resolved to keep digging, in more than one sense, until things were uncovered. So that Monday morning he began.

Simon decided to call in at the police station before he went to work. A small squad manned the station: two. The old stone police house still had the remains of a glass ball hanging outside that someone had thrown a brick at years ago and had been cracked and never replaced. It just said: " 'olice." The station itself looked like a house; it once was a house for the village bobby, and as Simon stepped up to the porch he felt compelled to tap on the front door and waited; nothing but silence. He creaked the door open and walked inside. He guessed someone was about as there were two squad cars outside, and inside the small corridor there was an aroma of newly made toast. He followed along to a waiting room that was decorated deep blue; the paintwork was flaky and deteriorating with age. No one appeared to be about. Simon coughed and waited nervously a while. He was keen to get away, and hadn't originally planned making this call in the first place but he had to get some things off his mind. A brass bell was sellotaped to the counter and a hand written sign that had been mutilated, said: *Please 'ing*, so Simon '*ang*. He heard someone coughing behind closed doors, then the door opened and an elderly, overweight policeman emerged still talking to someone in the other room. The toast smell became stronger as Simon graciously waited.

'Good morning. How can I help you, Sir?' The policeman was polite.

'My name's Simon Naylor. I …' but the policeman interrupted, 'I know who you are, Sir.'

'Oh, right. Good.' Simon coughed again, 'erm, of course then, you must have been familiar with my father.'

'Yes, I was.'

'I wanted to ask about him, that's all.'

'Ask what about your father, Sir?'

'Well, I was concerned about him. You do know he died?'

'Yes, I'm so sorry. Grand chap.'

'Yes, yes he was.' Simon noticed a grubby pencil behind the policeman's ear and wondered if it stayed there all day.

'So how can I help you, Mr Naylor?'

'If I thought that there was something suspicious about my father's death, who would I contact?' Simon waited for the man to remove his pencil, thinking surely he would write this down, but he didn't, he just said: 'If your father's death *was* suspicious, you would contact me. But seeing it wasn't suspicious, you needn't contact anybody.'

'Is that so?' Simon was disappointed.

'Everything was in order I presume. The death certificate and all?'

'Yes, yes that was okay.'

'Has there been a complaint then?'

'No, it was just something that someone said.'

The policeman shouted to the other person behind the half-closed door. 'Were you on duty the day when Harry Naylor died?' And Simon shuddered at the man's insensitivity.

A young man poked his head around the door and he was as thin as the other man was fat. 'I was on duty. I remember it well. I saw the ambulance so I followed; there was nothing much doing. I specifically remember where I was. I had just seen that woman at the papershop about her dog. It had bitten someone. This was my first death!' The younger policemen said, looking pleased with himself.

Bully for you, Simon thought. It was like he was talking about a celebrity death: "Where were you when Elvis died?" and "Where were you when

Harry Naylor died?" Simon wanted to say: *I hope my father made it easy for you. He didn't look too dreadful did he?*

'I remember your poor mother was beside herself.' The young man continued.

Simon muttered to correct him: 'Step-mother.'

'Well, whatever – anyway, I suggested we call a woman PC to come and comfort her until you arrived. But she said she didn't want anyone.' The young policeman was obviously proud of his good judgment.

'No, that would be Lucy.' Simon lowered his head.

'I'm sorry, but these things happen all the time, Mr Naylor. A daily occurrence for us. We may be village Bobbies but we're well trained and we know the law.'

Simon weakened. 'Oh no, I wasn't implying anything. I'm sure you know the law better than I do.'

'That's as well then. Is there anything else?'

Simon lifted his head and nodded.

'If it makes you feel any better, Mr Naylor, I spoke to your father only a few days before he died.'

And Simon's spirits were raised again.

'Yes, it was unfortunate really. But I liked him. Good bloke and all. I wouldn't have said anything unless you hadn't have brought the subject up.'

'So, er. What did you speak to him about?'

'Now, do you really want me to tell you?' the pencil was finally removed, fiddled with, and then put back behind his ear.

'Yes, I want to know as much as I can about his last few days.'

'Well, you did ask.' The overweight policeman sighed and the thin one still hung onto the door, staring at Simon. 'I had to pull him up one night. I recognised the Beama, only one around here like it - Series 6. He was all over the road but thankfully only a few yards from The Grange. I followed him safely home but pulled him up just before he entered the driveway. It was obvious he'd been drinking, and heavily. I cautioned him. Should have breathalysed him really. I did say if I caught him again I'd …' then Simon interrupted: 'Okay. Okay. Thank you. Goodbye.'

Simon heavily pressed the key fob and the BMW clicked unlocked. He pulled open the door, dismayed. He couldn't react to the policeman's assertions because he didn't really know his father. As he hung onto the opened door, thinking it would be best to get inside and drive to work, still saddened at his lack of knowledge of his father, Simon was aware someone was standing behind him. He quickly turned.

The larger of the two policemen was standing close, casting a dark shadow. 'Have you seen a counsellor or the like, Mr Naylor?'

'What!'

'We can recommend Bereavement Counsellors. I can get you an address and a phone number straight away.'

Simon looked into the older policeman's eyes and could see they were heavy, yet the man spoke with false empathy. 'It won't be necessary.' And Simon was now given the incentive to get in his car and start the engine, but the policeman held onto the car door.

'Well, sometimes folks don't know how to grieve, you understand. I've met many a chap in my time, like yourself, who can't deal with a death in the family; it can make them a bit deluded, you know – unbalanced - not thinking straight an' all.'

'I'm thinking quite straight, Sir.' Simon now spoke with a strength and courage that he didn't think he possessed.

The BMW sped away leaving the policemen alone on the car park.

During his lunch break Simon phoned the local paper. He knew one of the reporters, Andrea Briscoe, an old student friend; a "friend" in inverted commas. After a few brief pleasantries, Simon got to the point. 'I've inherited my dad's house in Chardwell and discovered on the banking at the back, the remains of an ancient chalk horse.'

'Sounds interesting. Go on.' Andrea automatically combed her fingers through her bedraggled hair, knowing, down the end of the telephone, her old "friend," Simon Naylor would be pristine.

'Well, it was netted over and turfed during the war to keep enemy planes away from a nearby airfield, and she was never restored. The cost you see.'

'Hope you're not begging for money, Simon. We're not a wealthy paper.'

'No. No, it's not just about money, although heaven knows I might need some.'

Simon did have an idea that the paper could solicit for help, but he would ask about that some other time. 'No, for now, I just want to know more about it. I've got a few documents, even the original blue prints and drawings, but only a few photographs. I have very little detail. I can't find much more on the internet: I want to know about its history. Who designed it and planned it in the first place? My father started something and I want to finish it; maybe do a restoration.'

'So you want me to plug it for you. Make a story?' Andrea was tapping her mouth with her pencil; already imagining the interest it could create, this was a rural paper and the restoration of a chalk horse had the makings of a good story.

'Well, that's what I was hoping. Some of your mature readers may have the know-how. Maybe we could meet for lunch sometime and I'll give you the details. See what you can come up with.'

'Yes, let's do it soon.' Andrea rubbed tired eyes, which were suddenly refreshed.

'There is another thing. This may stir up a hornet's nest. There's something wrong with the horse and I want to get to the bottom of it. There's a hush - hush campaign in Chardwell. They think I'm stupid…. So, if the paper can ask the readers if they have any information, more photographs, anything, I would be grateful. We may not be popular.'

Andrea liked a fight. 'Let's stir it up!' She also liked the idea of meeting Simon again; she hadn't seen him for a year or so, well, since her divorce.

'There's one more thing I should tell you, Andrea, and this is top secret. My father's death may not have been by natural causes.'

Simon had to wait until lunchtime to phone the family doctor. 'I'm sorry to bother you, Dr Campbell.'

'Are you all well and settling in?' Dr Campbell said.

'Yes, fit and well,' that was a lie; there was no mention of the bad back, cuts and bruises and the fact that he was aching all over and that some in the village were going to make settling-in difficult, and there was even an attempt to kill him.

'And Lucy. How is she?'

'Yes, she's good.'

'No, I just wondered. I wanted to ask you about my father. It's getting easier to talk about him now,' Simon used PC Plod's advice, 'and I've been thinking. Lucy tells me you saw Dad a few days before he died.'

John Campbell had to dig deep through his mind and found what he was searching for. 'Yes, yes. That's right I did.'

'Why did you see him? If you don't mind me asking?'

'Well, I'm sorry to say now he's gone, Simon, but I can tell you. He'd been having chest pains. Let me just put his notes up on my screen. Yes, here it is. I saw him three days earlier. He'd been complaining of pains. I went out to visit him, as I wanted to see what he'd done at The Grange. It was wonderful. He put a lot of work into the place didn't he?'

Simon didn't want to admit he'd barely set foot into the house until his father's death.

'He was quite unwell. In fact, I suspected he might have had a slight stroke; a transient ischemic

98

attack. They're like mini-strokes. He'd had them before.'

'So when you heard he was dead were you surprised?'

'Yes and no. He wasn't at death's door or I would have insisted he went to hospital. But you know how these things are. I see it every day. I'm sorry but it's a fact of life, Simon.'

'Or a fact of death!' there was sarcasm in Simon's tone of voice, as he didn't like the older man's complacency.

'Whatever, Simon. I confirmed him dead after the paramedics had finished. I wrote out the death certificate.'

'Nothing suspicious then?'

'No, not really. The police by law only have to be called if the deceased hadn't seen a doctor in so many days and because I'd just seen your father, it wasn't necessary. Any way there was a young policeman already there when I arrived.'

And the elderly doctor worried that this conversation might have been leading a way he didn't want it to go. 'I suggested hospital, Simon, but he didn't want to go. Lucy will tell you.'

'I'm sorry. I wasn't inferring anything on your part.' But Simon was. 'It's just Lucy. Well, never mind. I'm sorry to bother you.' And he politely rang off.

Simon didn't get away from work as early as he'd have liked. The traffic was heavy and an accident on the A59 held him up in a queue.

As he pulled into The Grange, Lucy was walking down the driveway, her auburn hair bobbling in the breeze in its usual way as she took Boris for walk. Simon pulled up beside her and let the window slide down. Boris jumped up at the beautiful car scratching his tiny claws on the door. Lucy didn't stop him.

'Ah, Lucy.' Simon growled and stopped himself from a complaint. 'Have you had a good day?'

'Yes, dear. The garden's looking well. The flags in the path come right up to the cottage door now.'

Simon looked across at the newly swept and washed York stone and was pleased Jonathan Miller was doing a professional job. 'I spoke to the police today.'

'Who?'

'The police.' He half-shouted and half-whispered, not wanting Melanie or Jess to overhear a thing.

'Oh, not that bunch of numbskulls.'

'Were you with Dad when they pulled him up the other week?'

'No dear. What did they pull him up for? Speeding?' She lifted Boris into her arms away from the car and he began to lick her face, then Simon's arm that was resting on the window. He pulled his arm away and coughed.

'No … I wish it was speeding. Didn't Dad tell you they'd stopped him for drink driving?'

'Nonsense, Simon. Your father hadn't touched a drop in three years. You know what he was like. Someone had said it was no good for his heart so he packed it up just like that and he never touched a drop since, surely you remember.' That was more shame on Simon's part. 'I'd have known if he'd have been drinking again. No, not your father. He was a strong willed man.'

'Yes, yes your right, Lucy.'

Simon was tired and he was hungry but he had one more job that evening. He wasn't one for a night out; usually after dinner when the twins were in bed, he would relax with Melanie and watch television or doze in the chair while she ploughed through the ironing. And tonight he wouldn't stay out long.

Simon knew where to find the butcher, Josh Bradshaw, and that would be at the Three Feathers.

As Simon walked through the village, he waved as Jonathan Miller ran past him, in his running gear. Simon quietly admired his vitality, knowing he must have worked all day at The Grange and then to run out training; either the man was mad or just a fitness junky, or maybe both.

Simon walked into the bar and ordered his drink; heads didn't quite turn. He was becoming well known, but this wasn't his time. There were people who Simon guessed to be local, who he'd never set eyes on. The clientele was different this time of night.

Simon was on his second pint of Guinness when Josh emerged. Simon knew he had arrived by the loud voice. Josh spoke in upper case, his voice deep and booming and Simon wondered if it was because of all the beef he'd eaten down the years.

Josh nodded at Simon standing alone at the bar and he ordered a drink. 'I'll get that,' Simon interrupted. 'I was hoping to catch you. I'd like a quiet word.'

That may be impossible for Josh.

The butcher didn't appear to feel threatened in anyway and stood close to Simon's side at the bar. Simon stumbled over his words purposely, to keep the butcher at ease. 'I've been thinking about my father.'

'Grand chap he was.' Josh slapped his chubby hands flat down on the bar. 'Grand chap, Simon's father, weren't he, Graham?' And Graham Langhorne, the landlord, joined them and leant on the bar.

'Were you good friends?' Simon just looked at Josh.

'Not so much that. But we did business.'

'Meat?'

'Amongst other things.' Josh sipped the cool froth from the pint of beer that had just been put in front of him.

'What other things?' And Simon sipped his beer and this time didn't look at Josh.

'Writing the family history, are you?' Josh spoke in a condescending manner.

'Maybe one day, but for now I'm interested in my father's life up at The Grange and I want to finish something he started.'

'And you think I can help you.'

'Yes, yes I do.' Simon now gazed into the man's puffy, beer and beef bulging eyes. The response he got would be laughable.

Josh took another mouthful of beer and gasped, 'Your father was a discreet man. He kept his cards close to his chest. And he was clever,' an instant hint that Simon should do the same. 'There's nothing I can tell you that would be of interest.'

'No, but it interests me to know what you argued with him about on the day he died, or what business you had up at The Grange.'

Josh just tapped his nose and Simon was angered, 'Were you aware you were the last one to speak to him before he died?' Simon and the landlord both looked curiously at Josh.

'I'm sorry to say I was. And I didn't ask any questions when the tab he'd accumulated hadn't been paid. Didn't want to worry your poor *mother.*' He knew this was a personal snipe.

Simon flushed. 'I'll settle it now,' and he pulled out his chequebook.

'Forget the money, lad. It's on me. The least I can do.' And Josh started to walk away with glass in hand.

'I've spoken to the Mercury, today.' Simon spoke louder. 'They're going to publish an article for me in the paper. Do some research and ask for info about the chalk horse.'

Josh paused and took another long mouthful of beer. 'HAH!' and people turned and stared. Simon knew others were listening. 'Yes, that's what my father wanted. I'm intending having it restored, you see. Now I reckon, and I've considered it carefully, and I think it would be good for local businessmen like yourself and this place.' He nodded towards the landlord and gestured. 'So if you feel in any way you could help me out we could get some sort of committee formed, do it all legal, proper and all.'

'You're barking up the wrong tree, Simon. That old 'oss is a loser, always was and always will be, so don't put your money on that one, and besides, I'm not a gambling man.'

'What sort of man are you, Josh?' Simon knew he was irritating him as he lifted his glass and drank the last of the Guinness. 'If you change your mind. I'd be glad of the help.' Simon put down his glass and left the bar; he was shaking, but he would undo this riddle.

CHAPTER 10

Danny wasn't to be trusted to cut back some of the shrubberies alone; he was learning fast, but Jonathan wanted to do this particular section of the garden himself. He was hidden in a border of dense bushes and trees, when he saw Danny at the other end of the garden talking to Simon. Danny should have been mixing cement for the garden wall, but he had stopped the cement mixer and was standing talking with his hands on his hips. Simon had a dour expression on his face. Jonathan couldn't hear what they were saying but he was worried. He wanted to interrupt but didn't want to appear nosey, yet if there was a problem, he should know.

'How are you feeling today, Mr Naylor?' Danny said.

'I'm aching more today than yesterday.' Simon rubbed his back and came in closer to the boy. 'Can you switch that thing off a minute, Danny? I can't hear myself think and I want to ask you something.'

Danny reached across the cement mixer and pressed the on-off button, stopped shovelling and stood wondering, hands on hips.

'Can we keep quiet about what happened on Sunday?' Simon nodded towards Jack and the body rustling in the bushes that he guessed was Jonathan.

'Of course, Mr Naylor. I did tell my Mum though, but she won't tell a soul.'

'Are you sure?'

'Well, just to make sure I'll tell her tonight or I could text her now, just in case.'

'Aye, please do.'

'It's not so much to be quiet about the horse, Danny, it's because I feel an idiot for falling. Thank God you were there.'

'Well, I wouldn't go on the bank alone if I were you.'

'Why do you say that?'

'I haven't been up there in ages but it seems a weird place, besides, the path isn't safe, let alone the loose rock.'

'It's not dangerous really, but on that section I completely lost my footing. It was the shale; it was as slippery as sin.'

As Jess left for school, she too stopped to talk to Danny, and then hurried down the drive for her lift, running awkwardly with her rucksack full of books. Simon had left for work and Melanie was just driving away with the twins strapped in the Land Rover.

Jonathan went straight to Danny.

'What's going on, Dan? I told you not to mess this one up.'

Danny restarted the cement mixer and split open another bag of cement with the sharp edge of his spade. 'Calm down. Calm down.' He thrust his spade into the bag and shovelled a load into the mixer. 'Everything's okay and, besides, I never mess up any job. I'm winning us credibility for this one.'

'What are you up to then?' Jonathan muttered as he started to fiddle with his secateurs. Jack Albright was at the cottage door near Lucy's place, watching them. He should have been laying a few more bricks in the garden wall but he too had stopped work and was eavesdropping. When he saw Jonathan watching, he pretended to straighten his line.

Danny continued. 'Don't worry, man. I'm keeping us in work. I may get us another job.'

'I don't like it, Dan. That's all. It's the girl isn't it?'

'No. No, she's just a kid. A mate of my sister's.'

'I don't want you dating the clients; she's all over you like a rash.'

'Is that a law then?'

'It is now.' And Jonathan turned.

'I can't help it if Jess fancies me. Just because your love life's on the decline you don't have the right to say who I date.'

'Don't I?' Jonathan showed uncharacteristic authority.

'Any way, it's him … Simon … Mr Naylor … we've kinda bonded.'

'*BONDED*,' Jack shouted across. 'Since when have you become a psychologist? Going "New Age" on us now are you, Danny. You wouldn't know the meaning of the word.'

'Shut up, Jack.' Jonathan snapped.

Danny dug into a pile of sand and threw it in the rotating drum. 'You're always talking me down. You don't trust me, do you? Jess told me we got the job because of *ME*. She fancies me like mad.' And another shovel full of sand took the vent of his anger. 'She asked her dad - Simon - to give us the job.' He put his shovel down and patted his own chest, then grabbed the watering can and poured water in the mixer splashing it over his boots and Jonathan's.

'Nothing like blowing your own trumpet.' Jack resumed his work.

Jonathan muttered, 'Come on then, pretty boy. I'm sorry. Keep shovelling.'

That evening when Jonathan walked in through his front door, he knew Katie had been back because the doormat was straight. He threw down his workbag and hurried to the kitchen, then the living room. The rest of the house appeared as normal: untidy. He ran up the stairs, two at a time, and hesitated as he stood close to the wardrobe door. 'Please, no … Katie, don't do this to me.'

Jonathan thrust open the door but everything was the same; her best clothes, her winter coat and evening dresses were all there. He leant on the door, held his face in his hands and groaned. He thought of how he'd barracked Danny for his relationship with Jess. What was he thinking? He had no right to impose his views on the young man. Danny was right, he was jealous and he was smarting. Katie's crusade had hurt and his ego was in shreds. Then he noticed at the base of the wardrobe an empty shoebox. He picked it up and saw the Niké logo, and realised her running shoes had gone. He went to the chest of drawers and slid them open, one by one. All her lingerie was still there, his favourite things, bras and pants in red satin and lace, neatly folded. He started to laugh uncontrollably, it wasn't funny but there was hope.

He ran the bath and crushed his soiled work clothes in the linen basket that was so full the lid wouldn't shut. Then, through the steam, mesmerised, Jonathan saw himself in the mirror. Through the haze, he could still see the image of his youth but, as he wiped away the steam and saw his lined face and the receding hairline, he sighed. He pulled taut the skin on his face with the flat of his hands to iron out the creases but he knew it was futile.

He envied Danny for his youth, also his good looks, but Jonathan couldn't see in himself all his own good points: his clear bright brown eyes: his sculptured lips: his intelligent forehead, even what was remaining of his honey blonde hair that any woman would want to bottle and sell over the counter, and a physique rare in a man of thirty-nine.

He would call Katie tonight.

That evening Simon went to his first village cricket match. He knew they played every Tuesday. The newsagent, Samantha Shakeshaft, had hinted he could soon get a game. Simon used to be a good batsmen and he felt the exercise would do him good, but it wasn't just the cricket on his mind.

Samantha Shakeshaft was the team secretary, and her late husband used to be the team's captain. Although he was, prematurely, long gone, Samantha still had influence and a reputation that didn't just belong to cricket. She didn't rush to speak to Simon as they intermingled around a small pavilion, yet he noticed she eyed him discreetly. He politely chatted to a few volunteers making tea.

Unbeknown to Simon most of the ladies watched him; they all thought they had him weighed up, this dark-haired, tall, attractive and sensitive man from Leeds.

'Come to pay your paper bill, Mr Naylor?' Samantha finally acknowledged him with soft creamy tones.

'Has Melanie not paid?' Using Melanie's name to remind Samantha that he had a wife. He dug his hands deep into his pocket and rattled some loose change.

'Just kidding ... just kidding,' and Samantha Shakeshaft laughed in a way that made it appear she'd been told a saucy joke.

Simon didn't think it particularly funny and he guessed her comment meant that his father's debt had been broadcast throughout the valley. He tried to smile and go along with it. 'No, I just wondered how the team was doing.'

A loud crack and everybody shouted, 'OWZAAAT...!' On the veranda a small audience stood up and applauded as they watched a young batsmen, red faced, rub his brow, remove his helmet, and leave the field.

'Hard lines, Jason.' Samantha patted the young boy on the back then, turning to Simon said: 'Would you like me to put your name forward, then? We could do with a fine man like you in the team.' She purposely looked him up and down.

'Yes, yes, that would be good. Thank you. I'd like to get to know some of the members a bit better.' He said, automatically holding in his stomach. Then he took a prawn vol-aux-vent that was handed him from a china plate covered in a paper doily by another attractive divorcee. He tried to remove bits of mustard cress before he had them straggling out of his mouth and embarrass him further.

'Yes, and I think some would like to get to know you a bit better, Simon.' The tone to her voice, softer still, as she eyed the other divorcee.

Simon blushed. 'Any way ... while I'm here. You said the other day that the chalk horse on my bank was nothing but a bother. Why's that, Samantha?'

'Money, Simon.... Sweat.... Gut wrenching hard work. Good pastry Mrs F,' and Samantha Shakeshaft winked at him and walked away, but he brazenly followed her to the perimeters of the cricket field. A round of applause came as the new batsman struck a four.

'I realise that about the horse, Samantha. But I figured if I could get some help, maybe sponsorship from some of the village tradesman, folks like you. It would be to their benefit - future custom and all.' He took another tiny bite from his vol-aux-vent.

'Now look, Simon ... you've worked in the city. You've no idea what country life's all about. You're still wet behind the ears. But I guess you're a good businessman and you know what money's like these days. I can't afford to shell anything out. I need the shop painting as it is. I'm even delivering a lot of the newspapers myself these days because I can't always afford the paperboys.' Then another four was struck and they applauded. 'So let that horse rest in peace.'

With the tone of her voice much changed and caustic, Simon purposely took a step backwards. 'But can't you see the interest it could generate. Tourists – Internationals - Coach loads would come to Chardwell. You can see the bank right across the valley. It's folks like you that would benefit. I'd get nothing, except for the satisfaction of knowing I've achieved something my father started.'

'Catch it…! Catch it…!' Samantha screamed as a young man headed for them at pace and caught the ball. There was another round of applause.

'Any way,' Simon resumed. 'I've approached The Mercury. Let's see what they can come up with.' He got eye contact again and saw the muscles in her face freeze.

He lowered his head and wandered back to the pavilion, then turning he looked back. Samantha Shakeshaft was walking swiftly towards a spectator on the edge of the park; someone who looked an awful lot like Jack Albright.

Standing alone on the veranda, Simon was handed a cup of tea. 'Are you well, Simon?'

The tea was gulped down quickly as he saw Sam Parkinson.

'Yes, Sam, and you?'

'Aye, can't grumble.' Sam took in a deep and meaningful breath. 'I'd watch that one, son.' Sam's head nodded towards Samantha.

'Is she usually that frisky?' They both watched Samantha standing close to Jack Albright, her hand on his shoulder.

'Depends which side you're batting for.'

'Ah … I see. Is that why Jack Albright's single then?'

Sam smiled. 'No, Simon, I didn't mean that. He's a ladies' man all right. Too much of one if you ask me.'

'So will Samantha be getting her fix of flattery then?'

'Yes, I'm sure she will. But they have attachments in other ways.'

Simon purposely laid the teacup on a wooden trestle table. 'Hmm…. So whose side are you batting for then, Sam?'

'I'm one of the good guys.'

'Well, check out the paper in the morning. There's to be a piece on the horse that'll interest you.'

Sam just grinned and didn't reply.

Jonathan called at his mother's house and this time managed to chop the kindling sticks alone in the shed. He didn't really want to speak to his mother because he guessed she'd only come up with some new and crazy scheme. He filled the bucket of coal, kicked the shed door closed and came indoors. He set the bucket down on the hearth, and for the first time that day looked at her. She had had her hair done.

'Your hair looks nice.' He would say anything to distract the conversation away from running and keep it under control.

'Yes, Katie took me this morning.'

'Katie…!'And he made the mistake of sounding surprised, because at the sound of her name, Jonathan was in love again. Then he saw an M & S carrier bag on the floor.

Alice Miller watched his eyes, 'Thank you for the new nighties. Just what I needed. Katie brought them, but I guess you didn't know that either…. Jonathan … I know it's none of my business.'

Oh, no here she goes again, he thought.

'I don't mean to interfere.'

'Then don't,' and he knelt by the hearth and swept up the coal dust from last night's fire. 'It's cool tonight, Mum…. Shall I set it up for you?' Scrunching up newspaper, then he took two firelights and broke them in half.

'Jonathan…. I'm not stupid.'

His face was reddened with bending down as he turned to hide his embarrassment. There was a healthy glow to his skin and her heart welled up for her son, as he always reminded her of her late husband.

But Jonathan was now thinking of Katie; surely, this was a concession on her part and, as soon as he could get away, he would call her and ask her out again. He didn't reply to his mother.

But Alice persisted. 'Jonathan, why didn't you tell Katie about New York? It was obvious when I told her, she knew nothing about it…. Oh, yes, she ummed and muttered but she was in the dark. Oh, no…! You weren't keeping that a secret were you?' That was meant as it sounded: a jab at him.

Jonathan was groaning inside. 'Secret …. no.' He was in a corner. 'We just hadn't spoken much about it, that's all.' That was close to the truth but he had to change the subject, fast. 'The job at The Grange is going well…. Jack's nearly finished the wall. The rest of the flags came for the path today.'

'Well, how much longer will you be working there, son. I've heard tales about Simon Naylor. They say he's a bad payer…. Be careful, Jonathan. Don't get yourself in debt with him.'

Jonathan was disappointed in the gossip and hoped this was just his mother's way of getting to him, for Jonathan really believed Simon Naylor was getting him out of debt.

'It's no good working for some fly-by-night from Leeds. What about your bread and butter jobs? Mrs Wainwright was wondering when you're going to go and fork over her border.'

Jonathan knew Mrs Wainwright's job would take an hour and a half and would only pay the price of his petrol bill for the day.

'Besides, I don't like The Grange, honey…. I never have. It's always had a reputation.'

'Don't talk silly, Mum. Any way Simon's already paid me up front for some of the supplies. And you shouldn't listen to village tittle-tattle. You shouldn't pre judge.'

'Well, I don't like you working at The Grange. Don't forget your old established clients, Jon.'

'It's not haunted, Mother!' And he playfully lifted his hands like a ghoul. 'Whooo... Whoooo.'

'Don't be sarcastic, Jonathan. You should listen to me sometimes.' She was venomous and he knew he'd gone too far, but he was always listening to her and he was tired of it. 'Any way, I'll send Danny to do Mrs Wainwright's border.'

'But she likes you to do it, Jonathan.'

She was impossible.

There was no more conversation between Jonathan and his mother that evening and as soon as he was home, he picked up the telephone.

'Katie'

'Hello, Jon.'

'I've just been to Mum's…. Thank you for what you did for her.'

'Well, I couldn't forget her.'

He wished he could.

'I feel a bit guilty about *her*.'

'Well thank you any way.' he was fiddling with a pen by the telephone. 'I was just wondering if we could talk. If I could come through. I'd like to see Moses.'

'Not tonight, Jon. I'm tired.'

'But when, Katie ... when?'

His plea touched her and she started to cry.

Jonathan felt bemused as he heard her sobbing. He wanted to reassure her but he didn't know how.

'Jon. I want to trust you.'

'Pardon?' Translation was at a premium through tear induced sentences.

Then more sobbing. 'Alice told me about ...' he thought she said New York.

'Katie, Katie please let me come round. I want to hold you, cuddle you, and kiss you. You know I can't stand it when you cry.' Oh, this was hard.

She snuffled and whined. 'Jon, please. It's hard for me too. I want to sort things out but everyone keeps interfering. Every time I think I'm getting closer, someone or something comes in the way.'

'Look, Katie.... I told Mum I don't want to go to New York. It was her idea not mine. I don't want to do any more charity work. I want to sort myself out, but you know what she's like.'

'Then speak to her. Tell her again!'

'Katie, I've told her a hundred times.'

'Will you come over then, Jon? Please. My mum's out.'

Simon threw his mobile on the table, grabbed Melanie and swung her round.

'Stop it, Simon. Put me down.'

'Oh Mel … this is going to be good - so good.'

'What is? What are you talking about?'

'That was Andrea Briscoe. They're running the story about the horse in tomorrow morning's Mercury. Won't make the front page, but Andrea's made a good story. She's asking for old photos. Is there anyone who can remember the horse - anyone who worked on it? They're printing the original plans. Oh Mel. It's good.'

'Simon…. I hope you know what you're doing.' She kissed him and straightened her pullover. 'I bet Andrea was pleased to hear from you?'

'Come on, Mel,' and he moved in closer and pulled her towards him. 'What's the harm…? Andrea knows the score. Besides, I want some fun. This lot here … half of them have never set foot out of Chardwell. They think were just "incomers" or "townies" or whatever they call us. They think we don't know how to hack it in the country. Well, maybe I don't know how to milk a cow or plough a field, but I know how to run a business and how to get things done.'

When Jonathan came home, he was humming some tune that had been playing repeatedly on Katie's CD player that the listeners had been too busy to change. Katie was like a drug to him. He wouldn't sleep. Oh, how she'd wept in his arms. He felt useful at last. Needed - wanted. Jonathan knew he hadn't to speak but to just hold her. That was the rule and it worked. He was glad her mother was out.

Moses was pleased to see him too but then he just purred and turned over on the bed.

The adrenalin that was surging through his body urged him to work. So Jonathan started to tidy the house, do some washing. It took him until midnight. Three weeks of mess. He hadn't made Katie any promises; he had just loved her and she'd loved him. He'd told her he would try, and that she must be patient with him. She was wise to wait. He must sort his life out. But they agreed to run together at the weekend, besides, Jonathan knew he couldn't bring her home just yet to the mess he'd made and he didn't expect her to clean up after him. There were still other things he had to do and by 1:00 am he was still awake and writing envelopes, writing cheques, clearing the backlog of bills. He was now penniless, but happy. He typed up two invoices ready to post. One a final reminder to a client for an unpaid job. If no money came in, he would call and get it; bang on the door if he had to.

CHAPTER 11

That morning the papers didn't arrive and Simon knew why, he also expected that from now on his beef would continue to be of poor quality and he told Melanie to find another butcher. He thought he wouldn't be invited to play for the village cricket team; he guessed he wasn't the right man for the charming Samantha Shakeshaft. He would soon find out who his enemies were. He would be right.

Simon stopped at a newsagent's in one of the suburbs of Leeds on his way to work and bought The Mercury. He sat in his car, flicked through the pages and read, full of anticipation, excited at the battle, sorry about the bad feeling, but waiting for the truth.

Jonathan's van stopped outside Shakeshaft's paper shop. Danny went off on his routine errands. First the pie shop, then the fruit shop, then the paper shop.

There were pies and fruit, but no local newspapers.

'The Mercury hasn't come.' Danny jumped back in the van and handed Jonathan a Gardeners' World magazine, and then turned to the sport's page of his own shock-horror- tabloid.

Jonathan was bemused as he saw a man just leaving the shop reading The Mercury. They waited for Jack.

'Did you get your paper, Jack?' Jonathan said.
'Er no.... There's none.'
'There!' Danny spat. 'If Samantha hasn't got one for Jack, there's definitely none for you.'

'What's he reading then?' Jonathan pointed.

'Probably yesterday's.'

'I told you ... you didn't believe me did you,' Danny complained. 'Go and check for yourself.'

'Oh never mind, Dan.'

'No.... You don't believe me do you? Just to prove it, I'll go back,' and Danny threw his tabloid down ready to get out of the van.

'Leave it, Danny....' Jack insisted. 'There's no Mercury. Come on, we'll be late.'

Simon had interviews that morning as the company were opening a new branch in Manchester; Simon would do all the hiring and firing. He'd been offered a position in Manchester himself; another promotion, but since he took The Grange, had declined. He knew he could easily commute, it was just an hour down the M62, but he needed the time to settle. He wanted time with his wife and kids, and he wanted the good life.

Today, Simon's easygoingness relaxed the nervous interviewees, and in some ways, he appeared more nervous than they were, but he wasn't. He'd never been a fluent speaker; words and sentences were always disjointed but still made in a manner that was likeable. People always had empathy for him and they never felt threatened. Once over Simon had considered his fractured speech to be a disadvantage and, in some ways it was, but he was articulate and that carried the weight.

It was Simon's disposition that attracted Melanie in the first place, and when he'd bungled a proposal she had laughed, and yet was even more endeared to him. She had said "Yes" straight away.

Today he would interview five people for the new position; their CV's were impressive. They all sounded incredible. Some of them were. One girl tried to let her legs get her the job; though Simon did think they were lovely, they weren't enough. One young man bragged when Simon asked him where he would put the company in his personal life. "At the top," he'd said. 'But what about your wife and family?' the young man was ashamed. The other three were agreeable and Simon would find difficulty choosing. They would have to go through a grilling before a hard-hitting panel. On that day, Simon would be "good guy".

Later in the morning, he opened an e-mail from Andrea Briscoe at The Mercury:

'Can you meet me for lunch? My call... I have some gen.'

Simon took Andrea's hand and kissed her on each cheek. Although they hadn't seen each other for some time, Andrea could see Simon hadn't changed, but she had. Andrea's Bohemian clothing and hairstyle had become more dishevelled, yet she was still likable. A bright red, crushed velvet blouse lay flat against her chest; her breasts no longer discernible. The greying strands in her long hair didn't suit her, and a blue paisley skirt was pulled up slightly as she sat to reveal the shapely calves of her legs. Simon couldn't help but notice her legs hadn't been shaved for sometime; Melanie had nothing to worry about. The Paninis were ordered and the drinks chilled, Simon sat with Andrea in the window of a glass-panelled conservatory overlooking the city. Simon was beaming. Andrea unfastened a string duffle bag and pulled out a laptop.

'Are the boys well?' Simon asked, watching her with intrigue as she pulled out the lap top from the unconventional bag and he started to remember some of the things he liked about her.

'Oh, yes. They're with their Dad this week. You were right, Simon. A hornet's nest.' The work appeared to be more important than her family as Andrea started to open each e-mail. 'There are six in all, some containing photographs of the horse in her former glory and a letter with each giving details of how relatives had worked on the horse over the years in pre-and post-war times.'

Simon glanced quickly at the names on one of the photographs they flashed up on the screen: Tom - John - Abraham.

'Some had helped net her over during the war; some had tried to restore her. There are copies of several old newspaper cuttings of the last attempt to re-do her in the 70's. Some poor chap fell to his death in one post-war incident. There were other minor accidents. I guess health and safety wasn't an issue then.' Andrea said as Simon winced, recalling his near death experience with the horse.

'I've printed these off for you and I'll run some of these stories next week if you like, they may encourage more. But I must show you this.' Andrea opened up the next e-mail as the Paninis arrived. 'I've had a few dodgy e-mails in my time,' Simon leant across and read, 'but this is bad.'

First of all, they guessed the bad language was meant to intimidate, but Andrea had been at The

Mercury for years. As a reporter, she'd been sworn at regularly. But it never stopped her from getting a good story. The "Stop the search or else...!" was the only thing that was polite to print, there were heavy threats, but nothing specific. Simon felt uneasy.

'There's another two like this if you have the stomach.'

Simon shook his head. 'Have you replied?'

'Yes, in like manner.... Did I do right?'

'Yes, yes I suppose so.'

'Oh and here's the good news.' Andrea cut the Panini in half and lifted it to her mouth, mindful that the strings of cheese didn't soil her blouse. 'We can run a full page; use all these stories - photographs. Maybe miss out the accident. We only want good press.'

That evening while Melanie was cooking Tesco's finest pork fillet, Simon walked next door to see Sam, armed with the photographs and print outs of the e-mails.

Sam had had his evening meal at 4:30pm. He'd started cooking it at 3:30. He was now resting in his chair watching Calendar News. He knew why Simon had come.

Sam pointed to the opposite fireside chair, as a Border Terrier sniffed at his shoes.

'Have you got some of what you wanted then?'

'Yes, and more than I bargained for.... It's wonderful, Sam.'

Simon took the photographs from a large brown envelope and handed them across. Sam sat forward in his chair and reached for his horned rimmed glasses. 'This takes me back.... It's just as I remembered her.'

'Almost identical to the blue print, isn't it.'

'Yes, she had quite a deep belly in my day. She was an old hunter, I think.'

'Do you know any of these folk?' Simon handed Sam a couple of the documents.

'No. Not him, but yes, him. I knew this chap. Went to school with him. Wondered if he was still alive.... He definitely is!'

Simon next handed Sam all the press cuttings.

'Dangerous job.' Simon pointed at one.

Sam didn't comment at first, and then he sighed. 'It's the eye, you see. Or so they say, as superstition goes. But these measurements look about right. The eye was a metre long. A man could stand on it,' or fall, as Simon knew to his peril.

'I know, Sam. We found the eye at weekend. It's more slippery on the shale.'

'Some around here would call you a fool, Simon.'

'Some are *already* calling me a fool.'

'Well, that's as maybe.... The eye was always covered in good turf, but not to be stood on. As you say, the bedrock underneath was dicey... unstable.'

'Don't I know it!'

'Well, some say the eye is the sensitive bit, like if you touch someone's eyeball they flinch - react quickly, you know. Well, it's the same with the horse. Personally, I'm not superstitious, Simon, never have been. But the young fellers that have stood on the eye over the years have all come to grief. Some misfortune of one kind or another.'

'The young man that fell?'

'Yes, well, that was a funny business.... You're up against it, Simon.'

'Did my father ever stand on the horse, Sam?'

'I doubt it. I used to sit up there on that old bench with him and dream. Watch the world go by. He used to like to get away, if you know what I mean.'

Simon thought of Lucy.

'Going up busts your lungs and going down busts your knees.... So, tell me. Who else have you spoken to?'

'The newsagent, the publican, the butcher, the baker and the candlestick maker!'

'And did you get any sense?'

'Nothing ... zilch.'

'Folks around here are a bit narrow. Lived here for generations. Take the landlord of the Three Feathers, Graham Langhorne. His father was a local magistrate, he became mayor and Graham always had this idea he should follow in his footsteps. But he's never succeeded. He's got pictures all over the pub of his father in his mayoral chains, opening bazaars and the like. They had friends in high places, and I mean high.... It's gone to his head. Thinks he owns the village. His brother's PC Alec Langhorne, the local bobbie.'

'Is he a big chap? I met him. I went to ask about my Dad's death, oh and the doctor too.'

'Aye well, be careful. They make their own laws.'

'I guess so. And Samantha doesn't like me anymore. There were no papers this morning.'

'No. Me neither. But I have my own supplier.'

*   *   *

Jonathan punched in the 1571 numbers into his phone and got three messages. One was from Katie, she sounded happy and was inviting him over for tea; his body tingled with the thought. The next message was from his mother's house-keeper, she was worried about Alice, saying she had taken to her bed. And then there was a message from Alice herself. She'd said not to be troubled, but if he did call, not to bring anything to eat because she hadn't eaten all day and wasn't hungry. She was just a bit unwell.

He checked his watch, and let his head drop into his hands. He just had time.

Jonathan unlocked the back door of his mother's house with his own key. The kitchen was empty. The house felt warm, and the heat heightened the smell of the old polished furniture. He glanced into the sitting room, but his mother wasn't there. Everything was immaculate as usual, except for some burnt newspaper in the grate. Black fragments had fallen on the hearth and looked messy; he shouted upstairs. 'Hi, Mum, it's only me.... Are you feeling any better? Do you want anything?'

He waited, but there was silence.

'Hello, Mum. It's me....' He crept upstairs and tapped on her bedroom door.

'Are you okay? It's Jon,' and he pushed the door open and heard her stir.

'Come in, son.... It's okay.... Come in,' she muttered.

It wasn't unusual for Jonathan to see his mother in her night clothes, he'd been nursemaid, carer and cook to his elderly mother hundreds of times: when she'd had one of her headaches, dizzy do's, or funny turns but, today, he was shocked as he hardly recognized her. If she'd been in hospital he would have walked straight by her bed.

He came close to her side and for the first time in his life, thought she really did look ill. Her hair was dishevelled and the pink lacy bed jacket she was wearing was partly unbuttoned, showing her freckled and bony chest, and the buttons that were fastened were done up wrong; she looked pitiful.

'Oh no ... you *are* poorly. I'll call the doctor.'

'NO.... No, Jon.... I'll be fine,' she insisted.

'But look at you.' He picked up her hand and felt the fragile bones, her skin was cold and clammy yet the room was warm.

'Where's Katie...? Is she with you?'

'No.... No,' he was embarrassed and nearly slipped up by saying he was going to her place for tea.

'Will she come and help me, Jon?'

He didn't know the answer to that one, so he said: 'Have you eaten?'

'No, nothing all day.'

'Do you feel sick?'

'I can't eat.'

'Oh, Mum.... I'll get a doctor.'

'Just leave it, Jonathan.... Get Katie, please. I want to talk to her. She'll know what to do.'

Jonathan was torn.

He went downstairs and fumbled around the lounge looking for the handset on the telephone. He would have to call Katie and tell her the truth; beg for her help.

Jonathan sat for sometime in a quandary. Why no doctor? Why not now, when she really needed him? She'd cried wolf so many times. Could she be bluffing again? Did she have some kind of second-sense, determined to come between him and his wife. Jonathan was angry and perplexed. He'd make her some tea.

While the kettle was boiling, he searched around for something to take upstairs to console her: bread and butter, maybe some soup - anything to entice her. Perhaps put the TV on in the bedroom. He hunted around for her reading glasses, and found an unfinished crossword she might like to try. The Mercury was on the coffee table, folded in half. Jonathan flicked through the pages, curious to see if he'd missed anything that morning. The paper felt thinner than usual and he could see it was incomplete, and realised the rest of it was the burnt remains that he had spotted in the hearth.

He telephoned Katie.

Katie threw the broccoli in the waste bin, and next went the cous-cous, then the chicken tikka. She wasn't normally wasteful, but this meal wouldn't be eaten. Katie thought she'd never eat again! She sat at the kitchen table with her red-striped cook's apron over the top of her black satin dress, put her head in her hands and wept. It was over and it hurt. A "*sorry, I can't come, I had to work late*" or a "*sorry, but I'm knackered*" would have been acceptable but, "*sorry, my mother's ill again,*" wouldn't do.

Then he had the cheek to ask her to come and help. Of course Alice wanted her, she always wanted everyone. And now Jonathan, who'd once again become her lover as well as her husband, had put his mother's wishes before hers - again.

Katie felt cheated. The intimacy they'd had, obviously meant nothing to him. She felt used. He was never going to get this one right.

She poured herself a glass of chilled wine and sipped, elbows on table, sobbing, shaking, drinking like someone who'd been denied for many months. Katie didn't realise it but the more she shunned him the more she loved him.

When they'd first met, she wondered why he'd never been snatched up. Jonathan was thirty-one at the time. It wasn't because he was a mummy's boy, because she believed he wasn't. He was manly, strong, funny, and he could be firm with his mother - sometimes, but somehow he'd changed. And Alice had never stood in Katie's way, she was happy to see her only son marry. She'd helped them buy the house, giving them a good deposit. She'd encouraged them to start a family. And Katie did like Alice; she liked her spunk, to bring up a boy alone; not molly-coddle him; turn him into a man. But Alice hadn't taught him to say "no." Jonathan couldn't, because if he did, that meant one day he would say "no" to Alice. And that was how it usually was.

When Jonathan started running for charity, he had compassion for every disadvantaged person that approached him; if he could help in any way, he would. It was an attitude that Katie had loved in him at first: unselfish, thoughtful. And, if she would be honest with herself and not down herself thinking he didn't care about her, she would realise that Jonathan wanted her the most. And tonight he'd begged her to come through and help Alice. But Katie wouldn't, and neither would she put up with this pretence any more, by keeping their separation secret; she would have to come clean. And although she didn't really want to, Katie decided to contact a solicitor tomorrow and see what she needed to do to get a divorce.

Jonathan took a tray of bread and tomato soup upstairs; Alice noticed his face was unusually pale.

'Katie can't come ... I'm sorry.... You're stuck with me.'

Alice slowly edged up the bed and her head pounded. She held her forehead.

'Let me get a doctor, Mum, please. I don't know what to do.'

'Just stay with me, Jon. Stay with me tonight. I might feel better in the morning.'

Alice lay in her bed reassured her son was in the next room, but truly sorry to drag him away from home and Katie. She knew he could never understand how she felt. And Alice could never tell him why she felt as bad as she did, and that it was pure stress that made her feel poorly; that fear had nearly torn her apart. And Jonathan was all she had. She would have loved to have had a daughter, and really believed that Katie fit that role well. Alice thought she was lucky to have Katie, and a good daughter-in-law was a bonus for her after the sadness of being widowed so young, bringing up a boy alone; a boy who'd only ever sat on his father's knee for a short time in his life. Alice had loved her husband despite only being married a few years; she'd married late in life and

Jonathan's father was much younger than her. He was a fit, healthy and happy man. Alice had nursed a sick father herself for years and she knew what it was like. She had reckoned she had done well to marry and conceive a son late in life and didn't expect a second chance if anyone else should come along and, somehow, it was frowned upon in Chardwell's archaic society. She also knew she had been infatuated with Jonathan's father to the point of ignoring and denying any bad in him, and Alice doubted she could ever have loved any one again like that; she also believed that no one would want to take her on board with a young son, but bringing up a child alone had been hard on her.

Jonathan was an energetic boy, that's where Jack Albright came in. He would take Jonathan out fishing, cycling, walking; usually in the hills, but when Jonathan started running, Jack couldn't keep up.

Jack had always assumed the role as Jonathan's guardian and he did the job well. And having never married, he had the time. And when Jonathan took on the landscape gardening business, Jack was the obvious one to help. He wanted to help.

Alice heard Jonathan knocking about downstairs until late, watching television, the kettle boiling, the toaster popping up. Then the toilet flushed and she heard him come to bed; she wasn't stupid and knew there was something wrong between him and Katie.

Jonathan lay in bed and his head ached as much as his mother's. His brain was sore from thinking. He'd manage to persuade Alice to eat a meal. She'd also had a milky drink at suppertime with a tot of brandy to help her sleep and a slice of toast. He would call Jack in the morning, tell him about his mother, and ask him to keep an eye on Danny awhile. At least the wall was nearly finished and Jonathan planned next week to start the re-planting and train Danny up a little.

The last few weeks of Jonathan's life had been hard. Despite the junk food, he'd lost weight because he hadn't been eating regularly and he'd run more. He hadn't realised how much the strain was beginning to show.

He clicked out the bedside lamp and turned over in bed.

CHAPTER 12

Sitting alone on the bench at the top of the bank with both hands resting on his walking stick, Sam Parkinson arched his back and pressed his bodyweight on the stick. Chardwell stretched out before him, the long line of cottages and houses rambling close to the meandering river as it's lifeblood along the length of the valley. The trees following the river and concealing it from view were lush with summer growth; swallows swooped below catching flies and midges. Sam wasn't looking at the view or watching his Border Terrier sniffing at the fence, he was just thinking; even worrying.

He heard distant voices, laughing, as if someone was fooling around and, as Sam looked down, he could see young Danny Wytherstone in the garden at The Grange below, talking loudly, probably teasing or being teased by Jack Albright. Sam heard the tapping of chisel against stone as they dressed it into shape to build the new wall. He saw Jonathan arrive in his white pick-up and join them and the talking became muted. Then Jonathan wandered away to the other side of the garden alone. Melanie Naylor appeared with what looked like a tray of tea and approached Jack and Danny. Sam could just hear the soft tones of her voice.

Sam liked this family; Simon Naylor was a decent man, Melanie seemed the perfect wife, and they deserved some happiness but, as he watched them for sometime, Sam had a deep feeling of foreboding. The dog sitting at his feet, lifted its head, sniffing into the air, but Sam was motionless.

They both heard the crash of broken glass from The Grange below. Sam watched Jack and Danny stop work and walk around to the back of the house. He saw Melanie follow them closely and then squeal. Jonathan was the last on the scene, walking slowly, shoulders bent, hands in pockets out of one of the shrubberies.

A few minutes later the dog sat up further, and pricked its ears at the scuff- scuff of footsteps on the gravel path coming up the bank. Sam watched and was surprised to see Graham Langhorne, the landlord of The Three Feathers.

Neither man acknowledged the other as Graham came closer, limping with the arthritic hip he had, gasping after the climb.

Sam bent his head low again, he didn't want eye contact.

'Sitting there won't do any good, Sam.'

'Maybe not.'

They were both watching the scene below. Graham stood beside Sam, catching his breath, with hands on hips, shuffling from side to side to rest his aching leg.

'Sounds like Jonathan's breaking things again.' Graham gasped.

'I doubt it.' Sam wanted to defend him.

'Is he doing a good job then?'

'He usually does.'

'Simon Naylor's wasting his time and money, isn't he?'

'Not in my opinion.'

'No. It wouldn't be.... But you've always been a meddler, Sam, haven't you.'

Sam didn't reply.

Graham put his hands in his pockets and limped on.

'Simon Naylor will finish this job, Graham. Mark my words.'

'Aye, words Sam – words…. That's all we hear, and haven't we heard it all before.' Graham turned and came back close to the old man. 'He's a stuttering idiot, Sam. He won't have the stomach for it. Can't imagine how he ever made a success in the city. Probably let his old man pull some strings.' And then he walked away.

Sam wasn't a violent man, never had been, but now he felt something well up within him that he couldn't and wouldn't restrain; things that had brewed inside him for years.

He was about to stand and go after Graham Langhorne when his judgement told him differently. He had been patient for years, why change now; he would be right to do so. And Sam continued to sit and brood, to connive and concoct.

'What's going on?' Jonathan watched as Melanie emerged from the conservatory with a lump of stone that should have been in the garden wall. Jonathan's eyes were fixated on the broken panel of glass and shuddered at the cost. 'Have you two been mucking about?' Looking at Danny and Jack.

'It's not their fault, Jonathan. I was with them.' Melanie twisted the stone in her hand and settled it down on the wall.

'Why do you always think it's us?' Danny stood forward. 'It came from your side of the garden, not ours.'

'Well, I haven't done it.' Jonathan blushed.

Danny ripped off his protective leather gloves and threw down the chisel. 'I know when I'm not wanted.'

'Settle down, all of you.' Jack said. 'Let's have a look around. Someone must be about. Some kids or something.'

'There's no one. I'd have seen them. We'll sort out the glass, Mrs Naylor. Don't worry. Tell Simon we're sorry.'

'You'll do nothing of the sort, Jonathan. This isn't your fault.'

Jonathan looked across the garden and knew there was no close access to Simon's garden apart from the public track up the bank. He wandered across to the path and leaning over the fence looked up and down the hillside but it was empty apart from a small rabbit scurrying up the track into the bracken.

'I thought you might call tonight.' Simon said.

Sam respectfully removed his cap as he entered The Grange. He smiled as he stepped over a small pushchair with a lifelike rubber baby in it. It was good to see The Grange as a family home again.

'Would you like a drink?' Simon asked.

Sam wouldn't refuse.

'Go into the study.... I'll just tell Melanie you're here.'

'Hope I'm not interrupting anything.'

'No. It's the girls' bath time. I can miss that for one night.'

Simon poured a beer from the fridge and joined Sam in the study. He was standing by the window looking at the view, distant clouds blackened the horizon. It was probably raining in Skipton.

'So has anything else come in?' Sam said, then took a drink from the cool beer and thought it tasted of tin. Simon rested his buttocks on his desk opposite him. 'Just more of the same I'm afraid. Maybe more will come in later.... It's early days. They're running another piece next week, I hope. Give people time to think and devise.'

Sam was baffled and thought he understood Simon's meaning but daren't say. So, Simon helped him, 'Devise more schemes against me and my family.

'I came home from work tonight and someone had chucked a piece of stone through the conservatory window. Frightened Melanie half to death. Good job the landscapers were still here.'

'I know, I heard the crash. I wondered what it was. Are you sure you want this, Simon?'

'No, I don't want trouble, Sam, but neither do I like deceit. It could be just coincidental. Yet I'm concerned that my father wasn't allowed to do as he pleased with his own land. I'm concerned of how he died.... I own this land.... I've inherited what should be a national treasure. I'm passionate about the horse. Folks have always had to fight for things like this. If you drive around the country and see monuments and buildings, we're glad someone took the trouble to fight for them. I went up to Newcastle last week, up the A1, and saw the Angel of the North for the first time. Have you seen her?'

The old man shook his head.

'It's wonderful. I know its brown and rusty but it does make you feel protected; I know that's sounds a bit cheesy. When it was being planned, folks went crazy, saying it was a waste of money, but it's beautiful ... it's awesome. What if Michaelangelo was never allowed to paint the Sistine Chapel or Brunel build the Eiffel Tower. I know my old horse won't be anywhere near as grand as those things, or hopefully, not cost anywhere near what they did. She already exists, she just needs restoring. I'll do it Sam.... I'll do it. And maybe in years to come folks will thank me for it.'

Sam's eyes watered. They did easily these days: a sad story, the birth of a child, and the death of a friend. He admired Simon's passion.

'How long have you lived in Chardwell, Sam?'

'Born here.'

'In your cottage?'

'No, I took that when I married.'

'What about your wife?'

'I lost her in '96.'

'Oh, I'm sorry.'

'Yes, but that's how it is. She was a good woman. She was from Bradford; not a local lass. Most of the villagers were prejudiced against my family for one reason and another. Mary still had a good life though. Not many friends, but that suited us ... we liked walking and she liked housework, baking, cleaning, ordinary woman's stuff.... As I said she was a good 'un.'

'Have you any children?' Simon relaxed back on the desk and realised he knew nothing of Sam; he'd never asked before, and never been interested. Simon had made mistakes with his father's life and, in future, he would always ask and take more notice.

'Aye, two fine boys ... well, men now. One in Hong Kong, one in America.'

'That's tough.'

'One of them rings me every day. They'd be back home if I needed them. One's in the police the other's a specialist racehorse vet.'

'They've done well.'

'Aye, I don't know where they came from. Mary always wanted to teach but left it too late. I guess the boys were pushed a bit more than most. They were friends of young Jonathan. The three of them were real tykes.' And Sam's eyes watered again.

'What do you mean about your family, Sam...? You said people were prejudiced.'

'I mean you have to be careful what you say to folks around here. They're all related. In-bred. Some of 'em are crazy.'

Simon fidgeted, uncomfortable with the frankness. 'So who lived here before my Dad?'

'Oh, some young family from the south.... They didn't stay long. Four or five years, maybe. Then they moved on.'

'Did they ever bother with the horse?'

'I doubt it ... they didn't bother with the house. It was them that let the place get into disrepair.'

'And before them?'

'Same story really ... but it's the ones before that. Well, that's what I've come to talk to you about. I meant to tell you the other day. It was the Langhornes.'

'Same as the Three Feathers?'

'Aye, same as.... Lots of them around here.'

'What relation were they?'

'Graham and Alec Langhorne were born here at The Grange. The sons and heirs.'

'Ah.'

'Yes, ah.'

Simon fidgeted uneasily and wondered why Sam had never mentioned this before. He set his beer glass on his desk and thrust his hands in his pockets. 'Come on, Sam. Dish the dirt?'

'Their family had this place for donkey's years.'

'Was this the Langhorne, the Mayor, you were telling me about?'

'Aye, yes, the Mayor.'

'So why did they leave?'

'Well, folks say they got into bother ... money I mean. This place takes a lot of running.' Simon knew that and it troubled him. 'They - the Langhornes that is, sold it off bit by bit- the paintings - the silver, you know how it is. Then the land. They had the farm at the end of the lane; that went too. Graham Langhorne gets hot under the collar about his fall from grace.'

'Did the white horse feature in any of this?'

'I was only a lad after the war ... everyone in the village wanted it back, except for the Langhornes; they were unwilling to contribute anything. But they bowed to pressure and agreed only if the village shared the cost, just as you've tried. A Trust was to be set up, the work was started, but everything was derailed. Even the local school wanted to set the kids on the level parts with hoes and rakes, but it was all stopped. Some considered it to be a white elephant rather than a white horse.'

Simon hovered uneasily around the room. The noise of the children playing upstairs echoed downstairs, shouting, laughing, and loud music started up as Jess hit the CD player.

Sam was relentless. 'The weather could be another problem, Simon. As I said before, she's made of Jurassic limestone. Then there's loose scree. It takes a lot to maintain her. Moss and lichen grow and turn her green. In winter, drifting snow and heavy rain's your main problem; brings the loose rock down in gullies; she erodes easily. When a storm brewed, we usually looked at the sky because we knew the old horse would suffer. You'll become nervous of the weather, Simon. You'll watch every forecast. It's a beast of burden this is. Gullies wash down and reshape her. Sometimes she loses her tail, or becomes sway-backed if you know what I mean. Then you'll have to be careful how you work on her. The steepest part's near the head - the eye, as I said before. She flattens out on the body. You can stand nicely on the body without too much trouble, but the bank rises steeply near the top. That's where you need ropes. Keep everyone safe. Just as a precaution, you know.'

Tiredness always made Simon worry, and now he worried even more as he fiddled with a pencil on his desk and listened.

'So stop it now, Simon.... Don't take this any further if you want to live happily in Chardwell. And don't take it on if you haven't got the spirit, remember that.'

'And there's no ready cash, anyway, Sam.'

The old man finished his beer and stood to leave, but Simon persisted.

'Tell me more about these Langhornes, Sam?'

'They've always scuppered all plans to see the horse restored. A bit like rebuilding Babylon, except that was Divine. This isn't. It's just downright evil.'

Simon laughed because he knew of Sadam Hussein's attempt to rebuild Babylon and print his name on the bricks. And where was he?

'So Graham Langhorne's bitter then is he?'

'Bitter and twisted.' Sam said.

A new day in the office and Simon must concentrate on his job, or he'd lose it. He tried to switch himself off from the horse but it kept coming back. He recalled the moonlit image and looked on his calendar to see when the next full moon would be; he'd planned to show Jess. Then he would control his thinking again, concentrate on the interviews he had this week. He had a young man in one of the offices that had been stealing and he had to be fired. He had several letters to transcribe, offering employment in the new factory. Then the horse came back again. Fears about the discovery that the local landlord was a head-case, and Simon had just managed to get on the wrong side of him. Then there were the poison e-mails, the verbal abuse, a brick through his conservatory window and the mysterious death of his father. His own near death experience. Was he just believing the flights and fantasies of these inbred people in Chardwell, with their superstitions and tribal grudges?

He rubbed his forehead and decided to make a call to one of his applicants and give him the good news that he had a job. That did the trick. Then he negotiated a pay deal with another. Simon got busy and his in-tray was emptying and his out-tray filling up.

Then the phone rang, it was Andrea Briscoe. 'We're running the next instalment in the morning.'

Simon sighed and reluctantly asked: 'Anything new come in?'

'No, just the same stuff. I'm surprised really.' Andrea was disappointed. 'Either there's nothing else, or your lot in Chardwell are keeping quiet for some reason. I can give it one last shot, but I daren't risk any more coverage.'

And that was it. More distraction and more disappointment.

CHAPTER 13

The day the second instalment went out in The Mercury was the first day of half term. Jess was ecstatic; she could see Danny all week. No newspapers were delivered to The Grange that morning, and Jonathan Miller was also denied his newspaper again. But he didn't care; he had enough to think about as that morning in the post he'd received a solicitor's letter telling him his wife wanted a divorce. It was also the day that Alice Miller had her first stroke.

Alice's housekeeper, Linda, found her in the hallway on the floor by the front door, and had called Jonathan at 9:30am.

Danny was left alone to clear and level the path with sand ready to lay more flagstones and wait for another delivery of stone. Jack's work was now finished; the boys could do the rest on their own. Jonathan left in a hurry.

He found his mother seated, if that's what you could call it. She was slumped in the hall chair where the housekeeper had just managed to lift her. Linda was now kneeling on the floor in front of Alice, trying to reassure her that Jonathan and the doctor would be here soon. And it was Jonathan who'd arrived first. His face was ashen.

Alice's heart jumped when she saw him and she held out her hand, the only one she could move. She tried to speak but the words didn't come out properly.

'Don't worry, Mum ... I'm here now ... you're safe ...we'll look after you....' He took Linda's place and knelt on the floor beside his mother, and couldn't help but straighten her clothes. Linda's worried expression did nothing to console Jonathan. The doctor was an age.

'Do you think we should call an ambulance?' Linda said, but Alice protested in an unintelligible way.

'Mum.... You need help.' Then a car door slammed, they heard footsteps coming up the garden path and Jonathan jumped up to see who it was.

'Morning, Jonathan,' the doctor said as he was ushered indoors. He was in no hurry. He'd seen it all before.

A medical bag was placed on the carpet as Dr Campbell started with routine checks. Blood pressure, heartbeat, looking into the eyes, asking Alice questions that she couldn't answer; she had terror on her face as she clung on to Jonathan's hand.

'We're going to have to get you to hospital, Alice.'

'I'll pack some things,' the housekeeper said, glad at last of something useful to do.

Tears started to fall steadily down Alice's cheeks; Jonathan had never seen his mother cry before, well, not in adult life, and he found it hard to speak himself. 'I'll come with you, Mum.'

Danny and Jess had lunch together sat on the new garden wall. Jess did most of the talking. She was sitting close to the Gothic archway that Jack had built. She imagined pink roses climbing over it in summer and someone, much like Danny, going down on bended knee and proposing. She would coyishly reject him and make him wait for an answer. She wore a red "Kiss me now!" T-shirt today.

Danny was happy but nervous. He didn't think he was good with girls and he didn't know how to react to Jess's enthusiasm. But he knew one thing, although he wanted to, he certainly wouldn't kiss her; not here - not today. He had a dilemma because Mrs Naylor had left early with the twins, expecting Jonathan to be there all day. Jess had been instructed to keep them well supplied with tea and cold drinks. Danny knew from his sister, Jess's feelings for him and he was flattered, but he was determined to remain distant. He couldn't risk losing his job and he couldn't risk a backlash from Simon Naylor. He had to be trusted, so he kept himself at a short distance from her and tried to read his paper.

Jonathan arrived back at work just after lunch. He'd left his mother sleeping in hospital. She was safe, but what the future held, he was uncertain. Danny was sorry about the news, but glad Jonathan was back. The stone was delivered just as Jonathan arrived so there was little time to talk. Jess disappeared.

That evening Simon admired the new stonework laid on his path as he softly walked up and down on the flagstones. Jonathan had randomly planted small clumps of Chamomile in the gravel beside them. The smell was intoxicating. Simon bent low and brushed the honey coloured stone with his hands, liking the feel and texture. Things were looking good.

Jonathan said another week would do it and it seemed like his estimate would be accurate.

Over dinner, Jess told her father how she'd helped Danny all morning raking the sand ready for the stone, and the sad news about Alice Miller having a stroke. Simon was concerned over Alice Miller, wondering if her illness would delay the refurbishment of his garden. He thought Jonathan had seemed subdued when he left that evening, but Jonathan hadn't uttered a word about his mother. Well, he couldn't, and Simon now understood why.

Simon had picked up The Mercury on his way to the office; the piece Andrea had written was good; a two page spread. There were some new pictures of the horse in her glory days, and a few well-chosen letters from readers, also an appeal from Andrea Briscoe for more information. He enthusiastically showed the paper to Melanie and Jess, but as soon as he and Melanie were alone. Melanie burst into tears.

'I couldn't play tennis today.'

'Why couldn't you play tennis?' Simon was shocked at her outburst. It was uncharacteristic.

'I don't want to talk about it.'

'What do you mean? Are you unwell?'

'No ... I'm not unwell.' And she blew her nose.

'Then please, Mel, you're not crying for nothing. What's the matter?'

'It's you and that Samantha woman.'

'What Samantha woman?'

'The woman at the papershop. They're all saying you've been flirting with her. Saying you wanted to get to know her better.'

'What!'

'Tell me the truth, Simon. What's going on?'

'Oh Mel.... Nothing's going on.... She's lying.... Making trouble.... She's like that.'

'So how do know what she's like then?'

Simon was in a corner. 'Melanie ... Melanie.... I'm sorry. I was fooling around that's all, trying to get to the truth about the white horse. I just played along with her. It was stupid ... stupid, I know.'

'This isn't like you, Simon.' Melanie started to fill the dishwasher, clattering the china. 'Then you go hanging around with Andrea Briscoe....'

'Stop it, Mel.... Stop it now.... This is ridiculous. It's village gossip - tittle-tattle. And Andrea's helping me, that's all.' Simon stood closer.

'What's the matter with you, Simon? Are you having some kind of mid-life fling?' She threw in the powder and banged the door shut.

'No.... Nothing. I love you, Mel. This is ridiculous.' He took her in his arms and she leant her head on his shoulder and relented. 'How can you believe this rubbish....? There's ill feeling in Chardwell, against me....This is all my fault, what's happened.'

'Well, some are saying you're here to cause trouble. I was so angry ... I had to walk away. And then Jess told me the friend she had, you know, that Samantha woman's daughter, she said she wouldn't speak to her. Jess reckons it's some rift over young Danny. But Jess knows something's going on, she's not stupid.'

'I don't want trouble, Mel. I want the truth, you know that. I'm fed up with these narrow-minded clowns.... It's all because of the horse, but for you I'll stop. I'll stop it now.'

'No, Simon ... it means such a lot to you.' She suddenly noticed the kitchen door still open and went to close it away from any small ears that might be listening.

'It doesn't mean as much to me as you and the children.' He shook his head.

'No, I'm sorry. I've overreacted. I should have trusted you. You must push on ... I'm being selfish. I let things fester all day. It's not everyone, it's just a few.'

Simon propped himself up in bed that night and knew he wouldn't sleep. He stared out into the darkness and he was just drifting when he became aware that the security light had come on outside. He wasn't concerned; it would be a cat or even a fox. Then he heard a noise downstairs that made him freeze, yet the need to protect his young family made him stir. Melanie sat up in bed and, from across the yard, Boris was yapping.

'Stay there, don't move.' Simon whispered.

'Oh, Simon, be careful. What is it?'

'Call the police.' He muttered as he tumbled out of bed, and then slipped on a bathrobe to cover his bare chest. Glancing quickly around the be-darkened room, he found an old silver candlestick and crept out of the bedroom.

A stench hit him first and churned his stomach. Simon was terrified. He stood motionless; his heartbeat erratic, but there was silence. Then out of the silence, he heard the noise of footsteps running across the gravel drive. Simon rushed to the window, just in time to see a shadowy figure moving quickly across the lawn. He put on every light he could find and, as he stepped down the stairs into the hallway, he could see what the smell was. Poured through his letterbox was a mass of pig slurry, oozing through the letterbox and down the front door onto the hall carpet.

Jess was standing behind him now in her pyjamas and she held onto Simon's arm. 'What will they do next, Dad? What's wrong with us...? Why don't they like us...? It's that horse isn't it. It's bringing nothing but bad luck. Danny said it would.'

'It's not bad luck, Jess. That's what they all want you to believe. There's something wrong with that horse and I'm going to dig until I find out what it is.'

Across the yard at the Garden Cottage, Lucy's light was on. She was peeping through the half-opened curtain, her head clad in yellow plastic hair rollers. Simon telephoned her straight away to pacify her, and then went across the yard to assess the damage.

By the time the police arrived, Simon could have arrested a dozen criminals single-handed. The saboteur would now be in bed and drinking his Horlicks, with a smug grin on his face.

'Not much we can do tonight, Mr Naylor.' PC Alec Langhorne said as he glanced around the oak panelled hallway and seemed to show more interest in the décor of the house and the huge oil paintings on the wall than the slurry on the carpet.

Simon thought: *not much you'll want to do, anyway.*

'You've stirred up some ill feeling, Mr Naylor.'

'I've every right to do what I want on my land.'

'You've made assertions and accusations right, left and centre. How do you expect people to react? Folks don't like being questioned.'

'Well, not in this way, that's for sure. No, they just dump muck on my house.... If folks would give straight answers there'd be no more questions,' but Simon knew it was futile.

The following morning Danny came to The Grange alone. Jonathan was still in a state of shock over his mother and didn't want to speak to anyone. He dropped Danny off at the gate and promised he'd be back later once he'd been to the hospital.

Danny was happy to be left in charge again, at least he could put some more flagstones down; a chance to shine and show he could be trusted. And as he walked up the path to The Grange to restart his job he couldn't comprehend why pig slurry was smeared all over the new flags, the garden wall, and right around the corner, over the front door. His young heart sank.

Simon was waiting at the door and Melanie was keeping low in the background, hoping to shield from the young man the dark circles under her eyes. Jess didn't appear.

'How's Jon's mother?' Simon politely asked first.

'Oh, she's survived the night.... Man alive...! What a mess. What's happened?'

Simon hovered around the young man as he threw down his tools. Danny noticed for the first time ever that Simon was unshaven.

'You wouldn't have wanted to be here last night, Danny.'

The boy rubbed his brow.

'You told Jess folks are saying we've caused trouble.... What are they saying?'

Danny was embarrassed and hesitated.

'It's alright, son.... I trust you. Just say what you've heard.'

Danny bent low and moved aside some of the clean flags, then swept away the slurry with his boot, grimacing at the smell and gasping with bending, he tried to be diplomatic. 'I'm not sure if I should say, Mr Naylor, but Jack said there was some superstition about the horse being uncovered.'

'Oh, for pities sake ... I've heard it all before. Don't tell me you're superstitious as well Danny?'

'Not a bit,' the boy shook his head.

'And Jonathan.... He's from Chardwell, isn't he? What does he say?'

'Don't know ... I've never talked to Jonathan about it. You said to keep quiet about the horse and your fall on the bank, so I did. As far as I'm concerned he doesn't even know the white horse exists.'

'Doesn't he know much local history? Doesn't he read the papers?'

'Jonathan doesn't seem to be able to get any papers these days.' And now Danny was confused but Simon was intrigued.

'What do you mean?'

'Well, Samantha said the local papers haven't come these last few mornings.'

And slowly Simon was putting a hazy outline of a picture together. 'Danny, will you help me ... I don't think I can do this alone. I need allies.'

'Anything, Mr Naylor.'

'Good. I'll get back to you. But still keep quiet, won't you.' and he winked. 'I hate to ask, but could you help me clear up this mess a bit.'

'I'll do what I can, Mr Naylor.'

Jonathan was relieved Alice had had a good night. The doctors said the next 36 hours would be critical. She was sitting up in bed as he walked in; everyone watched him. The nurses all knew Jonathan as Superman and one nudged the other as he walked in; they liked him even more in his jeans and grey marl T-shirt. An old lady beckoned him, and Jonathan smiled at her, and was about to go across and help when Alice waved and moaned louder. He stopped and went over to kiss his mother. The conversation was mostly one way.

'Have you had breakfast?'

She just nodded.

'Let me help you with your tea.' And Jonathan picked up a blue plastic feeder cup; embarrassed to do this for his mother. The elderly lady in the opposite bed continued to beckon him so Jonathan went to find a nurse. As he wandered down the corridor and took in the smell which was a strange sickly mixture of toast, talcum powder and disinfectant, he was shocked at the number of sick and elderly people; some were sitting in a day room, already dressed, some were just fragile shapes under the sheets. He was disturbed at his own naivety; his life had gone on as normal, yet everyday this was happening; all these people.

He found the nurse and went back to his mother. 'I'll see you again later. I'll go and check the house

... feed the cat.... I'll get you the paper. I'll see you tonight.'

Alice just muttered and Jonathan discerned she had just said, "yes" "yes" "yes" "no" "yes". Then she said what he thought was "be careful" then she said what he thought was "The Grange" then she said: "No horse." he didn't know what she meant; he was just relieved she didn't ask after Katie.

Simon didn't need to call Andrea Briscoe at lunchtime. His mobile rang and it was her.

'Good news and bad, Simon....'

'Go on, bad news first.'

'Two more dodgy e-mails.'

'From the same person?'

'The filthy language sounds like it. Don't worry, I've saved them.' She didn't really want to tell Simon that the threats were stronger, and she hoped he didn't ask what they said.

'Is that it then?'

'No, there's more. We've got the blasted thing the wrong way round. She should face the other way.'

Simon reached across his desk to check his newspaper from yesterday. 'No.... Surely not. How's that happened?'

'Does it really matter how...? It's just that we've been inundated with phone calls. Pensioners ringing up, jubilant that they've got one up on The Mercury.' Andrea thought it was funny but Simon couldn't laugh.

'Don't worry, Simon. We'll run another story.... Make light of it.... Have some pictures of you and me, maybe get the kids up on the bank with a cardboard cut-out of the horse, we can use captions like "*They don't know the back end of a horse from the front.*" We can turn this on its head. It'll make a better story.'

The despair in Simon's tone of voice was discernible. 'Right, so what's the good news?'

'You'll like this ... the local agricultural college phoned this morning saying, if we want help, they're interested. I spoke to the tutor. He wants you to contact him. He says he can take the horse on as a project for the students. They have trainee surveyors there. Lads who can mark her out properly, and the right way around. There are agricultural and horticultural students who he can set too on clearing the weeds. It may only take a few weeks. Think of it. Twenty or so young farmers and gardeners; all that free time. The only proviso is you provide any extra equipment and feed them. It's good advertising for the college.'

Simon wanted to weep.

Jonathan arrived at The Grange and he couldn't believe the mess; he'd never seen anything like it, but when Danny didn't offer any explanations, Jonathan was suspicious.

'Why do you think they did it?' Jonathan walked up and down the slurry-ridden path and watched Melanie still scrubbing the front door and porch. 'What a mess. Do you know anything about it, Dan? Does Simon know who did it?'

Danny just shook his head.

'Come on.... You kids know what's going on around here. Is it something to do with us? The stone chucked in the conservatory looked like it implicated us.'

'Look! I don't know anything, Jon. Okay.'

When Simon came back early from work he was glad to see Jonathan. 'Can we have a chat?'

Jonathan was worried, 'Of course.... Keep on with the paving, Danny.'

He edged to one side, away from Lucy who had just started up her turquoise Mini. She pulled up beside them and wound down the window. 'Sorry to hear about your mother, Jonathan. How is she today?'

'Well, she's had a good night.' Jonathan didn't realise Lucy knew his mother. He was bemused and Lucy interpreted his look. 'Oh, she came to visit Simon's father once.'

That was news to Simon.

Jonathan continued: 'Here...! My mother came here? It's just that she hardly ever leaves the house unless she's with me. She's very lame as it is,' and he stopped himself from saying: "*she does all her contriving from home these days.*" Yet, it didn't surprise Jonathan that his mother hadn't mentioned coming to The Grange. They never talked about trivialities.

'Oh yes, dear. I know she's lame, but she came with Barney's Taxis. She's a lovely woman - lovely. I'll get her some flowers.' Lucy wound up the window and both men stood and watched her edge precariously out of the driveway, waiting for the screech of brakes as they always did when Lucy left the premises.

'Can you come inside, Jonathan, please?'

156

Jonathan lifted his heels and checked his boots were clean as he entered and followed Simon to the kitchen.

Simon went to fill the kettle. 'I'm sorry about your mother, Jon.'

'I think she's over the worst. I hope....' Jonathan looked about him at the fine house, noticing how good the garden looked from the view out of the huge kitchen window.

'What's the damage?' Simon had true empathy in his voice.

'One side.... The usual, you know ... speech and paralysis. The nurses are confident some use will come back, but whether she'll ever get home - that, I don't know.'

'Sit down please, Jon.' Simon had compassion on his face and gestured towards the kitchen chair. 'This mess - this slurry. Danny's worked hard today, I don't know what we'd have done without him, but can you do anything to clean the stains off the stone? I'm sorry to have to ask. I'll see you right.'

'No, that's okay. I don't mind a bit of muck. I can try a power-washer. I'll bring it tomorrow if you like. Should bring most of it off but it might leave a small stain. We could get some masonry cleaner, that might work, or as a last resort, maybe get some people in to sand blast it, but that would be expensive.'

'Can you try the power-washer please, Jon.'

'If nothing else, you may have to leave the rest to the elements and see how she goes. A hot summer and a wet winter might do it.'

Simon cringed at the thought of all his beautiful stonework being corrupted in such a way.

'Er … is there a problem, Simon? I've never had anyone sabotage my work before. Though some might have wanted to.'

'Don't worry, Jon. I have an idea who dunnit ... and it's nothing to do with you, or for you to worry about. But if you can help me clean it, I'd be grateful. No, I really wanted to ask you if you're still running for charity?'

'Running!' His relief was apparent. 'Well, yes and no.... I've an idea I might do a half-marathon this weekend.'

'Still keeping busy then?'

Jonathan didn't mention his plan was to retire from the running, but what was the use, now his wife was gone, he may as well carry on. So he just nodded and took the mug of tea Simon had handed him.

'You've done a good job here. You've nearly finished.'

Jonathan was pleased one thing was going well.

'There's something I want to ask you about running, charity work and all that. I want to pick your brains.... You'll have to bring your wife around one night, we'll have a drink. Yes, bring your wife.... What's her name?'

'Katie.'

'Yes, bring Katie.'

Jonathan stared; not a muscle in his face moved. He thought Simon seemed happily married, a bit older than him with a young family; everything in his hands. And what Jonathan said next, he couldn't help; there was no holding it in any longer. He'd unburden his problems, wisely or foolishly, to this new client.

'I don't think my wife will come out with me anymore.' He sipped his drink as Simon stood over him. 'She's gone.... Well, we've split up.... You know how it is. But never mind that....What did you want to ask me?'

'And I thought I had problems.' And Simon couldn't burden Jonathan with any more. 'We could maybe discuss some regular maintenance work. I can do the lawns myself ... I'll enjoy using the ride-on, but I don't have a clue about the garden.'

That evening Jonathan phoned Barney to tell him about his mother. Barney had already heard and he was sorry. Alice had been his best fundraiser. She had done all the paper work; she was the brains, and Jonathan had done the legwork.

Barney asked if he could help and Jonathan just suggested a visit; maybe ask some of the kids to send cards; draw some pictures; she would like that.

'I've been thinking about a half-marathon this weekend.'

'I thought your mother said you were retiring.'

'I was....'

'Was, as in past tense?'

'As in, yes. I want to raise a bit of cash for the hospital. I couldn't believe it how many old folks were in there. The place needs help. I can't do any more for my mum, except visit, but the hospital needs cash. By the way. When did you take my mother to The Grange?'

The long silence aroused suspicion.

'I can't remember taking her to The Grange.'

'Well, you, or someone in your taxi did.'

'Must have been me then. Oh, I remember now, she said she wanted to meet up with Lucy.'

'Ah.' And Jonathan relented and rang Katie.

CHAPTER 14

Alice Miller would never go home again. She would have to stay in hospital for some time, until all the rehabilitation she could do was done. She would have physio on her arms and legs, but she would never walk again. She could squeeze the soft rubber ball they gave her in her weak and swollen hand, but only just. The speech therapy helped a little, but words were still disjointed and Alice would eventually have to go into a nursing home. She wasn't too troubled by this because she'd been struggling at home as it was. She hadn't told Jonathan and he hadn't noticed. The good thing was the promise that he'd visit her daily, and could spend more time with her because he wouldn't be chopping firewood, getting the coal in, or shopping. And then of course Katie would come too, but not with Jonathan; they would never arrive together.

Alice couldn't trouble herself about them anymore.

She didn't know that Jonathan had moved into her house where he'd been reared, and Katie was back in their marriage home, still alone, apart from Moses. She didn't know Katie had apologised to Jonathan and deeply regretted her actions, yet still had a troubled mind and a prideful spirit and insisted they stay separate.

Jonathan never begged Katie to get back together, if he had have done, she might have listened to him, but Jonathan's spirit was crushed and he just capitulated.

Going back to their home was a huge step as it was for Katie. She agreed to keep their failing marriage a secret from Alice as Jonathan had insisted. That grated on her, but it was his wish. She'd pleaded with him to get things out in the open but Jonathan worried it would finish his mother. Katie couldn't understand his secrecy, it was almost deceit. She was used to intimate talk; well, she was a woman. She had always confided in her mother and friends at work, and they all said she was crazy to leave Jonathan, as many wished they had him, but Katie just said they didn't know what he was like to live with.

Neither could Katie understand Jonathan's relationship with his mother; they'd always been the same. When Katie first met him and he eventually proposed, it took him months to tell Alice. If he'd failed any of his exams, he could never tell Alice; if he'd lost a client or given up in a race, he never told Alice. He never told her of any disappointments, only good things. Jonathan didn't understand the concept of an open and frank relationship and Alice was just the same. She didn't tell Jonathan many things, and often there became an uncomfortable situation between them when one or the other found out. It drove Katie crazy. The silence was worse.

Danny didn't ask any more questions as to Katie's whereabouts but guessed what the trouble was between them, and kept silent. The job at The Grange was completed, the slurry was, in the main, removed from the stone, the planting finished and the garden looked stunning and Danny and Jonathan were back to cutting grass for every member of the

Chardwell Women's Institute. Alice's friends supported them well.

Jonathan ran a half-marathon for the cottage hospital and raised £1,200. He'd disagreed with Barney and said he couldn't – wouldn't – run as Superman, he felt anything but super, and for the first time ever, Barney failed to persuade him. He'd said: 'The kids always love you as Superman ... and so do the women. You'll raise more cash that way.' But it was all to no avail.

Jess liked her father's idea to get the horse restored. She was told about the twenty young farmers and surveyors coming to help, and swiftly, in Danny's absence, wavered in her love for him as twenty young farmers beckoned. In her mind Danny appeared immature, but in her heart it was really his complacency with her, that he'd snubbed her, and never tried to kiss her when he could have. She had wanted him too much.

Danny sensed her dis-interest, and felt hurt. He knew he couldn't compete with twenty young farmers. What an irony that now as the job was finished at The Grange, he could have legitimately asked Jess out. He wondered how he could possibly wheedle his way back into her life; surely, Simon Naylor wouldn't mind him seeing Jess, if he dated her properly.

One evening Jess was over to see his sister, and Danny wanted to ask her out. But Jess had started to tease him in front of their friends and his sister, even laughing at him, pretending she was happy, and acting as if she could live without him. He would have to do all the chasing. Yet, despite her showy display, that evening she begged him for a lift home. And, as they drove home alone, not speaking and the car CD player booming, she turned it off and asked him something: 'Dad wants you to pop in sometime to see him.'

'Why?'

'Some stuff about the white horse.... He said you'd promised to help.'

'I did....' Danny slowed down as he drove the twisty lanes back to Chardwell. 'Jess.... Now that I'm not at The Grange...' he stopped the car in the lay-by, 'I was wondering...'

Jess's heart was racing because she guessed he was trying to make a move and the realisation of it was nerve racking. She was shaking. She must keep calm.

'What have you stopped for?' She managed to keep up the charade.

He twisted around in the car seat, leant across, took her head in his hands and tried to kiss her, but she pulled away. 'Oh, come on Jess. I know you want to.'

'Don't Danny ... I don't want to.' She lied.

He sat frustrated; sorry he'd been snubbed. He felt foolish; stupid even. He was about to restart the engine when she turned to him. 'I maybe will consider a date, Danny.... Do it proper, like ... but will you do one thing for me?'

At that moment in time, he would do anything.

'Will you talk to Jonathan....? Dad wanted to ask him if he'd help raise some funds for the horse, but then he heard about his problems and didn't want to worry him anymore. But he needs the help, Danny; he can't do this on his own.'

'Oh, I don't know, Jess. Jon's never in such a good mood these days.'

'I thought you wanted to take me out!' and she pretended to sulk.

'I do ... I do....'

She turned and this time held his face and kissed him.

'Then talk to Jonathan, please ... please ... please ... do it for me.'

Later that evening Danny called at Jonathan's house and he was surprised to find Katie at home. She didn't invite him in but just stood on the doorstep, her hair dishevelled and she was wearing a sloppy cardigan that hung around her slim body and some tracksuit bottoms that had seen better days. She just said: 'Jon's at his mother's place.'

'Oh....' And Danny reluctantly backed away and left, not coming up with anything constructive to say and drove to Alice's house.

Jonathan heard the turbo engine of Danny's car as it came up the street. He was ready for awkward questions and was glad he was already dressed to go out training.

'Can I ask you something?' Danny leant on the front porch.

Jonathan hung his head around the front door but unlike Katie, was pleased to see the boy, but if he stayed too long, it would be too dark to run. This time he was invited in.

'What's up? Do you want a sub?'

'No....' Danny fidgeted.

'Come on spit it out....' Jonathan sat on the sofa and started to tie his running shoes.

'Well, I wondered if I could come running with you.'

'What?' Jonathan was stunned.

'I need to build myself up a bit, get fitter, you know.'

'I'm sorry ... is this a wind-up?'

'No, I need to raise some cash and you earn loads of money running don't you?'

'Not for myself, dummy. Any way I don't always raise "loads" of cash.'

'It's not for me.... It's to help someone else.' Danny was hurt.

'A charity you mean. You - help a charity?' Jonathan observed the young man, clean-shaven, clear and healthy eyes; he was always dressed in pristine condition, with every designer label he could afford. Today he was wearing jogging pants that had never intended to be jogged in, Danny may have played football in them but that's all. On his feet were trainers that would have cost the earth, but would never be comfortable in a marathon.

'You want to come now, then?'

'Yeh, sure.'

Danny didn't like doing the stretches Jonathan taught him but he'd insisted they couldn't run without them, he felt foolish standing in Alice's back garden, stretching his limbs. He was glad the wall was high. They ran together slowly at first, Jonathan was glad of the company. He talked as they ran, but Danny barely replied, and a "yes" or a "no" was all he could manage as he gasped for air.

166

They jogged along the lane to The Grange, glancing at the new garden as they ran by, looking over the hedge to see if Simon had cut the grass, and he had.

'One push to the top of the bank.' Jonathan mumbled as they ran.

They leapt the stile and Jonathan jogged slowly up the stony path and waited on the seat at the top for the boy.

Danny was walking when he arrived at the summit, grabbing at strands of bracken and tall weeds to pull him up. He fell on the bench, breathing heavily, looking down the steep bank, wondering why he was doing this. 'How do you do that? Get up here so fast?'

'Training....' Jonathan said; he would let the young man rest.

Then with renewed vigour Danny started to question Jonathan. 'You know about the chalk horse under this cliff, that Simon wants to restore?' Danny pointed to the bank below them as he leant forward to rest his back.

'What chalk horse?'

'Ah right ... I see "*what chalk horse,*" eh. You're playing dumb?'

'What are you on about?'

'You must know about the chalk horse, Jonathan, don't lie.'

'I'm not lying ... I don't know what you're talking about. You must be delirious with the running.'

'Oh, I get it.... You're in league with the butcher and the baker.'

'Who?'

'Look, Jon....' Danny untied one of his trainers, and pulled it off and rubbed his foot, 'either you're stupid, or you've been living on another planet for these last few weeks.'

'Stop ... stop.... Just a minute. What's this all about?'

'Well, I wouldn't have believed that you were in on it. You of all people.'

'In on what?'

Danny shook his head, disappointed that Jonathan too was obviously against the horse and he intended not to say another word about it, and shoved his trainer back on and said: 'Right, let's run.' But then Jonathan wouldn't leave it and stood with his hands on his hips looking down. 'Is this something to do with you raising money? Danny, I do want to help you, but I honestly don't know what you're talking about.'

'You're not superstitious then?'

'Superstitious. No, why?'

And now Danny really believed that Jonathan was in complete ignorance. 'How long have you lived in Chardwell?' He knew the answer, but he just had to be sarcastic.

'I was born here.'

'Amazing...!'

'Why...? Oh come on let's run.' But this time Danny stopped, and he stepped a few paces down the bank. 'Can you see that clearing there, where the rock's exposed. That's the remains of a white horse ... a hillside carving ... a chalk horse.'

Jonathan leant over and could just see the patch, deep in the undergrowth.

'Simon Naylor told me all about it.' Danny persisted.

'Then why didn't you tell me?'

'Well, it was none of your business. Besides, Simon told me to keep stum. There's some trouble in the village about it. That's why they had the garden vandalised, and the stone through the window. Anyway, you've had your mind on other things these last few weeks. My discussions with Simon were in my private time, so don't worry. They're getting twenty lads in from the agricultural college to help clear it. They'll do the labour but he needs some cash. I'd like to help.... He said he would value my help. I'll do it in my spare time, a freebie, you know. So do you fancy helping, we need someone to supervise and we need to raise some money.'

Jonathan thought of all the times he'd run up on this path and didn't know about the horse. He watched Danny playfully slither about on the gravel obviously ready for another run.

'Well then?'

'Well what?'

'Will you help?'

'Dan....' Jonathan held his hand out to the boy to encourage him back up the bank. 'Let's go before we get cold.'

Danny never stopped talking after that. He told Jonathan the size, and all the dimensions, of how she'd been covered over in the war. He didn't tell Jonathan about the e-mails. Jess had told him to be careful of negative talk.

'Did you never get to see any newspapers?'

'No, it seems I've been banned from reading the papers - remember.'

And Danny knew that was true. 'So, will you help?'

'Look, Dan.... I run for worthy causes ... kids that are sick, cancer charities, the hospital ... I don't do buildings.'

'It's not a building.'

'Well, what is it, then?'

'It's an ancient monument.'

'A monument…! There's nothing there!'

'Leucippotomy, they call it.'

'Lucy what?'

'Well, it's an ancient art … a hillside carving. An artefact, then. They're all over England. Please, Jon, please help us. You're not doing much these days. Just do one run with me. Together we'll raise some cash. Please help him, Jon.'

'Leave it, Dan....'

'Just do this one.... Then I'll ask no more.'

'Shut up Danny. I've heard enough.' And he stepped up the pace and left the boy standing.

As Jonathan showered he was brooding. He'd enjoyed Danny's company, despite the argument; that was nothing new, they were always arguing about football, jobs to do, money. They'd had a beer together sitting on the sofa, with their feet up on Alice's coffee table and watched the rest of a football match. Alice's place was starting to change; somehow, the chintz wallpaper and anaglypta didn't fit with Jonathan's life style. A few magazines were scattered about and a large green rubber plant was wilting in the corner. Danny had written in the dust on the television: 'Clean me.'

They agreed to run together every other night and Jonathan laughed, thinking he would never keep it up. He recalled Danny's crazy story about a white horse buried under the bank and believed it was just some wild notion. Jonathan had been born in Chardwell, schooled in Chardwell, worked in Chardwell and knew nothing of it. His mother never spoke of it; no one ever did. He thought it wasn't like Danny to lie to him and, if this was true, he was dismayed at his lack of knowledge. He was pleased the boy was interested in running; to help get him fit would keep him out of trouble. He knew when the next race would be and wondered if he could get him signed up and fit by then; it was only 10k. Then he felt guilty at the way he'd ridiculed him over the "white horse" story. He would like to help Simon Naylor. Simon had been good to him. He had settled up the final invoice as promised and on time and even had a contract to do the borders at The Grange once a month and that was just enough. He liked working at The Grange and Danny was right, he wasn't doing much with his life.

He stopped the shower, and for the first time in weeks, felt he had something to look forward to; he would help the boy.

Jonathan dried himself and went to find something to eat. The cupboards were almost empty; he must go shopping. The TV was dreary, so he decided to tidy away a few things; the housekeeper was coming back tomorrow and he didn't want her to know he was living there, and didn't want her to tell Alice about any mess. He stuffed some of his mother's mail in her desk: endless catalogues and brochures for clothes she would buy but never wear. He had already opened some other letters, he had to arrange Power of Attorney any way, and Alice would never spend her own money again except on bills for the nursing home. Jonathan knew where Alice kept all her documents; she'd told him a hundred times: "If anything ever happens to me," and he always joked with her. "What will happen, Mum? Are you going to get taken by aliens or turn into a werewolf," and Alice would scold him for ridiculing her, but she loved him to tease her.

He found the documents he needed for the solicitor and while he had the opportunity started to browse through all her other stuff: bank statements, stocks and shares, building society statements. He raised his eyebrows at the figures and yet he knew as soon as she went into the nursing home it would diminish. Thankfully, Alice had been astute years ago and had already signed her house over to him. At least that was safe. Jonathan became absorbed as he discovered things about his mother that he never knew; she was certainly a good businesswoman. As he sat at her desk, flicking through papers, rubbing his head at others, finding endless insurance documents, he became absorbed. As he peeled open one old envelope, loose photographs and letters fell in his hand, all yellowed with age. His heart shuddered when he read the private papers. And something in their content made him grieve even more for his ailing mother. He composed himself and rang Danny.

'Tell Simon, I'll do it.'

Danny, flat on his bed, jumped up and paced around the bedroom. He rang Jess on his mobile and knew he now had a girlfriend.

'He'll do it, Jess.'

'Are you sure?'

'Well, he argued as usual and complained he didn't know a thing about it but I know he'll help. I went running with him tonight and he's already agreed to train with me every other night. So can we go out then?'

'Yes, yes, you can take me bowling this weekend. Oh Danny, this is great.... You are sure he'll help with the horse?'

'Yes, Yes, Yes, Yes. He always does this; moans and says he's not going to do anything, but if I act stupid, he always feels obliged to help. Yes, he said he would do it Jess. So where can I pick you up. Can I come and get you now?'

There was silence. 'Jess, are you still there. What's wrong?'

'Nothing....' she was reticent, 'it's just that I think we should keep quiet about us. For now, anyway.'

'Why...? I'm not really working for your dad any more. And Jon won't notice.'

'Then let's just meet in the park near the monument, please, Danny.'

'You'll have to tell your dad sometime, or are you scared what he'll say?'

'Er . . . no!'

But she was.

CHAPTER 15

In clandestine fashion, the Chardwell White Horse Committee met in a pub on the outskirts of Skipton, far away from Chardwell. The members were: Simon Naylor, Sam Parkinson, Andrea Briscoe, Danny Wytherstone and Jonathan Miller. The strategy was as follows:

The work should start on the horse immediately with Simon as Chairman. Andrea would be chief researcher and with Jonathan's know-how, find more sponsors. Sam would provide background information and Jonathan would also be Project Manager with Danny as his assistant. Some of the times and dates were planned to coincide with the students and, for Jonathan and Danny, most of the work would have to be done on evenings and weekends.

Simon was nervous. He'd pushed this horse so far and in a short time, and was finally beginning to achieve something, but he felt uneasy, contemplating the trouble it could conjure up. Jonathan too wondered what crazy mood had driven him to agree to help; yet he hoped the voluntary work on the horse would be a good advertising platform. He had little time to delve into the history of Chardwell's White Horse and little desire, his function was to organise and advise on the work, and hope some of his sponsors would have a change of heart and support a very different project. With Barney's help, that could happen.

*   *   *

On Danny's first half-marathon he hit the wall early. The lactic acid in his legs made them feel like they weighed an extra stone. He lost all thoughts of finishing, and the mood swings that Jonathan had warned him about were kicking in: Was it worth it? This wasn't for him, and he couldn't do it. He didn't have faith in his own abilities, yet he had trained with Jonathan day and night. He was certainly fitter than he'd ever been in his young life. Jonathan had told him to start slow and go slower, he'd thought he'd done that, and he couldn't go much slower. Jonathan had said that running was a mind - thing as much as a physical one and to split the race, theoretically, into small sections and it would be easier. None of this was working. But Jonathan was patient and had run by his side, encouraging him to go on.

Melanie and Jess had already started selling t-shirts and coffee mugs on the internet and now had a stall of bric-a-brac in the market place, close to where the race ended. The Mercury had an advert every night for White Horse Memorabilia and, today, Jonathan and Danny ran in the new White Horse t-shirts: black with the sketchy outline of the horse on the front.

Several girls whistled and called at them as they ran. Spurred on by the admiration, Danny continued, but around the next corner away from the public, he stopped and put his hands on his hips.

'You okay…?' Jonathan had to walk back towards him and gasped beside him. 'There's only 4k to go. Pass through this last 2k and it'll get easier. You'll run on adrenalin after that.'

Danny was muttering something that could have been a swear word, when a group of girls dressed in Rocky Horror costumes passed and whistled. And so he started running again.

'Are your feet okay?' Jonathan said; his face red with exertion and the short strands of his blonde hair, damp and straggly at the ends. He was running slowly, and he knew if he left Danny to run alone he would stop.

'It's not just my feet.' Danny jogged on and he too wondered what moment of madness he'd had to allow himself to come up with this scheme in the first place. He wondered how Jonathan could do this for so many years when he too clearly suffered in every race.

As they slowly jogged another 2k, Jonathan was proved right and Danny did break through the wall and they left The Rocky Horror show standing. They passed some student doctors dressed in white theatre gowns and some lads from the rugby club. Danny suddenly started to feel the adrenalin surge that Jonathan had promised, and it felt so good.

Through the finishing line, Danny spotted Jess and heard her screaming words of encouragement. He was ecstatic, yet he felt like he would die. He wanted to fall to the ground but resisted and bent low resting his hands on his thighs. Jonathan stayed with him all the time.

Someone handed them water. Danny poured it over his head and the next thing he knew, Jess was with him, kissing and hugging him. Now he remembered why he had done it, and he worried where Simon was.

*   *   *

Work began on the horse on the first week in July; the twenty students promised were down to eleven. Jonathan wasn't surprised, but Simon was disappointed. There were four girls and seven young men, all enthusiastic. The college had backed out under protest and not wanting to stir discontent and remain neutral to public interest, relented. But several students, bent on making a name for themselves, forged forward in their spare time. Jess was aggrieved that the students didn't arrive before she left for school but, as usual, planned to hurry home in a hope that they would still be on site, but school holidays were fast approaching and the chance to make new friends; new male friends was her foremost thought; and her love for Danny was being put to the test.

Simon took two weeks off work and gave a safety meeting every morning. Hard hats were distributed and Simon gave constant reminders for all to be careful. Ropes and harnesses were used as an extra precaution. Only four people would work on the horse at any one time, the others would act as anchors.

The surveying was the first job, and re-pegging out and marking the boundaries, Simon knew his initial estimate of the boundary was flawed and, of course, the wrong way around, and he was frustrated at his misconception. He'd seen her under moonlit skies, just as Sam had said, and now she would face in the opposite direction. He started to wonder himself if all he'd seen was just pure imagination: a mirage. He'd sweat over the plans day and night and re-read the letters to The Mercury. He was certain he

177

was right, yet its precise location niggled at him. He recalled his fall when he tried to bury Midge. Then when he and Danny had found the eye, Simon realised it was the same place, but as he looked at the new marker posts he guessed where he had fallen was near the back end of the horse and the shaley rock wasn't even part of the body.

He discussed his overriding thoughts with Sam, who agreed with him; it was always the way he remembered her. This was surely a scheme by someone to sabotage their plan. Then a deeper memory came to Sam as he recalled the last attempt to uncover her in the 70's and there had been a dispute then as to which way she stood; some had resisted, saying it would be unlucky to have her face the other way and some of the team back then campaigned hard to restore what Sam believed to be the right way.

And so Simon spoke to one of the surveyors.

'I want to change it. Before we get too far.'

The young man sighed and called a halt.

'I know everyone says this is the wrong way around. I don't care what some might say. She'll stand this way – the way I saw her. I want you to re-mark her. It'll give folks something to talk about. This is my project and I can ride my mare whichever way I like. Her head will face west.'

And so it was achieved: three days work surveying, pegging out and realigning.

Jonathan, Danny and Simon worked together on the evenings when the students had gone home, tirelessly scrabbling about on the rocky slope, relying on the ropes when they needed to, crawling about on hands and knees, walking easily on the flatter parts. They knocked in each marker with small mallets, their wrists aching with every blow. Simon's soft, pen-pusher's hands were blistered and torn by the end of each day.

The reams of old netting were found and peeled off and thrown to the bottom of the bank, leaving a clear area that was full of nettles and brambles that had spread since 1945. No one was pushed to work, they were all volunteers, but all worked happily and willingly.

Sam sat at the bench at the top of the bank every day; he never missed; he was the first to arrive and the last to leave and despite his age, appeared to have more conviction than most. And then, piece-by-piece, some of the stone was revealed.

The bulk of the weeds were strimmed off, where it was safe to do so, and then they sprayed the land with weed killer.

Sam had said the initial sculpturing had taken four men four days, but Simon couldn't beat that, even with his army of workers.

Melanie spent whole weekends baking and making meals and storing them in the freezer for her army of workers, bringing teas and cold drinks up and down the lane in the 4x4. Sam generously supplied fish and chips and take-aways, if the work went on later into the evening.

Jess was always on hand when she was off school and Danny started to feel jealous of her interest in the seven male students; their dating was hit and miss.

After several days, a head emerged, then the belly, but the legs were badly defined and hard to discern. Every day if Simon drove through the valley, he would stop in the lay-by and view her from a distance, but he was always disappointed.

Jonathan had said to be patient and let the weed killer and the sun do its work. They would leave her bare for a few weeks and give them chance to rest their tired limbs.

Andrea Briscoe continued to receive abusive e-mails but, slowly, as the Chardwell folk realised this horse was going to be completed, the support finally came in: the hairdresser's, the building society, the teashop and a local B and B. People were already starting to drive through Chardwell and use its facilities. Simon posted an information board with leaflets on the lane under the hill, along with a contribution box. The post office agreed to sell more t-shirts and beakers.

It was then that Alice Miller stopped speaking altogether. Whatever Jonathan said to her was ignored; she just sat like a rag doll, droopy eyed. Not that he discussed much with her. He didn't want her to worry about issues he didn't want to worry about himself. He had questions about this project on the White Horse that he didn't want to ask in case he might not like the answers, but what did it matter anymore. He feared that the two people he loved more than anything, he was soon going to lose. There was no point in worrying Alice about his divorce. He still hadn't told her he'd moved back to her house and was now resident in his old bedroom where he'd slept as a boy. He couldn't move into his mother's bedroom, despite there being more space, and although Jonathan knew she'd never return home, he just couldn't bring himself to do it. At least Alice could die with one less worry. But Alice's manner with him troubled him. She clung to his hands and all he could do was to speak softly and quietly to her, reassuring her. And yet, neither opened their hearts as to what was really on their minds, there was an unspoken understanding of each other's plight.

When Jonathan had told Katie about his work on the horse she wasn't surprised and the roller-coaster he'd put her on, was still rolling. He'd once said that wild horses wouldn't drag him away from her, but this one was. He'd promised he would change and he hadn't. Oh yes, he'd paid the bills on time and kept her financially secure, but he still spent all his free time visiting his mother or at The Grange or out running with Danny. She couldn't see how anything could heal this rift.

And then the rain came, the wettest summer for forty years. Money was slow coming in for Jonathan, and he hated working in the rain. He knew his clients would call and tell him not to come, but what could he live on if he didn't work in the rain. He would ignore the telephone if it rang before he left for work and hope, when he got to a job, the rain would either stop or the client would find him something else to do. Jack Albright was unemployed, but he didn't mind because he still had his pension. Danny worked with Jonathan when they could, in rain soaked clothes; their boots coated and weighed down with mud. Danny was glad of one day a week at college but if it rained that day, he pitied Jonathan.

As for Simon, well the rain meant more worry. The horse was exposed and was ugly. There was still a lot to do and fine edges needed realigning. The remaining weeds on the horse were dying quickly and it turned Simon's ugly horse, yellow. But the wet weather leached out much of the weed killer and then encouraged more to grow, and Jonathan had to re-spray the whole of the horse again.

As the rain fell heavily one evening Simon felt like he had a sick child and he worried for his mare out on the hillside; and this was the middle of summer; goodness knows how he would feel as winter lurked. He found himself regularly watching the weather forecast and looking at the sky, just as Sam had said. He became an expert at reading the barometer, but there was nothing he could do. From a distance his white horse was like a yellow and brown image that a child had drawn; there was no sophistication in her and Simon was disappointed, hoping as soon as they could work on her they would get the lines just as she was before. He was now responsible for other people's money and he had to be careful how he spent it. One particular night the rain fell in torrents and at five in the morning Simon was awake and out walking under the bank. Floods of water had washed over the horse, dragging muck and gravel down the hill, leaving deep rifts on the body and totally removing the tail and the two back legs. She looked alien and totally illegible. And so he talked to Sam.

'What can I do, Sam?'

'When the snow comes and the thaw, it'll just be the same, Simon. Your father had the idea of putting some terracing across her. Boarding up areas to stop the erosion, and holding the worst of an avalanche.'

And then came the same question: 'Why didn't you tell me this before, Sam?'

'If I'd have told you everything, you wouldn't have started.'

Simon thought: *too right.*

'But she'll look like a zebra, if we put boarding across her.'

'You won't see it from across the valley. She'll be like an impressionist painting.'

'Well, I'll see it. Besides, how much would it cost, and plus all the extra work. I can't expect Jonathan to keep flogging his guts out all the time and I don't know if the students will want to stay much longer. It would be more time consuming and I wanted her finished by autumn.... Is there anything else you're not telling me, Sam?'

But Sam said nothing because he didn't want to lie.

The boarding was expensive but Jonathan agreed it was the only way; more hard work driving posts in, crawling about on their hands and knees in the gravel, tapping in by hand the pegs and boards and levelling out the shale. The terracing from close up did nothing to improve the look of this ugly horse, but Sam was right; from the valley you couldn't see any trace of them. Simon read articles of how the Chinese and other races used terracing to utilise their land and it was done just the same. It was then that Simon yearned for his father's wisdom. The loss was hitting him hard and more grieving came. Melanie was compassionate and knew he was tired and disappointed and she became a source of strength. She said not to give in, and he wouldn't.

Katie saw little of Jonathan, but one evening, she heard the doorbell ring. She set the piece of toast she was eating down on a saucer, grabbed a cardigan and went to the door, but there was no one there. Then the phone rang, but the caller hung up, and then it rang again, but this time the caller remained stony silent. The number was always withheld. For one crazy moment, she thought it was Jonathan fooling around, but night after night, it continued. She stopped answering the phone and all the time wishing Jonathan was here. But pride once again stopped her from calling him. One morning she got up for work and found a tin of white emulsion paint tipped on the windscreen of her car. She called the police.

The young officer she spoke to was concerned, but could do nothing. He suggested she rang BT to monitor her calls. Katie had had enough, so she took Moses and went back to her mother's. When Jonathan found out, he was incensed. He called to see PC Langhorne who only enforced what the young policeman had said. He told Jonathan he was stirring up trouble; what did he expect.

Jonathan had always been popular in Chardwell for his charity work but he too started to notice a definite turn in loyalty by some of the villagers and it puzzled him. The morning's run to work took him to the paper shop and the cake shop. And it was Samantha Shakeshaft that first troubled him, as Jonathan realised she only gave him newspapers when it suited. Jonathan even suspected Samantha was trying to avoid him and that wasn't like her; Jonathan usually had to try and escape her constant flirting. Danny had also become an object of abuse by the local police. He was constantly being stopped, yes, he had done some dubious cruising in the past but, now, with his new found running skills and his charity work, he had other things to waste his petrol on; and then there was Jess. One evening they were out together, secretly driving to a quiet location where Simon couldn't spot them, when they were stopped. There was never anything wrong with his car to justify the police pulling him up and hounding him, but Danny was always told to get out of the car. He was sick of PC Langhorne being on his back but afraid if he complied Jess would think him weak, so he refused.

'Just get out of the car, lad.'

'There's nothing wrong with the car and you know it!'

But, as Danny sat defiant, Alec Langhorne wandered to the back of the car and pulling his asp from his uniform, flicked it open and smashed it onto the rear light. 'Get out of the car, NOW...!'

Consequently, they were always looking over their shoulders; every one of the team was suspicious, but all determined. Jonathan felt as Simon did; he wouldn't be coerced or blackmailed by anyone, whoever it was.

One evening, Jonathan and Danny worked with the students on the last of the boarding. Jonathan walked to the summit for more boards and saw Sam asleep on the bench at the top of the bank. He smiled at the old man. If money were paid for hours they'd spent on site, then Sam would earn the most.

Sam stirred as he heard Jonathan sorting through the boards and watched him for a while.

When Jonathan looked up he saw Sam wakened, so he went across and sat beside him. 'Go home, Sam. You've had enough.'

'I'm okay.' The old man rubbed his eyes. 'How's it going?'

'Well enough.'

'Many more to do?'

'I don't think we'll get it done tonight. But tomorrow the lads can finish it.'

'Is everything alright with it, Jon?'

'What do you mean?'

'Ah ... nothing.'

And Sam stood to leave. 'Be careful Jonathan, won't you.'

'Sam.... We're all careful. Always. But what are you so worried about?'

'Is it that obvious?'

'Yes, it is.'

'Have you not spoken to your mother about this?' Sam lowered his eyes, and deep furrows on his brow appeared.

His reply was hesitant. 'Er… should I...?'

'Yes, you should and I don't want to be responsible, Jon,' and he turned.

Jonathan watched Sam walk away and became heavy in heart. He glanced down at the horse below and could see Danny waiting for him. He smiled at the boy and took a deep breath.

Jonathan wasn't a regular at The Three Feathers, but Katie had agreed to meet him there one evening for dinner and talk on neutral ground; not a talk of concessions or pleas, but a talk on how the divorce would go. The meal was ordered and it was an age arriving and an uncomfortable silence struck them. Their eight years of a marriage had been colourful but in forty-five minutes waiting for two steaks, it appeared as nothing. She told him about the paint and Jonathan tried to piece together what this was all about. Then the landlord, Graham Langhorne, tore a strip off him.

'It's no good wining and dining while your mother's critical in hospital.'

They were harsh words and Jonathan gritted his teeth. And for the first time in weeks, Katie had empathy for him.

'I saw her before I came out.' Jonathan had to defend himself. Then looking at the meal that was set before him he said: 'I ordered well-done.'

'Not by my instructions.' And Graham Langhorne threw two sachets of mustard on the table. 'And what are you wasting your time on that hillside for, when kids are dying.' And Jonathan wanted to say: *and what have you ever done to help the kids that are dying?* knowing full well, in all the years he'd been running that Graham Langhorne had never coughed up a penny.

'That old mare will be rubble in Simon Naylor's back yard before the winter's out. You're wasting public money.'

'Aye, and none of yours.' Jonathan said. He knew the publicity that the horse had cultivated was bringing folks to Chardwell, and no doubt The Three Feathers. 'And what kind of service do you Langthornes provide when your brother, the police constable, ignores paint being chucked on my wife's car and you can't even get my order right.'

Katie cringed at his words.

'Enjoy your steak, Jonathan, because it'll be the last one you get here.'

All the boards were put in place and the stone levelled. Simon knew she was near completion. The students finished and Jonathan and Danny agreed to work on the perimeter fence. They'd turfed the sketchy edges to define the shape and at last, the horse appeared as elegant as she was in all the old photographs. All the yellowed weeds were removed from the body and the bare rock was finally revealed, but the eye was still to be made. Simon believed she was neater and better defined than ever, but he still had a niggling thought that had bothered him for weeks now. As Simon drove home, he stopped his car in the lay-by and looked at his folly from across the valley; the sky ahead was thundery behind the horse and dark clouds loomed. It had been showery all day. His fear that the rain would cause more erosion would put his boards to the test. Simon hoped his father's contribution and his idea would work. He sighed heavily; he would have to speak to Sam and all in the committee, because his chalky white horse was actually a grubby and dappled grey mare.

CHAPTER 16

'We'll have to paint it!' Sam insisted, cupping his beer glass in his hand.

Simon threw his body back in the chair, exasperated, and Jonathan had his head in his hands. Danny was at the bar buying more drinks. Andrea Briscoe had a pen, paper and a calculator in her hand.

'How can you paint a ploughed field, Sam?' Simon felt cheated.

'Well, how about chalk chippings. We can get them from the quarry.' Jonathan said, determined as ever not to give up.

'It's been tried before, but can you imagine the cost. How many tons do we need?'

Simon shuffled through his file and found some of the old documents. 'Thirty tons, it says here.' And he continued to flick through the pages of his folder at a loss, as if searching would reveal some hidden advice – anything – even some help his father had written that he'd missed. There were a few notes in his handwriting that Simon had clipped to the documents, all of little relevance, but they would be kept purely because it was a reminder of his father. He continued glancing through the documents only half-looking and half-listening to what the others were saying.

'No, chippings won't do.' Sam said, much to Simon's relief. 'It was tried before that's true, and it failed. One night of heavy rain and they'd all disappear down the bank and end up in Simon's

189

back garden. The boards wouldn't hold them all. No ... paint's the answer.'

'What about white plastic.' Andrea said, and being a woman, nobody commented. 'Well, cement then....' again no response.

Jonathan took the beer glass Danny had just handed him and sipped the froth. 'If we use masonry paint - spray it on with the knapsack sprayers like we did with the weed killer, it'll only be like marking out a football pitch.... I read about a horse further north where they'd done this. Some local decorators sprayed the thing.'

Simon still didn't reply to this crazy scheme. Funds were already low and he was running out of patience.

'Danny and I could do it. We could abseil. It would get the work done quicker. Rely on the ropes rather than our balance.'

Danny looked up, mortified of what Jonathan was now implying. But Jonathan persisted. 'We can do it.... We'll get some proper tackle.... I could train Danny.... We'd do it together. Paint the horse and whiten her up a bit. It'll last for years.'

'Who do you think you are ... Spiderman?' Simon muttered, shaking his head, defeated, and not understanding why the others were laughing.

'No, he's Superman. Didn't you know that?' And Danny joked.

'Well, he's right.... It is the best way.' Sam repeated as he sat beside Simon, closely looking at him, but receiving no response.

Simon knew the idea was a good one and Jonathan's enthusiasm and logic made it more appealing, but he wondered how much further and what other crazy schemes he would have to do to get this horse finished.

'Do you think we could get some sponsors ... paint companies ... DIY shops and the like. We could approach them.' Andrea said hoping this suggestion would be taken on board. 'We could agree to have their logo somewhere, maybe an ad in the paper.'

Simon wouldn't commit himself to this either but continued to rummage through his folder. He was uneasy at Jonathan's suggestion to abseil, he was talking like it was a game and it scared the living daylights out of him. But Jonathan had done skydiving, parachute jumping, ghyll walking, every pursuit one man could possibly do for worthy causes. For Simon, each time he had watched the men working on the steep slope he had feared for their safety and couldn't stress enough every day that someone give the safety talk. Yet they were all safe and the horse was nearly completed. Simon then looked at some of the old photographs taken back in the 70's. He looked at the volunteers; young men all laughing, happy at what they were doing, yet never knowing they wouldn't complete it. He saw again Tom, John and Abraham, names he remembered from the early research. Then he realised, as he looked closer, that the young man in the middle of the photograph looked familiar. He checked the list of names below the photograph, just Christian names; he saw the man was called John, and Simon thought he knew him. Searching his mind, desperate for answers he became enwrapped in a bubble-like trance as he focused on the man. Then it came to him; the moustache gave it away. The man looked like Jack Albright. He looked closer at the others but didn't recognise anyone else. Then he found the newspaper cutting of the man that fell to his death and it sobered him. He started to read it again; half-listening to Jonathan talking and Danny still laughing at the Superman comment, but their voices became muted as he concentrated on the cutting. It read: *"Local Man Dies in Restoration."* And the name and the face jumped out at him: "T*hirty-nine year old local man, Abraham Miller, died after a fall*." Simon started shaking as he looked back at the yellowed photograph to find Abraham, and he picked him out in the line of men, and looking at the blurred image, pitied the man. It said he was thirty-nine, and Simon thought it no age. Abraham had a young face; a handsome face. He was standing next to the man who looked like Jack Albright, who had his arm across his shoulder. Abraham had a happy expression, with a fair and receding hairline, and then Simon thought he would stop breathing, as he looked up at Jonathan who was still talking and joking about Danny abseiling. Simon looked into Jonathan's eyes, and observed every strand of hair on his receding brow. Then he felt the folder close in his hand as Sam quietly pushed his own hand on top.

Simon was pleased the journey back to Chardwell would be in the darkness; he was agitated and wanted the night to conceal his anger. He was in the 4 x 4 with Sam beside him. They watched Danny and Jonathan drive away in Danny's hybrid car and Andrea Briscoe was just leaving in her Alpha Romeo. Simon started up the engine.

'Right Sam.... Start talking.' The 4 x 4 squealed out of the car park. 'Man alive, Sam! What's going on?' He pulled out onto the main road. 'You saw me reading.... Is Abraham Miller a relative of Jonathan's?'

There was silence.

'For pities sake, Sam.' He pushed his foot hard down on the accelerator. 'My father's dead.... Jonathan's mother is desperately ill in hospital.... His wife's left him.... Danny's being hounded by the police and my own house attacked. What's going on? I know it's no superstition. What's wrong with the horse?'

The old man pushed his cap forward on his head, to cover his eyes and stayed silent.

Simon slammed on the breaks. 'For pities sake, Sam. Speak to me.' Both men jerked forward.

'I said if you had the money and the spirit, Simon.'

'I'm fast running out of both, for crying out loud,' his face was reddened. 'Who is Abraham Miller?'

Simon couldn't bear the silence. 'I won't move until you tell me, Sam. Who is he?'

The old man choked as he said words he hoped he'd never have to say. 'He was Jonathan's father.'

Simon gripped the steering wheel and punched it with his fist. 'Oh man.... Please tell me this isn't true.'

'No, it's true.'

'Then why is Jonathan here? He said he didn't know anything about the horse.... I don't understand. How can he be so cool about it? Isn't he afraid?'

'I don't think he knows, Simon. He's never known. I had no idea you were going to ask him to work on the horse. This is Chardwell's best kept secret.'

Simon moaned and restarted the engine.

'Everyone loves Alice Miller, and she's had her reasons not to tell Jon how his father died. She's a strong and influential woman.'

The following morning Simon phoned Andrea Briscoe's office.

'I need to talk in confidence, Andrea.'

Andrea got up and closed the door to her office and found herself running her fingers through her hair to tidy it.

'Remember the guy who fell off the bank back in the 70's?'

Andrea had been eating a toasted bagel which lay deserted on a paper napkin; she sipped from a polystyrene cup filled with strong black coffee.

'Does the name Abraham mean anything to you?'

'The guy that fell … yes, I've always just known him as the "Abraham" bloke.'

'Does the name Abraham *Miller* mean anything to you?'

Andrea went to her filing cabinet and pulled out all she had on Chardwell's White Horse. She flicked through the files and found the copy of the photographs she was looking for. 'Er…. Yes and no.'

'Come on, Andrea …! Abraham MILLER.'

'Oh no…! What's the connection?'

'I hardly dare tell you.' Simon still cringed as he thought about it. 'They're father and son. And there's more. One of the men looks and awful lot like Jack Albright, the man in the middle of the photograph called John - get it – Jack was a slang name for John back in those days. He works with Jonathan as a builder and he's Jonathan's uncle. He's worked at my place and I know him well. He's retired now but still does a bit part-time. The other man, Tom, I don't know at all, there's no surnames under the photograph.'

The long silence was anticipated. 'So why didn't we notice this before? Why didn't we see it? Why didn't Jonathan tell us?'

Simon rubbed his brow and tired eyes through lack of sleep. 'Because he doesn't know about his father. It's all secret.'

'Well, how did you find out?'

'Sam. Stupid - stupid Sam told me before he clammed up and went all sulky.' Simon wanted to swear and resisted. 'I knew about Abraham, but his Christian name was so outstanding, I mean, who on earth's called Abraham these days, and Miller's a kind of non-descript name. I too just thought of him as the "Abraham bloke". When we did the research months ago, Jon was just my gardener, he was no way associated and, stupidly, I didn't see the connection. I'm in trouble, Andrea. I don't know what to do. It was me that got Jess to persuade Jonathan to help us. It's all my fault.'

'I'm sorry, Simon, but I'm still confused. Why doesn't Jonathan know? How come? How old is he? I mean, how can you live in a village for thirty odd years and not know about the horse. Not even know how your own father died. I don't believe it, Simon. It doesn't add up.'

Simon knew to his cost that you could live a life and know little about your father, especially if you couldn't be bothered to ask questions or your judgement had been coloured by the whims and fancies of others, and it saddened him. 'Believe it, Andrea ... It's true. His mother for some reason decided not to tell him - *never* to tell him. Sam insists he doesn't know why, but I think if we knew the answer to that one we might know who doesn't want us to build our horse. Danny said Jonathan runs on the bank every other day almost. He would surely have said something if he'd have known.'

'Well, it would scare the living daylights out of me if I knew, but Jonathan's never scared is he? Oh boy.... And now he's on about abseiling!'

'I know. But why should he be scared, if he doesn't know, besides, Jonathan's not scared of anything. He jumps from aeroplanes remember.'

'That poor woman.... No wonder Alice Miller can't speak.'

'I know.... Don't rub it in.'

'So what do we do? Do we come clean?' Andrea said.

'No, how can we do that when the woman's kept it secret all these years. It could kill her.... I'm going to see her later.... I'm taking Lucy with me ... I must apologise. Can you imagine what torment she must have been through? This explains a lot of the resistance, Andrea. Sam said this is Chardwell's best kept secret.'

'Do you think Jonathan's mother could have sent the dodgy e-mails?'

'I can't imagine a little old woman using language like that, can you?'

'No.... No, but maybe somebody did it for her.'

'What, and drove my father to his death and smeared muck on my house and got the police to smash up the headlights on Danny's car. Oh, I don't know, Andrea, that's a lot for one little old lady. Anyway, it's all gonna have to stop here. I've lost the spirit Sam's always going on about. That old horse will just have to stay grey.'

Andrea put the receiver down and threw the half-eaten bagel in the waste bin. Her coffee would go cold. She knew Simon had talked of giving up before and had changed his mind time over. But this time the stakes to continue were higher.

She fiddled with her pencil, leant back in her chair and sat looking at a blank screen on her computer. She had promised Simon she would start and hunt for more sponsors for the paint. She already had lists of companies she could cajole with the promise of a full-page spread if they co-operated. Jonathan had done a rough estimate last night and had said they needed at least 3,000 litres. So despite Simon's decision to stop, Andrea decided to carry on; she had the potential of a good story here when all was told, and she hoped the problem with Alice Miller would be resolved and they could at least get Jonathan off that bank.

Lucy handed Simon a large bunch of pink roses and carnations to give to Alice; she said they would mean more coming from him. This was her idea and Simon wished he'd thought of it. He'd already had to be adamant that they went to the hospital in his own car, despite Lucy insisting they went in her Metro so she could take Boris out for a run. The little dog was now jumping around in the back of the BMW, something Boris had done before when the car belonged to Simon's father, and no doubt he would continue to pluck the backseat with his claws, as he had done back then. Lucy was dressed in an orange and green flowery blouse with mustard coloured trousers. Simon was embarrassed as he walked one step behind her down the hospital corridor, the air behind her smelt of cheap perfume. He was totally lacking confidence, and relying on Lucy's hospital know-how and her good nature to help him.

He handed Alice Miller the bunch of flowers but she just smiled and waved. Lucy took them from his hand and rested them on the windowsill. Simon rubbed his brow, pleased they were alone in the small room, but feeling hemmed in.

'I'm so sorry about the stroke, Alice.' Lucy took the initiative while Simon stood nervously over her.

Alice knew why they'd come.

A young nurse brought another chair and Simon pulled it up to the bed.

Alice looked closely into the young man's eyes. She peered at his face and thought he had an honest one. She had liked his father.

Simon bent his head low. 'We've come to apologise, Mrs Miller.'

But Alice didn't respond; her heart was beating far too fast.

'I think you know why.'

Alice did know why, as several co-conspirators had told her about Jonathan's exploits on the horse.

Simon continued. 'I'm sorry. I was slow to discover the truth.'

Alice now bent her head low and nervously fiddled with a blue crotchet square on the blanket over her legs.

'If I'd have known sooner I . . . I.' but the old woman rested her good hand on his arm to pacify him. 'It'll all stop now...' he continued, but Alice shook her head.

'I'll not say a word to Jonathan. I believe he doesn't know ... I'll just tell him that we've run out of money and the horse will stay as she is: grey.'

Lucy wanted to help him, as there was an uncomfortable silence. 'Simon and his father only wanted what was best, Alice. You must understand that we didn't know the truth.'

A nurse came and offered them tea, and Simon put his hand up to decline. 'I'm just so sorry.' And he stood up ready to leave when Alice muttered. 'No.... No.'

Simon's eyes widened.

'Don't stop,' she drawled. 'But don't tell him ... please. Let him do it!' How she got the words out, she didn't know. It was tearing her heart in two. She could see this man genuinely cared and it wasn't his fault, all this trouble over the horse.

Simon could barely speak. He couldn't believe what she was trying to say. 'You mean you want us to go on?' he had to check what she'd said, but Alice just nodded.

'Ah no, I can't.' Simon shook his head. 'It's troubled me ever since I heard about Jonathan's father. I couldn't bear the worry.'

But Alice repeated. 'Let - him - do - it.' And she turned to look out of the window at some chaffinches on a bird table. She wouldn't look at Simon again.

Alice Miller had feared for her son, for the last thirty-nine years, as any mother in her situation would. She was so proud of Jonathan; she loved him dearly, and she loved Katie. And in the moments of despair, she realised her world was getting smaller. The detached house that had been her home for the last forty years, she would probably never see again. Alice realised her home and boundaries would spread no further than the walls of the nursing home that was waiting for her when she'd recovered as far as she could. Alice knew one day her space would diminish even further to the bed she was lying on, then to the box in the ground. She hadn't been idle in her thoughts all these weeks; when she had heard about Jonathan working at The Grange she had detested each day of it. When she was told he was running on the bank every other evening she worried and insisted he called her often, not to check on her as he thought, but just so she would know *he* was safe. She had images remaining in her mind, after all these years, recalling the police coming up the garden path and telling her of Abraham's death. Of Jonathan, as a child, sitting on her knee and her weeping on his little face, and him clinging to her, and all she wanted to do was protect him. She knew in some ways she was being unreasonable but she couldn't help having his safety in mind. And when she was told he was now working on the horse itself, fear had gripped her beyond recovery. But Simon Naylor she liked and she trusted. She had told his father about Abraham and he must have been discreet in not telling a soul, not even Lucy. But now she had too many fears of her own and wouldn't let fears over Jonathan grip her any longer and, although she had tried and fought it for thirty-nine years, she would fight it no more and let others do as they wished. And neither would she stifle Jonathan's desire to help others; this was his decision and he must live with it.

Simon pulled out two chairs in the hospital diner, still self-conscious to be in Lucy's company. He set two coffees down on the blue Formica table.

'I didn't know what Alice said when she visited your father, Simon. I left them alone. But your father was troubled over the horse as I can see you are.' Lucy sipped the coffee and didn't feel the frothy milk rest on her top lip. Simon had to look away.

'What shall we do, Lucy... what would my father have done?'

'He'd have carried on, Simon. Jonathan's father's long dead.... You have Alice's consent.'

'I don't want to lie to Jonathan. But I'm uneasy about him carrying on. I can't let Danny do it alone and me and Andrea are useless when it comes to manual work.'

'Well, you can't tell him.'

'I'll have no need to tell him, I'll make up some excuse, get him off that bank, if not I'll make sure the lad's safe up there. There's just the paint to do and it's finished.'

The call to Andrea Briscoe was almost anticipated. Andrea knew Simon would change his mind again, but to have Alice's consent amazed them both.

'So what about the paint?' Andrea reminded him of a small detail.

'Yes, the paint.'

'Don't worry, Simon ... I've already started hunting and I think I've got a sponsor. It'll mean logos and boards of all different colours and sizes outside your house. We'll try and do a deal with them about that.'

'You're a star, Andrea.... So who is it?'

'Only the biggest DIY chain in the country...!'

Simon fell back in his chair amazed at his good fortune and that, finally, things were starting to unravel and go his way and he wished his father was around to see his progress.

CHAPTER 17

The tubs of white masonry paint were stored in Simon's workshop for safekeeping, it took Jonathan and Simon an hour to clear the workshop and haul the tubs indoors.

The conversation was broken with each journey backwards and forwards to the 4 X 4.

'I just think you've done enough ... that's all.'

Jonathan couldn't believe what he was hearing. The look of disappointment on his face touched Simon, but he must persist. 'You've done a great job.... But I'll pay some willing decorators to come in and do it. Get it done quicker so you won't be troubled.'

Jonathan noticed a reticence in Simon's voice that often happened when he was stressed, and today he was stuttering.

'Decorators!'

'Well, you said you'd read about some lads near York who might do it.'

Jonathan kicked one of the paint tubs into place with his boot. 'It's a shame though.... I started it - I somehow wanted to finish it!'

'And you've done a brilliant job ... but have a rest.'

'Is it something we've done wrong?' Well, he had to ask.

Simon hadn't anticipated it would be so hard. 'Ah no.... No.... You're a vital part of the team, and I hope you'll stay that way. I just thought you and Danny might have had enough.'

Simon knew Jonathan had spent many evenings tweaking the outline of the horse, sending Danny to the other end of the valley to view her from a distance and then ring back on his mobile telling him which bit needed re-shaping. And now the horse was elegant and beautiful, apart from her colour. Jonathan had lifted and replaced turf to mould her legs, head, and ears; all the difficult corners, he had planned to re-seed some areas around her so the lines were smooth and clean; he was proud of his work, and hoped some more paid landscaping work would come in after this.

'Is it Danny...? Has he done something wrong?'

'Look, Jon.... Nothing's wrong - okay.'

'Then in that case I want to finish her if you don't mind.'

Simon cursed Jonathan's stubbornness and conceded.

Danny was just kissing Jess in the backseat of his car when his mobile rang. Danny fumbled with his free arm, put down his can of cider on the floor and glanced at the small screen on his phone. He put his finger to his mouth for Jess to be quiet: it was Jonathan.

'Are you busy?'

And this question brought a wry smile to Danny's face as he considered Jess. Yet, it irked him to think that Jonathan thought he had little to do in life but work with him.

'I *was* busy....' Danny attempted and failed to sound agitated, but Jess giggled and he tried to quieten her, but the cider had gone to her head. He wouldn't give her any more; they had to be careful.

'Have you got a girl with you?'

'What if I have?'

'Oh, sorry.'

'Yeah.... None of your business.' But Jess laughed again.

'You're with Jess, aren't you?'

'No.' Danny lied and hated himself for doing it. 'It's just our Amy. She's messing around.' And he pulled away from Jess. 'So what do you want?'

'I've got the climbing gear ... here ... now... and the paint's come. Do you fancy a bit of abseiling on the bank.'

'What, NOW, as in right now, you mean.'

'Yes, now.'

Danny was angered. 'Ah, I don't know mate. Just because you're having relationship problems, don't expect my life to be the same.' But Jess was listening and whispering and nudging him. *'Do it.... Come on, do it.'* Danny was now scared as Jess tried to take the phone from him so he pulled his hand away and jumped out of the car. Definitely no more cider for her.

'Okay.... Where...? When...?'

'Meet me up at the horse in half-an-hour.'

Danny clicked off his phone and was reluctant to get back in the car.

Jess was wriggling around the back seat. 'Wow ... Danny.... Abseiling? Pretend you've just met up with me and Amy.... Pretend I'm interested.... Dad will like me to help. I can come and watch.'

Danny tried to think of every excuse to keep her away. He didn't want to abseil, he didn't want Jess to see him make a fool of himself and to see his fear. He jumped in the front seat away from her and started the engine. 'Look, Jess. I've made a mistake.... I'll run you to the shops.... Drop you off there. We shouldn't be doing this. I'm sorry. We shouldn't have had the cider.' But she laughed even more and flung her arms around his neck as he tried to drive. How could he possibly take her home in this state? He was now glad Jonathan had rung. He would be in trouble.

'Oh come on, Dan.... Take me home. I'm okay.'

'You mustn't go home like this, your mum will see you're tanked up ... we'll get done for this. I'll take you back to ours.... Amy's home.... You spend a night with her. Here...' and he handed her a ten pound note. 'Get a DVD and a Maccy D and some fries - anything, but don't go home like this.'

Jonathan set the tackle down at Danny's feet then pulled the harness around his waist.

'Never forget your hat, Dan. Always check the gear regularly. Don't take any risks. Have you been drinking?' Jonathan stepped closer and looked him in the eye.

'Just a can.... I didn't know you were going to ring.'

'Are you lying or what? Because we'll not do this if you're smashed.'

'Look, I'm not smashed, okay.... Don't preach. It was just one can.'

'Well, you shouldn't have driven.... Don't let the police anywhere near you, or you've had it, you know that.'

'Shut up. I'm not over-the limit, okay.'

Jonathan pulled hard at the harness and Danny felt the rope tighten around his groin. 'Now let me hold you.'

'I don't trust you, Jon.... Why abseil...? Why not just use the ropes like before.'

'Because it'll be quicker. I've spent enough time on this horse as it is. I want to get back to serious stuff. Besides, Simon's keen to get it finished.' And Jonathan laughed. 'We'll start the painting tomorrow.'

Danny stood up straight again, they stood close to the base of the bank, not too far to fall. He was scared; maybe the can of cider was a good idea after all, because it gave him some false courage; or maybe not as he felt light-headed. Danny had worked on the bank all these weeks and had hated every minute of it. He'd had a few near misses himself and Simon's fall earlier had done nothing to allay his fears. Jonathan didn't appear to have any fear. He was reckless with his life so how could Danny trust him with his own, but he would have to.

Andrea Briscoe was a researcher. She knew where to look, but time wasn't on her side. Stories needed writing; leads needed to be followed up; this wasn't her paper and despite her position, Andrea was still answerable. She'd neglected other work for weeks now, working on this story with the horse, but continued to punch in some names and glare at the screen, learning nothing; printing out reams of documents, intending to read them at home later; she read and re-read; same old stuff, and nothing new. She read again about Abraham's death, but very little was found in any of the old papers; the same story, just written in different words. Some had Abraham's age wrong; some mentioned his grieving widow and young son, but nothing else. Andrea browsed the internet all morning. She must stop soon, her head was buzzing. She had a story to write about local business opportunities being encouraged in the area. Her gardening editor was leaving and she was supposed to be finding a replacement, and she knew nothing about flowers. She even wondered if Jonathan could write and planned to ask him next time she saw him. Andrea could help him with the editing; he'd maybe have the time in the evenings when the horse was finished, as she knew his marriage was on the rocks.

Something had struck Andrea weeks ago, she hadn't mentioned it to Simon but it troubled her. She'd realised they'd all had aggravation except Sam and she thought it odd. She punched in Sam Parkinson's name and flicking through pages of old news items, found nothing. She tried just PARKINSON and then CHARDWELL and finally came across something that interested her. Parkinson was a common name, but to link it with Chardwell narrowed down the field. She would work on this all night.

They worked all the following morning in the hot sunshine. Jonathan was sweating under his boiler suit, he was lathered in paint and his back was aching. Jonathan was the anchor as Danny did most of the work that morning; Jonathan was pleased he'd got the lad trained. The paint sprayed on quickly and effectively, the spell of good weather helped. Danny, along with his boots, was covered in white masonry paint. And as they worked their boots were now heavy and covered in layers of dust that had clung to the white paint. Danny didn't think he'd ever get clean. They'd pegged out and marked the eye, intending not to spray it; there was no need to waste the paint as Jonathan was to turf the eye later. It would be the last official job and would be celebrated with a bottle of Champagne and with The Mercury photographer present.

Sam was standing at the bottom of the bank shouting instructions. Jonathan at the top, anchoring the ropes and watching the boy was safe.

'Let me down.... I'm knackered.' Danny's hands were red and blistered his arms were aching as he safely abseiled down to Sam at the bottom. He landed and wobbled momentarily on the solid earth and ripped off the empty knapsack sprayer.

Jonathan checked his watch and knew Melanie had a meal ready for them as she always did when it was just the three of them. He was glad the house would be quiet with the children at school.

Jess was disappointed the men were working on one of her school days; she was pleased Danny was abseiling now and it made him more appealing to be secretly dating him with the credentials of a marathon runner and charity worker. He hadn't been as attentive to her since the binge-drinking incident and it troubled her, yet she too was glad that Jonathan had broken up their party. It was her idea and it was a mistake. And she was now ashamed of her behaviour and worried what her father would say if he found out. Danny hadn't mentioned any more dates and she wished he would; but they would have to be more careful.

Andrea met Simon for lunch and handed him a folder. She'd whittled down the documents and had just a few papers that she wanted him to interpret for himself. She was nervous and, for a hardened journalist, that was unusual. She hadn't told Simon her findings but just said it was urgent they met. Simon kissed Andrea on each cheek as they stood at the bar, but Andrea was in no mood for pleasantries and ushered him close to the window, to a seat away from onlookers. Out across Leeds the lunchtime traffic was building.

Simon read each document carefully; just four old cuttings from newspapers and one excerpt from a book titled: "Memoirs of a Village Bobbie". He looked up at Andrea and said: 'I'd better go now...! Thank God you've found this.'

'Be quick, Simon.'

Danny felt he'd eaten too much. Melanie was a good cook but the pastry landed heavy from the home made steak pie. He shouldn't have had two pieces; that was just greedy. He trudged back up the path, zipped up his boiler suit, and pushed on his hat. He helped Jonathan with the tackle, picking up the gear from over the bank and re-setting it to paint the next section. He was pleased it was Jonathan's shift to do the spraying.

Jonathan filled the knapsack sprayer with the white paint, tipping some on his boots.

'Are you ready, then?'

No one answered Jonathan's mobile and that was no surprise. Danny's phone went straight to voicemail and that meant Danny was either talking or out of signal. Simon left a message and the thought that they were back on the bank top worried him the more. Every car in Leeds appeared to be at a standstill. Simon blasted his horn and cursed at an old man in a large Merc hogging the carriageway. Every light was on red and every junction, stuffed with traffic. He tried ringing Melanie, but still no reply. He would just get the boys off the bank and go and see Sam.

There was no time to stop and view his horse from the lay-by, today he just glanced upwards as he sped on and could see the horse was half-painted; she looked wonderful, elegant, Jonathan had made a masterpiece. Simon should have been delighted, but he had a knot in his stomach. He drove his BMW recklessly to the back of the house and as far as he could up the hill, bouncing the precious car on the rocky track under the bank and jumped out.

Simon heard the rushing of the stones, and saw the dust. He heard someone shouting, then screaming, he saw Jonathan's blue helmet tumble to the ground, flipping up and down as it bounced on the rocks. Simon ran as high as he could up the newly painted chalk bank not caring that his best suit would be covered in paint. He watched Jonathan's body tumble like a rag doll down the hill. Simon scrambled up as far as he could to break his fall and stop him, aware of Danny slithering down, shouting and muttering.

Jonathan fell at Simon's feet, face downwards, and covered him with dust and paint.

'Oh, dear God, no ... Jonathan? Are you Okay?'

Jonathan moaned. His leg was folded beneath his hip like it didn't belong to him. His hands were smothered in rock dust and paint, his hair matted with blood and paint and dirt. He was motionless. If not for Danny slithering down and nearly falling on top of Simon, he would have stood mesmerized.

'I tried to stop him....' Danny screamed. 'Oh man. Jon, are you okay?'

'Don't touch him, Dan, mind his head.' And the boy leant over and knelt almost prayerfully at Jonathan's crumpled body.

'The rope just snapped!' Danny was close to tears.

Simon fumbled in his pocket for his mobile: 'It didn't snap, Danny. It was cut! Here ... run to the top. Get a signal. Call the ambulance.'

For the first time ever, Danny managed to run all the way to the top of Chardwell Bank without stopping. 'Oh, hello, ambulance please.... Chardwell Bank.... The Grange. I have a friend with head injuries.... Possible spinal injuries.... He's fallen on the bank at the back of the house -The White Horse. Do you know it?' Then he ran back down to Simon and knelt at Jonathan's side.

Simon scraped gravel and muck from around Jonathan's head and face. He carefully pulled the knapsack sprayer from around his shoulders. 'Don't try and move, Jon, if you can hear me. You'll be okay.... You're safe now. Help's on its way.' But there was no response. Simon laid his head on his back to try to hear breathing and could feel Jonathan's body trembling under his hands. He was breathing heavily.

'It was all my fault.... It's all my fault....' Danny was totally defeated, almost crying, but Simon got eye contact. 'No...! It's not your fault. It's *my* fault. Did you leave the ropes and the tackle?'

'We've er... Oh, man...! We've just had lunch.'

Simon looked up at the bank and saw nothing. 'Did you leave them up here over lunch? Unattended.'

'Yes, yes. No one comes up here. No, Sam was here. Oh, I don't know.'

CHAPTER 18

The police were the first of the emergency services to arrive at the bank. A young policeman was struggling his way up the slope with PC Alec Langhorne a way behind him. It was an irony that when Simon wanted them out of the way, they barged in.

Simon didn't move from Jonathan's side, and he kept his hand on his shoulders to reassure him and spoke tenderly, not knowing if he could be heard. 'I'll look after you, Jon. Don't worry.' And Simon didn't look up as he muttered to the approaching policeman. 'You can come in a hurry when you want to, PC Langhorne.'

'I'm just doing my job, Mr Naylor.'

'And what job's that?' Simon, still kneeling, mumbled, while all the time protecting Jonathan's fragile body from more aggravation.

'I'll inform Mrs Miller about Jonathan's fall.' PC Langhorne said.

'If you mean Katie, she already knows. I've called her.... If you mean *Alice*, you'll keep well away from that dear lady until I get instructions from the family. If you disregard my wishes you'll know about it and so will your brother at The Three Feathers!'

PC Langhorne laughed nervously at Simon's manner as he'd never seen him as assertive as this.

The young policeman started to ask Danny questions, and Danny showed him the rope. PC Langhorne went across to look at it.

'Doesn't seem much wrong with that to me, Mr Naylor. Except the condition. These are old ropes.' He shouted back. 'I'm afraid there could be negligence on your part, if this lad dies. Shoddy equipment too. Must be his stuff. Typical of Jonathan Miller.'

It took every ounce of self-restraint for Simon not to punch him.

Jonathan was lifted into an air ambulance that had landed in the meadow beside the bank. The paramedics took time to brace his neck and spine before putting him onto the stretcher. Jonathan moaned as they lifted him, they gave him immediate pain relief and took him straight to Leeds. He would never remember this trip.

Simon and Danny had watched the paramedics, both helpless and remorseful. They saw the helicopter, labour slowly, as it took off in Simon's paddock, the noise alerting the village. Cars stopped in the lane and people wandered out into their gardens watching. The police draped around the public footpath and the perimeter of the horse some yellow strips of tape, forbidding entry. The tape said: "Crime Scene". Simon was also told not to enter and then they left.

Katie sat in the window of her house waiting for Simon, she had always expected this phone call, but not from him. She'd thought they'd tell her Jonathan had been knocked down by a car while out training; had a seizure in a marathon, or had a parachute that had failed to open. And then every bad thing she'd ever accused Jonathan of and every foolish action against him came back to her mind; she thought she wasn't worthy of him. '*Don't let Jonathan die*,' she prayed, '*I couldn't bear life without him*,' and that was no lie.

Simon planned to drive Katie to Leeds and Danny insisted he went with them, he knew Katie better than anyone and, in his young and lovable way, he knew he could bring her some comfort. While Simon was alone with Danny in the car waiting for Katie to get some more things, Simon questioned him.

'Which part of the horse were you on, Danny?' His voice was dead and lacking passion.

'It was straight after lunch.... We were near the top. Couldn't have been any higher. Oh, man ... he fell a long way.'

'Were you near the eye?'

'We'd just left the eye. Jon had said there was no need to paint that piece. The turf was coming next week.' Danny was still close to tears.

'Will you come up there with me again? I need your help. We'll see if Andrea can come. Just the three of us ... tonight. Don't tell a soul.'

'I don't know, Simon. ... I'm scared.... It's evil, all this.'

'It's not evil, Danny.... Get that out of your head. There's something up there that someone doesn't want us to find. I don't know what it is, but Jonathan must have been close. His poor father died up there Danny and Jonathan must have been close to finding something as well.'

Danny was shocked at the revelation and it didn't help his decision to meet back on the bank any easier. 'I have an idea who doesn't want us to find things, but it's confusing.'

They stopped talking and watched as Katie ran to the car with a carrier bag full of things; her face was blotchy with tears.

'I'll pick you up tonight, Dan.... About midnight,' and Simon restarted the engine.

'I'll see how Jonathan is, then I'm going to Jack Albright's. Can you tell me where he lives?'

Katie wasn't allowed to see Jonathan straight away. He was taken to theatre with a suspected fracture of the spine, ruptured spleen, head injuries, broken pelvis and broken leg. A young doctor took Katie to one side and explained his injuries. 'The next forty-eight hours will be crucial - blood clots and the like. Jonathan was lucky to survive the fall. He's a healthy bloke and that'll help.' She sat with Danny in a small room, neither speaking, drinking needless cups of tea. They looked at posters on the wall about the effects of drink and drugs, reading to pass time but not comprehending. Then Danny would speak and Katie would smile. Then silence again. It wasn't until Katie's mother arrived did Danny feel he could leave, yet he hated to leave without seeing Jonathan again.

Katie sat by Jonathan's side all evening; he hadn't responded since coming out of surgery, and even in the coma his countenance was strained. He lay bare-chested, with bruising on his face, stitches over one eye; they'd shaved off sections of hair where more stitches were in place; Jonathan wouldn't like that, she thought. He still had remnants of paint in his hair and on his body. She just held his hand and talked to him constantly, hoping he could hear her. He was heavily sedated. She saw the nurses cast worried glances to each other and wished she hadn't.

Katie rested her hand on his arm, his skin was warm. 'Don't die on me please, Jonathan.... Be strong ... I'll come back to live with you. I'm so sorry I hurt you. I've been stupid.'

She lowered her head and rested, exhausted, on his chest and wept.

Then again, she sniffed and blew her nose. 'You're mother seems better; she's speaking again now. The horse looks wonderful. Simon says you've done so well. It's all credit to you, Jon. I'll come running with you when you get better.' And she held his hand again. She longed for him to hold her and respond; she would cry more at home, when she was alone. Then she thought she felt his hand respond, perhaps a twitch, but maybe it was just wishful thinking.

'Moses caught a mouse and dropped it in the kitchen,' she tried again. 'It was still alive and he let it go. It ran under the washing machine. I'll have to put a mouse-trap down. He's useless; he just sits there all day waiting for it to come out.

'We've decided not to tell your Mum today. It'll only worry her. I'll probably tell her tomorrow when you're awake and feeling better. Simon's gone to find Jack and tell him. He may come and see you later.'

Katie had struggled with the decision whether or not to tell Alice. If Jonathan died that would be soon enough, but if he could fight for life and win through then it would be good news she could give her. Katie felt more bad news would finish Alice.

Simon parked the BMW in a small cul-de-sac, just off the main council estate in Chardwell. He clicked the lock and wandered up to a small group of red brick flats; in his hand was a scrap of paper with Danny's handwriting, stating Jack's address. He walked up the path and looked to the windows on the second floor, netted with curtains. He passed a kitchen garden full of neat rows of broad beans and lettuce, not a weed in sight. In the opposite garden an elderly lady was cutting some roses. She stood up awkwardly and held her back, smiling at Simon.

'Do you know if Jack's in?' Simon politely asked.

'Yes, he's just come home. He's been bowling in Skipton.' The information disturbed Simon as he guessed he was to bring bad news.

He rang the bell, stepped under the lintel, and waited with a group of gaudy coloured gnomes. He read a plaque that said something about being closer to God in a garden. And Simon knew he needed to be as close as he could right now.

Jack looked genuinely surprised to see Simon and smiled as he hung on the opened door.

'Can we talk please, Jack?' Simon glanced back at the elderly lady, and Jack took the hint and gestured for him to enter. They wandered up a concrete stairwell and the smell of boiling cabbage hit him.

Simon met Andrea at Danny's house in the 4 x 4 and drove them the few miles back to The Grange.

219

Danny was dressed in his green army combats, somehow thinking they would give him courage, and they did. In darkness, they approached The Grange. Danny and Andrea were concealed in the back of the vehicle under an old carpet. Simon saw a police car and he waved. It was parked at the foot of the public footpath leading to the bank where Jonathan ran every other night. The policeman flagged him down, and stepped out. 'Everything okay, Sir?' but Simon lifted a take-away bag up and said: 'My wife can't sleep.' That was pure deception, as he hoped Melanie and Jess were both fast asleep; they mustn't know of his dangerous plan.

The take-away was shared in Simon's kitchen, well away from sleeping women.

'We'll walk ... it's a good night. We'll cover every inch of that horse until we find what we are looking for.'

'What are we looking for?' Danny chewed on some prawn crackers then pulled his favourite black beanie over his hair. He was edgy.

'I don't know.... Any anomalies ... but when we find it, we'll know. I don't know where to look exactly but I know where to start. Keep quiet as we walk. We mustn't let those donkeys sitting smug in their patrol cars hear us. This is supposed to be a crime scene, but they don't care.'

Simon picked up some brand new tackle from the boot of his 4 x 4; he pulled the ropes through his hands, checking every section. He checked the new harness he'd bought and the karabiners. 'There's no abseiling today, just steady scrambling with the ropes as an anchor. One of us at a time on the bank, while the others hold the ropes and keep watch,' he insisted. 'There'll be no more accidents.'

Simon checked the torches, but hoped they wouldn't have to use them, then took the long and tedious climb up the bank. Danny was there first, his young eyes adjusting quickly to the dark. They stepped over some yellow tape that the police had arranged all around the horse to mark it as a crime-scene. The footpath had been closed, but no one was guarding the horse. Simon wasn't surprised.

The wind was gusty with a few specks of rain touching their faces, despite being a warm day the night was cold.

'Just hold me, Danny.' Simon slithered down the bank on all fours, glad of the ropes as a safety net, but not relying on them as Jonathan had done to his peril. Danny was uneasy, recalling how he'd thought he'd safely anchored Jonathan most of the day. And now he was standing in the exact spot where he was when Jonathan fell. Simon went straight to the bare patch that they had left for the eye. He didn't care that he was scuffing up the paint. He reached the eye, and took out a small hand trowel tucked under his belt. He started to rake the gravel like an archaeologist, slowly, quietly, piece by piece. He slipped momentarily and Danny's heart jumped as he felt the weight of Simon's body. Andrea grabbed the rope with her hand.

'I'm okay. Don't panic.... This piece is as slippery as sin.'

'That's where you fell last time.' Danny half-shouted, in muted tones, 'be careful!'

'It's solid rock.' Simon hands were already grazed and he thought of his wife and children sleeping. He balanced himself and started again to rake at the rock, opening up a wound at least a metre long. He could see hazy outlines of the shrubs and bushes beside the horse. The white paint on the horse illuminated the task.

'Throw me the torch down, Andrea.' But Danny grabbed the torch and, excited, slithered down the bank and lay face down on the slope beside Simon. 'Get back up, now...!' But he was ignored.

Danny pointed the beam at the rock. 'I saw that bit the other day.... It's not rock, it's concrete. I should have said something.' Danny shuffled across on his hands and knees clearing some of the rubble off the concrete. Then Simon found a cleft and a metal rod. 'Here.... What's this?' And he pointed and poked the hand trowel into the cleft, but nothing would budge. He mumbled up to Andrea. 'Go back to the house, Andrea. In the shed there's a crow bar, can you bring it please, be quiet, but hurry.' Andrea was reluctant to leave them alone and went back to The Grange, trying to compose herself as she walked back down the track in the dark, terrified of who might be lurking in murky corners.

Danny and Simon worked on the face of the horse then sat and waited for Andrea's return. They heard footsteps on the path and hoped it was her; neither dare move.

'Mind your heads. I'm coming down.' Andrea re-checked the rope and then anchored them to a tree at the top, and slithered down, the three of them now clinging to one rope.

Simon took the crow bar from her hand and prized it into the cleft but nothing would budge, repeatedly he tried, but he was exhausted; the mental anguish of Jonathan's fall had tested his fitness. He was no strong man and he knew Jonathan would have had this open in no time.

'Let me try.' Danny said and he took the bar from Simon, easing himself on his knees, mindful of his footing; he was trembling. He shoved the bar into the cleft and it scraped loudly as it moved. They all sat motionless and waited but there was no movement from the police cars below. 'Push the spade in, Simon.... Lever it.'

The concrete lid slithered off, leaving a dark chasm. They pulled at the lid, slipping and scuffing with Andrea holding tightly to them both.

Danny was the first to grab the torch and press the button and shone the beam carefully into the pit. 'Mother of thunder...!' Danny fell to his knees. Simon grabbed his arm, and took the torch that had dropped from Danny's hand and shoved the beam into the open chasm and saw the skull of a man.

Katie sat with Jonathan all night. Her mother had visited and left. He was peaceful and still heavily sedated. There was little in the way of family to help, but Jack Albright came, he knew Jonathan better than anyone and agreed it best not to tell Alice just yet.

Katie left the room for a break. Her heart was heavy. Jack was happy to stay awhile with Jonathan.

He found it hard to talk at first but he couldn't bear the silence. He sat watching the digital numbers on the machinery over Jonathan's head, rapidly fluctuating. Blood pressure – pulse - heart beat. He watched the heart rhythm pulsating, but beating consistently. A beeper went and a nurse came running. Jack was terrified but it was only the IV bag that needed changing; no worries, and the nurse soon left.

Jack sat in the bedside chair and started to talk. At first, he told Jonathan off. 'What a blasted fool thing to do, to mess around on that bank anyway.'

He stopped.

'Oh, Jon.... We all love you.... Just be strong.'

He sniffed back tears.

'Boy, you scared the life out of young Danny.' More silence. Then he joked about them cycling and playing football when Jonathan was a boy, and falling off his bike, 'Do you remember breaking your arm?'

More silence and Jonathan didn't move.

'I'll help the lad with the regulars; at least we can get on with the grass cutting. Keep some money coming in for Katie.... Alice will see you're not short of money.'

Jonathan's face was deathly pale and still, almost lifeless. The only dead person Jack had ever seen was Abraham Miller, and here, now, Jonathan looked just the same. The bruising, the blood, it all brought back distant images that Jack had tried to erase from his mind. And despite what the machinery was telling him, Jack really believed Jonathan was slipping away.

'Oh, Jonathan, your poor father did love you.... But he never got to see what a fine man you made. All that running and all those prizes, all those charities.' Jack looked down at Jonathan's face, but there was still no movement. 'They were older you see. Your mother and father. I think your mother thought she'd never marry; she thought she'd be left on the shelf. He was a bit of a rogue your dad. Oh boy, Abraham was the wrong name for him. I'm surprised your mother married him…. He was fun though, Jon, just like you…. Boy, she coped well after he died. He was always fooling around … fooled around too much some would say. He never got depressed or stuff like that. He could see nothing but good in everyone and gave away as much as he earned. Drove your mother crazy, when she was scratching around to pay the bills. She's a brave woman, Jon.'

Jack stood up and wandered over to the window, holding back tears, and for an elderly man, that wasn't easy. He stared out across the city. A few cars were slowly coming in and out of the hospital: ambulances arriving, sirens blaring loudly and ambulances leaving in a hurry.

'We never told you about your father - how he died. We were scared, you see. There are some not-so-nice people around here you know … you're too good for them. Alice is stronger than I am, Jon. I said we should tell you but she insisted we didn't.'

He turned back to Jonathan and took a deep breath, groaning as he did so. 'I can't bear to think of you dying and not knowing the truth.' He said under his breath. 'Oh, we did everything to stop you finding out; even managed to stop the papers when Simon Naylor started with all this talk about re-doing the horse. Didn't think he had it in him. You see your dad fell just like you; just the same, like father like son. What an irony…. We kept that secret thirty-seven years. Can you believe it? You'll never know the truth if you die. Your Mum felt it best just to have a quiet life and not trouble you with this, but

225

I know more than her. You've always wanted to know, haven't you? When you were a kid, you never stopped asking and it broke my heart not to tell you. But there, I've told you. I wish you were my own. I'm so proud of you. But you deserve to know.'

Jack rambled on and on, sobbing and muttering many words, saying things he shouldn't have said, and stuff he thought he'd never say. Admitting things; telling new stories; incredible stories. But he said them.

He came back and sat by the bed touching Jonathan's arm. The words now were barely legible. 'We'll find out who did this ... you shouldn't have fallen, no not you. ... You fell off that horse just like your poor father.'

He was still crying when he heard footsteps. Katie returned with two paper mugs of coffee in her hand.

She placed them on the bedside table and rested her hand on the older man's shoulder. 'Come on, Jack, you're tired ... have this and then go home. We'll be fine. It's how it should be, just Jon and me.'

Jack took a handkerchief from his pocket and blew his nose.

'Jon's strong ... he'll get through this.' Katie said.

But Jack didn't reply, because he didn't believe her.

Andrea Briscoe wondered what on earth she was doing at this time of night in this dangerous and inhospitable place clinging to a rope with the wind and rain in her face. 'Can you get inside, Dan. You're the smallest.'

'Oh man, you're kidding.' He had guessed they would say this. 'Why me?' And he scrambled to the edge of the pit and Simon shone the beam inside. 'The cavity goes under the rock ... look at the brickwork. It's like a man-made cave.'

Danny shuffled in on his back.

'Don't touch anything, Dan. It's all evidence.'

He just thought: 'Too right, I won't touch anything.' His breathing was heavy. 'Pass me the camera then.'

Andrea dangled down the camera to the young man. 'What can you see?'

'I don't know. Muck ... rubbish ... not much ... it stinks in here.'

'Come on, Danny. Hurry up. Get some pictures.'

They heard the boy scrambling about and the camera flashed several times. Simon hoped the police at the bottom of the lane hadn't seen it. 'Pull me out. I'm coming out.'

He handed them the camera and Simon grabbed the torch and quickly turned it off, and hauled the young man out.

Even under night-light they could see Danny's face was ashen. He fumbled down into his pocket. 'There's been a fire in there ... everything's burnt. Papers - equipment. I don't know what. There's a lot of bones for one man. There could be two.' He wanted to be sick. 'I didn't touch anything else.' And he thrust his hand in his pocket, 'but I found this.' And he handed Simon a small metal object.

CHAPTER 19

They were all sitting around the computer monitor waiting for the images to load. Danny bit his lip and hoped he'd done well, as each image projected on the screen in front of them. There was the burnt paper and skeletal remains just as Danny had described, and he was right: there were too many bones for one body. But burnt fragments of Hessian obscured the rest and there was clearly some kind of metal equipment poking up through the remains.

Before Simon could save and click onto another file he heard the soft footsteps of Melanie in her dressing gown come and stand behind them, her hair dishevelled; she was surprised and embarrassed to see Simon with Andrea and Danny.

'What's going on?' She came closer to look at the screen and hoped she hadn't caught them on some degraded web site, but what she saw didn't console her any the more. 'What on earth are you looking at?' She backed away and rubbed her eyes wanting to rid herself of the sickening images.

Simon quickly stood up and turned to her, 'Don't worry, Mel,' but she was worried and angry. 'What is this stuff?' She was shaking.

Danny shrunk back to stand close to the window and wondered how Simon would explain this one, but Simon took her by the hand and pulled her away. 'We've been out on the bank tonight, Mel. And we've found a pit full of old bones.'

She held her hand to her mouth.

'Look, honey ... I didn't want you to see this, please don't tell Jess. Go back to bed and we'll talk about it later. It's okay. We can handle it.'

'And you think I'll sleep...!' Melanie wandered away but didn't go to bed; she went to pour herself a glass of brandy and sat huddled over the remains of the fire in the lounge.

The search of the images was resumed; the saving and printing them; several copies of each; they needed the evidence, both private and personal.

'We'll have to call the police.' Simon was reluctant, as he paced around the small study; excited he was having some of his questions answered.

'Not yet.' Andrea said. 'Once this is all out in the open we'll have no control of it. We need time to think. We need help, but I don't think we'll get it with the local police.'

Simon knew she was right. 'Look, Andrea. I want to know who cut those ropes and who tried to kill Jonathan.... Heaven help us if he dies.'

'Yes, but I think we should wait until tomorrow lunchtime and in the meantime we could run the story. If I can write a short piece for tomorrow night's edition, we'll get it in the papers before anyone has time to refuse us. If you and Danny go back up there in the morning and pretend you've just found the pit. It'll give you more time to see it in daylight. Then call the police; hopefully you'll get up there without being spotted and see what crawls out of the woodwork.'

Early the following morning Simon and Danny went back and had a better look. The police car stationed at the bottom of the public footpath had gone and PC Alec Langhorne was probably eating toast back at the station.

They took more photographs but didn't move a thing. In broad daylight, the scene still seemed macabre and Danny struggled not to vomit. Soon everyone in Chardwell would know something was amiss. Simon didn't call the local police but found the number of the Skipton Police Station. He just said that he'd found two bodies and suspected foul play in the way Jonathan Miller had fallen. Because of the bones, the murder squad were called in and a blue tent was put precariously over the pit and the approaches to the footpath were properly taped off.

By seven in the evening, Simon sat at his desk with three documents upturned on his desk. They were the ones that Andrea had researched and copied and had forced Simon to make the desperate and futile race back to Chardwell before Jonathan's fall.

Simon had been on the bank with the police all afternoon and was desperately tired, he'd been awake all night, and he'd not gone back to bed but rested with Melanie on the sofa for an hour or so. He'd rung the hospital first thing and was told Jonathan was stable. He'd sent Danny home and he was now sleeping, not anxious or curious as the older men were, but glad to be away. Andrea Briscoe was long gone; she was used to late nights and early mornings, dosing herself with black coffee to keep awake. She had a good story to write but she wouldn't reveal all; just tell that a body had been found on Chardwell Bank under the White Horse. The rest would come later. They set the bait and waited.

The first thing that surprised Simon was that the evening's paper was delivered, with the headlines: *Human Remains Found on Chardwell Bank*. He loved the story Andrea had written; being astute and not giving too much away.

When Simon heard the doorbell ring he was startled and his tired body jumped as he reacted. But he knew who it would be; Melanie opened the door and was talking to Sam.

Simon was shocked to see the old man's face. He looked ill. Sam took his cap off in his usual way and scrolled it nervously around in his hand.

'Come and sit down, Sam. Can I get you anything?'

Sam declined as he stood before Simon's desk. Simon momentarily rose and shook Sam's hand, then resumed to his sitting position and purposely looked at the downturned documents.

'I wish you'd have told me first.' Sam muttered.

'No time, Sam…. I saw you were out. You're car was missing.'

'Have you heard how Jonathan is today?'

'They say he seems comfortable, but I doubt he's anything but that. He's comatose, I'm afraid. At least he's survived the night. He's still in intensive care but not responding. He's well out of it I'm afraid. They said it could be the drugs that are doing it.'

'What will happen to the bones?' Sam looked at the documents on Simon's desk and wished he could turn them over and read.

'The police will take them away. They'll do some DNA tests, check dental records and all. See who they are.'

'They...?'

'Yes, oh didn't you know, Sam. There's not just one body.... There are two.'

'It didn't say that in the paper.'

'No, no it wouldn't.'

Sam fidgeted with his cap and sat on the chair in front of Simon's desk still looking at the documents. He felt faint.

'Do you know who they are, Sam?' A question Simon thought he already knew the answer to.

'I think I know one of 'em, but I'll be blowed if I know the other.'

'And will the DNA prove it, Sam?'

'Yes.... I should think so.' Sam's voice shattered.

'And who is it?'

'He's my brother... I hope.'

'Is he the other young man in this picture?' Simon handed him the old photograph of Abraham, John and Tom.

'Aye, that's him, alright.'

'Why didn't you tell me, Sam.' And Simon turned over one of the documents and pushed it towards the old man. He picked it up to read:

DOUBLE TRAGEDY FOR CHARDWELL

Tom Parkinson, local builder has gone missing on the same day as his friend, Abraham Miller, fell to his death on Chardwell's White Horse bank. The police are concerned about Mr Parkinson's mental health as he was distraught over the death of his friend. Mr Parkinson's family are desperate to hear from anyone who may know of his whereabouts. The police would like to speak to him in connection with the fatal accident.

Sam clung to the document bearing a photocopy that Andrea had unearthed from a 70's edition of the local paper. 'I needed justice, Simon.... I've had thirty-seven years of shame. I needed it to end. When Tom went missing, everybody assumed he had something to do with Abraham's death, but it was all nonsense. Tom and Abraham were close; they were just young friends. Tom went out that night because he knew there was something suspicious about Abraham's fall. He could see that the ropes had been cut, but, like yesterday, the police just ignored it. But he never came home again. So everyone assumed he had something to do with it and this whole village has shunned our family ever since. I didn't know what had happened to Tom, but I did know he could never have killed Abraham. When you found the bones, I knew it was him. I've hunted for years on that bank, looking for something, clues, anything, but it was futile. The bad weather this summer must have loosened the scree that was camouflaging the pit. When you were interested in the horse I wanted to push you to get it done, you have more vigour than me, Simon. You also had the means.

'I never intended Jonathan to get involved. I knew there was something up there to make someone kill, but I didn't know what. And now my heart weighs heavy to think you may have found it. I had no money and very little spirit left, Simon. All those lads back then were doing just the same as you, trying to restore the horse but someone didn't want them to do it. They even tried to get them to put her the other way around, just the same, so I always knew the problem was near the eye. They were just a few young men having fun.'

'Did your brother tell anyone else there was a problem, Sam?'

'I don't know. You see, he saw Abraham fall, just as I saw Jonathan fall. I dropped to my knees in shock.... I just couldn't bear it. I know what you thought, Simon. But I think the world of Jonathan. I would never do him any harm. The boys went for lunch and I fell asleep. I sat on the bench. It's my fault. I should have watched the stuff. When I woke up, I thought I saw PC Langhorne on the footpath. I just thought it was a coincidence that he was near-by.'

'It was no coincidence, Sam.' His voice faltered.

Simon turned over the next document and handed it to Sam, it read:

Excerpt from Memoirs of a Village Bobbie. By Alec Langhorne. Published 2000

Page. 25: Chardwell has always had its mysteries, and there was none so greater than the mystery of the White Horse. Village gossip and old folklore has cast a shadow on the White Horse. She was never to be rebuilt. Arguments abounded about the original site: Did she face east to west or west to east. Then gossip was rife, of the tragedy of a young man who fell to his death. Some had said the ropes had been cut, but that was all nonsense.

Sam looked at the next cutting waiting for Simon to turn that over as well, but he didn't. He purposely put his hand on it and put it away in the folder.

'My mother died with the shame, and I wasn't going to do the same. I did this for my family's reputation. Those ropes were cut Simon, and you know it.'

Sam pulled from the inside pocket of his jacket a wad of letters and threw them down on the desk. 'These may give you some evidence.'

Simon was reluctant to read them, but as he carefully opened each letter, he saw the same abuse and the same warnings they'd all had. Only Sam's letters went back much further.

Katie wasn't with Jonathan when he first opened his eyes. He was being man handled by three nurses who were trying to clean him of the white paint. Jonathan had opened his eyes earlier and had closed them again. He knew Katie had been in the room because he'd heard her clear her throat like she often did when she was anxious. He didn't want her to see him awake so he'd closed his eyes again like a child trying to hide.

He moaned for the first time as the nurses washed him; he could still smell the paint and he wondered what they were doing as he drifted in and out of consciousness. Then one of them spotted him open his eyes. He wanted to close them quickly, but Jonathan would never do anything in a hurry for a while.

'Hello, Jonathan.' The nurse spoke softly.

Jonathan moved his lips but he couldn't smile, he just bit the inside of his lip and shut his eyes again.

Jonathan was aware that Katie was soon back in his room and so was the doctor.

The doctor shone a light into his eyes; it was cruel. Jonathan guessed they had to do it, and then he was alone again with Katie. She had her hand on his, with her head bent low. She didn't see him but he wanted to touch her hair that was caressing his chest. But his hand just twitched. Katie saw him open his eyes and she started to cry and smile at the same time. Again, he moved his lips and half closed his eyes. He wouldn't try to speak to her yet as his throat was so very dry.

It was the nurses that woke him again; all over his body he felt an incredible pain. Jonathan wondered why he still had his knapsack sprayer on, yet he could touch the bed with the flat of his hands and, realised, it wasn't the sprayer he could feel but a lump in his spine. He tried to tell them how much he hurt, but he knew if he spoke, the words wouldn't come out properly. He just moaned.

During the night hours, Jonathan lay awake. He played a game with himself to check every part of his body was still there. He would join every bone together and try to flex his muscles, thinking in his mind that his leg bone was connected to his hipbone, and his hipbone was connected to his thighbone. He went all around his body, repeatedly, and then he would sleep, waken, and start all over again. He would try to speak to the nurses when they came back and he succeeded but, as he suspected, his voice was croaky, so he just whispered only a "yes" or a "no" to their questions. All morning when he was alone, he practised speaking until his voice was clear.

Katie sat in the hospital restaurant with Danny. It was his turn to stay with her. Katie had mixed feelings about Jonathan's recovery. She felt bitter that he was talking to the nurses but not responding to her. She thought he hadn't forgiven her for the way she'd treated him; maybe he was right. She bought Danny a cup of coffee and they sat at the blue Formica tables.

'He's just being awkward, Katie.... You know what he can be like.'

'Don't, Danny. I know you mean well. He's punishing me ... he's doing it on purpose.'

'He loves you, I'm sure.' This was a difficult thing to say to his boss's wife.

Katie bowed her head low guessing Danny didn't really know what had happened between them, as he continued to mutter empty words. She wished he'd stop so she changed the subject. 'What did the police say?'

'They want to talk to Jon, as soon as they can. That's if he ...' and he faltered again.

'He *will* recover, Dan, he will!'

And now it was Danny's turn to bow his head and feel uncomfortable with this conversation. 'They've brought in the Big Boys - men in suits, from Leeds. There's two bodies, Katie. I can't tell you anymore.' Danny could, but those were the rules. 'Look, I'll go and call Simon, and tell him Jon's responding.'

'Responding.... Yes, but to who?'

Katie went back to Jonathan's room alone. She sat motionless looking at his face, willing him to speak. Some colour had returned to his complexion; he needed a shave and some gingery stubble was curling from his side burns. She had always been attracted to the chiselled structure of his mouth but, today, his lips were tightly shut. She took some ice and dabbed his lips; he loved it when she did this.

He pursed his lips and tried to sip the cold water, and then she kissed him.

The trick worked, because as she pulled away from him he said in a soft, low voice: 'Did you catch the mouse?'

The police were roaming around The Grange like insects. Every scrap of evidence was bagged and tagged. Simon told of his suspicions; he was careful of whom he spoke to, but he had no proof. He had ideas but had no motives. This was now a possible murder inquiry and the attempted murder for Jonathan.

The detectives made themselves comfortable at The Grange. Lucy and Melanie plied them with tea and cakes; it was a PR trick of Simon's to get good service. But supplies soon ran low and Simon encouraged Melanie to shop in the village again.

Melanie went to the butcher's to get some pork pies and to see Josh Bradshaw's reaction. He gave her a complementary basket of home baked pies and sent a food hamper, full of tins of cooked meat, delicacies and biscuits for Katie Miller. He insisted he would do anything to help the poor woman. Josh's last words to Melanie as she left the shop were: 'I told Simon not to meddle with that horse.'

Through a process of elimination, Simon was sure he could disregard three of his suspects. He was glad he still had an ally in Sam and realised he'd only acted in desperation to clear his family name. Simon considered Josh Bradshaw the butcher and Samantha Shakeshaft the newsagent to be allies of Alice Miller; they'd both acted discreetly to obscure

238

from Jonathan the cause of his father's death. But Simon was still left with worries about others.

He'd planned to visit Jonathan that evening and he would take the hamper for Katie, along with the promise of some financial support. He was sure at some stage he would have to discuss compensation with them and he cursed himself for not writing any disclaimers, yet his conscience told him he would have to help.

Simon gelled his hands with anti-bac, knocked and entered the room. His heart welled for the desperate man he saw lying there, his body and face battered and bruised. The room was decorated with get-well cards from Barney's Kids and well-wishers.

Jonathan was lying still and he looked like he was asleep, but he wasn't. Katie was in a chair away from him. She put down the novel she was reading, looked up and smiled.

Jonathan heard a man's voice and opened his eyes. He knew it was Simon.

Standing tall at the bedside and apologetic, Simon said, 'How yah doing...?'

Jonathan whispered: 'How d'ya think!'

'Yes, I'm so sorry mate....' Simon wanted to touch Jonathan to console him but didn't know where he wasn't hurting. 'Don't talk if it's difficult.'

'Everything's difficult, if you know what I mean.'

Katie shook her head, annoyed at Jonathan's attitude; he was obviously going to make it hard for them all. 'Look, I'll leave you two alone. I need to spend a penny, anyway.' She was tired and wanted to scream.

When she'd gone, Jonathan whispered: 'So, what happened?'

'Are you sure you're ready for this.'

'Can't do much more harm.'

Simon couldn't help but look over his shoulder. 'Someone cut the rope, Jon.'

Jonathan closed his eyelids and suddenly felt afraid. The anaesthesia and the morphine were wearing off and reality was hitting him hard. He had feared that was the case and now it was confirmed. 'Same as my father then?'

'You know...!' Simon was astonished and he slowly eased himself into Katie's chair.

'Yes, I do and evidently *you* know as well.'

'Yes.' Simon repeated, 'but how did you find out?'

'My uncle... Jack Albright. He thought I was dead I think, but I was awake. I heard it all.' Jonathan faltered as he chose his words carefully, 'He said my Dad fell off the horse.'

'Oh, Jon.... If I'd have known sooner, but no one told me. I'd have never let you near the place, and then when I found out, I did try and stop you, but you were – well, insistent. Oh, man...! I should have stopped you.'

'How much does my mother know?'

'She doesn't even know you've fallen. But I told her I found out about your father, but as for the rest, she knows nothing. She said I should go ahead with the horse and I promised I wouldn't tell you. She said you must do as you pleased.'

Jonathan wanted to laugh at the irony, but it wasn't funny.

'What shall we do?'

The door opened and Katie came back to the room but Jonathan continued. 'Tell my mother I know the truth, and tell Katie.'

'Tell Katie the truth about what?' She spoke up as she went to tidy some flowers in a vase by the window.

The following day Katie had much to do. Firstly, she must speak to Jack Albright and then she must go and see Alice, and she didn't relish either. But Jonathan begged her to do it.

She went straight to the day room where Alice was sitting and feeling abandoned. Alice had been left completely isolated for two days, apart from the nurses, playing Scrabble. And she was now sick of Scrabble. She'd asked the nurses to call Jonathan but none of them seemed to want to co-operate. Alice cursed the nurses, she cursed Jonathan, and she cursed Katie. When she saw Katie walk into the room, she was overwhelmed and garbled a: 'get me out of here.'

'I'm sorry, Alice. I'm sorry.' Katie kissed her.

'Has my son forgotten me?'

'He's unwell, Alice, and he didn't want you to catch anything.'

'Unwell, my foot…. Jonathan's never ill. When he's ill, heaven help the rest of us.'

Katie unwrapped a blue woollen bed jacket and handed it to her as a peace offering.

'I hope that's not got lace on it…. You know it irritates my skin.' Then Alice smiled at her daughter-in-law and knew she was a treasure.

'You're back in good spirits, I see.' And Katie hesitated as she tried to remember how she'd planned to tell Alice the bad news.

But Alice persisted. 'So, what's wrong with him?'

'Oh, this and that.'

'If you don't tell me what's going on, Katie, I'll disinherit the both of you.'

'Look, Alice, it's not good news. This is hard for me…' Katie whispered.

'If you're going to tell me you've split up, I know, I'm not stupid.'

'No, it's not just that.' She hesitated again and looked straight into Alice's tired and watery eyes. 'Well, I've come to tell you that Jonathan's in hospital, but he's doing well and he wants to see you.'

Alice was now subdued. 'What's wrong with him?'

'I'm sorry, Alice, but he fell.'

And the words killed her again.

CHAPTER 20

The few healthy members that were left of the Chardwell White Horse Committee sat in the Three Feathers purposely whispering, shuffling around useless bits of paper, and doing anything to attract attention. Danny was at the bar ordering drinks; three John Smith's Extra Smooth. He took a sip from one glass as he waited for the other two to be poured. He checked his watch and hoped he could get this over and done with; he was meeting Jess in an hour and he wanted to take her bowling. He watched the bar maid pulling the pints and had to turn his head away from staring at her cleavage. The landlord, Graham Langhorne, was soon to speak to him. 'How's that mate of yours going on, young Danny?'

Danny didn't like being referred to as "young" despite the fact that he had only just turned eighteen, and neither did he like Jonathan being referred to as his "mate".

'He's recovering. He'll be in a while; they're bringing him to the Cottage Hospital this week. It was a close call.'

'Shouldn't have been messing around up there anyway.'

'It's as well he was, if you know what I mean.' Danny raised himself a little in stature to stand up to the older man.

'That's as maybe,' then Graham Langhorne came in closer. 'Did *you* find the old bones then lad?'

'Can't say, Graham.... Top secret.'

'Come on, Danny. We're all wishing Jonathan well. We've had a whip round for his wife. Is she still with him then? I've heard rumours, you know.'

Danny could have floored the man but resisted, it was hard not to let his feelings show. And what Danny said next would also stick in his throat, but it had to be done. He leant in even closer to Graham Langhorne. 'They're getting back together again.'

Graham whispered back. 'No more running for him then, eh? He'll be a cripple. Be as near useless to that pretty wife of his, if you know what I mean.' And he laughed.

'Maybe...' again, Danny hated the things he was admitting too and was a reluctant participant.

'So back to these bones then.... Did you find anything else?'

'That's top secret too.'

'Come on, Dan. You can tell me. Man to man so to speak. Let me top that up with a whisky?' and he started to pull the pint glass away from Danny's hand but he held it tight and purposely looked around to see who was watching them, 'The answer's, yes, I did find the bones, but don't tell anyone.'

Graham tapped his nose.

'And it wasn't just bones I found.' Danny picked up the trinity of pints, held them precariously in his two hands as he wandered back to the table, and muttered under his breath some indiscernible words.

Simon leant across to the young man. 'Did he buy it?'

'Sure did ... stupid old fool.'

Danny left in a hurry but Andrea was invited back to The Grange for supper. Before they left The Three Feathers, Andrea slipped into the ladies' toilet. Simon wandered around the back corridor and waited. On the walls he saw some old black and white photographs, just as Sam had once told him; photographs of his beautiful, ivy-clad Grange. Simon stopped, with his hands in his pockets, peering into each frame. There were photographs of groups of men, who he guessed were the Langhornes' relatives in times past, some standing with horses and hunting scenes. Then there was one of the Mayor, who Sam had said was Graham and Alec Langhorne's father; he was with some other dignitaries, with his mayoral chains draped around his neck. On one photograph, he could clearly see members of the aristocracy.

Simon heard the cistern flush and was about to walk to the back door to wait, when Graham Langhorne wandered down the passage towards him.

'You'll not get many visitors like that up at The Grange these days, Simon.'

'No, I doubt it.'

'Yes, well that house didn't always belong to ne'er-do-wells.'

'Can't take it, can you, Graham?' Simon didn't look him in the eye but continued to glare at the photographs.

'And will you Simon, when you struggle to pay the bills and you're back in Leeds. That horse'll finish you off.'

'Then I'll enjoy her while I can.'

All work on the horse ground to a halt, and the white horse was now a major crime scene. Police and forensics were up and down the bank raking stone, looking for more clues but finding nothing else. Simon's poor mare had become a beast of burden and the disturbing of all Jonathan's hard work, turned her piebald: half-grey and half white. The pit was excavated and found to be a small cave, three metres by two metres, lined in red brick. Historians were called in and the pit was soon discounted as an ancient monument; not even a tomb. No, this cave had been constructed with one purpose and that wasn't to hide dead bodies.

The DNA and dental records proved one of the men to be Sam's younger brother, Tom. Sam cried when he was told the news. His brother appeared to have a fractured skull from a blow to the back of the head. Cards now flowed in from well-wishers and Sam was sorry he was the only remaining member of his family to hear the sad news. The local vicar promised a small and respectful service, and would completely exonerate Tom Parkinson's involvement of any misdeeds causing the death of Abraham Miller.

The other body remained for the time being, nameless. But Simon and the police had a good idea who he was and, eventually, some poor woman, if she were still alive, would be told the remains of her missing husband had been found on a hillside in Yorkshire.

Later that evening, Simon sat in his office, and looking again at his list of suspects, he underlined two. He could now cross off the family doctor who had been nothing but good to poor Katie and Alice.

And Simon realised he'd allowed his imagination to get the better of him. His own father's death was probably of natural causes and his suspicions were raised out of fears of being accepted in Chardwell, and clouded by the sensitivity of the persecution, but he knew all of it wasn't his imagination. He knew Alice had her co-conspirators in the butcher and the newsagent, and she certainly wouldn't have been behind any violence towards her own son or the damage to everyone's property; no, there was still evil at work and Simon would find the perpetrators.

Jonathan's recovery was slow. Katie sensed a difference in him and she continued to think it was her, he was rejecting. He was moved to the Cottage Hospital with his mother down the corridor, sleeping in the chair, sorrowful and in ignorance. That morning Katie came into Alice, all smiles.

'Come on, Alice.... Were going for a trip.' A wheelchair was set in front of her and two nurses shunted her in the chair and covered her legs with her blue patchwork blanket.

'No.... No.' Alice complained, thinking she was to be taken for her hair washing and man-handled over the wash-basin. She thought Katie had been roped in to coerce her.

'For once in your life, Alice.... Do as you are told.' Katie was bold, and that's how she would continue.

'You'll like this trip.'

Wheeled at pace down the corridor, avoiding the bathrooms and shower rooms –relief; passing the X-ray unit - and more relief. Avoiding the front door - disappointment. Then down the corridor to the men's ward and Alice was reversed into a small side ward.

Jonathan lay flat on his bed, his head raised slightly onto a soft pillow. He was waiting and he was smiling.

It was hard for them both to respond to the inner feelings of love that overwhelmed them. Jonathan tried to move closer to his mother, but could only move his arm. Alice tried to nudge the wheel chair closer to her son, but was prevented by paralysis.

She took his hand with her good one and lifted it to her face.

The conversation wouldn't flow too quickly but there was no need for many words. Katie stood back, and the nurses left.

Sam stood over the open graveside, a few wreaths of flowers coloured what was a gloomy scene. Jack Albright was by his side. Both men had their hands deep in their pockets. This was a funeral without tears, but with much sadness. A few locals had come to pay their last respects to Tom Parkinson; Simon had taken the day off work. The young vicar didn't know the man he had just laid to rest, but he understood the circumstances and he knew Sam well.

'That puts an end to that chapter.' Jack said, not looking at Sam but staring at the coffin and remembering his young friend, Tom Parkinson.

Sam just said 'Aye,' because he knew in his mind, it would take him some time to put an end to this chapter.

'Grand day for it, anyway.' Jack persisted.

Sam just said, 'aye,' again.

'I'm the only one left now, Sam.'

'Aye,' again.

'Kinda makes me feel edgy.'

'It will do.'

'What do you think will happen now?'

'Just let the police do their job, Jack.'

'I always knew he was innocent.' Jack admitted.

Sam knew this was true because unlike most of the folks in Chardwell Jack Albright had never snubbed Sam's family, despite losing a friend and cousin in Abraham.

'I think Simon's got something up his sleeve.' Sam said.

Jack twisted around and looked at Sam waiting for more, but he said nothing.

Danny and Jess waited in the study expecting a lecture. Simon had spotted them on his way home. Jess hadn't expected her father to leave the house again that evening, but starvation had occurred and Melanie had sent him out for another take-away. Simon had intended stopping in the lay-by to view the damage to the horse, when he spotted Danny's car. Danny cursed his stupidity to stop with Jess so close to home and, what's more, they were kissing. Thank goodness they had tinted windows and no booze with them. Simon had banged on the car door and terrified them both.

'Home, now! I want to speak to you both.'

'We've done nothing,' Jess whispered to Danny as they waited. She could hear her father in the distance, ordering the twins back to bed. Then they heard his footsteps marching down the tiled corridor, firm and determined. Jess knew he was in a mood.

Danny was like a lamb to the slaughter and had agreed to come back to The Grange. Simon had insisted.

'Right, you two....' Simon barged in as large as life and Danny felt compelled to stand and took his new beanie off.

'I've got something to ask you.'

Jess rolled her eyes in disbelief, wondering what penance he was now planning to discipline her with.

Simon went to his desk and sat down.

Danny wanted to run; he would lose his job, he would lose a girlfriend, he would lose a friend and all credibility; he would never be trusted again.

'Well, come closer then,' Simon beckoned them to the desk and pulled out his White Horse folder that was getting fatter by the minute. Jess rolled her eyes again almost disappointed at his distraction to the horse.

'Right, which one of you's going to volunteer to help?'

Danny's shoulders dropped. Jess's face flushed, she sighed and for once she was stuck for words.

Simon jumped up and went to a large cardboard package on the floor and pulled out two metal detectors.

'Right. Are you coming? We can get this done before dark.'

'Where, Dad...? What are you on about now?'

'We've not much evidence to go on so we're going to find some. The police are one step behind us, Jess. This place used to be owned by the Langhornes. They were a proud family and their

250

relatives don't like us being here. They have real skeletons in their cupboards.'

'So what else are we looking for, Dad...? Haven't we found enough or are you finally losing it.'

'No, Jess, that's where you're wrong and that's what everyone else wants me to think. But tonight, Jess, were going looking for an aeroplane...! Go and get ready.'

Danny stood motionless uncomfortable and intimidated by Simon's stature and he turned to leave, but Simon stopped him. 'Hang on young man,' and Jess left quickly, knowing Danny was going to get a grilling. She banged the door closed.

'Look, Danny. It's hard for me to say this.'

'I know what you're going to say Simon, and I'm sorry. I shouldn't have.... Well you know?'

'Yes, I do know Danny and that's what worries me. But I know what Jess is like. She set her cap at you right at the start. But I wished you'd have been more level-headed. I trusted you.'

'I've not touched her, Simon.'

'I should hope you haven't, and you'll not get the chance. You're now eighteen - an adult, she's still only sixteen - a kid.'

Danny held his head low, looking down at his trainers. 'Did Jonathan not tell you about us?'

'Did he know? Oh boy, I wish he had.'

'Well, I won't see her again, if that's what you want.'

Simon slowly approached the younger man and rested on the edge of the desk. 'If you finish with her, do you think you'll break her heart then, Dan?'

Danny never thought he'd ever get the chance to break anyone's heart. 'Er ... I don't know.'

'Well, do you think one of us should? Break her heart, I mean.'

'I'd rather it was you than me, Simon.'

'Then you shouldn't have started what you can't finish, should you.'

'No.... No, I guess you're right.... I'm sorry.'

'Oh, Danny, she's bad enough to live with as it is. Do you want to keep seeing her?'

What was he supposed to say: "yes," because he liked the fun, or "no", because he didn't think that much about her.

'Right ... I'll make this easy for you. Keep seeing her if you want to. But be careful mind, I'm watching you. And if there's any hint of malarkey, there will be trouble. I'm getting some decorators in next week to re-do the front door where the muck was spattered. Maybe she'll fall for one of them next.'

And that's exactly what would happen.

They struggled over the wall to a small woodland full of deciduous trees adjoining the bank. Simon had intended asking Jonathan what he should do with the place. He'd gathered a few logs from some dead trees over the summer, and looked forward to the winter when he could burn logs from his own woodland, but how to maintain it was another matter.

He would often walk Midge in this woodland and fetch firewood. The old dog would scratch around for rabbits, but since Midge's poisoning, Simon hadn't set foot in the place.

The gate was long broken and the woodland floor was deep with undergrowth and years of fallen leaves composting naturally. It was just a small plantation of oaks and silver birch trees, with a few conifers that were planted years ago by someone who wanted a woodland walk. Simon had seen deer in this woodland, also jays and squirrels.

The plan was to work methodically up and down the bank until they found anything metal. Simon had one detector and Danny had the other, with Jess in tow. They worked separately, on opposite sides of the woodland, and as soon as Simon was out of earshot Jess questioned Danny.

'What did he say to you?' She whispered.

'Oh, nowt.'

'Come on, Dan, he must have said something.'

Danny tried to distance himself from her, and with his newfound fitness walked quickly up the leafy slope but she was soon to follow him.

'Did he know about the bingeing?'

'No, don't worry. Jonathan never said a word.'

'Huh.... Why not...?'

'Jon's not like that. He wouldn't talk.' Danny had guessed it was only because he'd been discreet about Jonathan's relationship with Katie.

'Well, I'm in for it when you've gone, anyway.'

'I doubt it.'

'Oh come on, Dan. What did he say then?'

'Just leave it out, okay. I can still see you if that's what you want.'

'No kidding. Is that what he said?'

Danny carried on walking up the woody slope, scuffing up leaves and mud onto his trainers. 'Not in as many words, but it's okay.'

Jess picked up a handful of dry leaves and threw them playfully at him. 'So, what's this aeroplane he's on about?'

'You'll know if we find it.'

'Well, how can you lose an aeroplane?'

'Look, I don't know, Jess. Let's just do it, okay, and keep him happy.'

They could hear Simon scratching about in the undergrowth on the opposite side of the woodland. He knew Jess would be plying Danny with questions. And he laughed.

And then the beeper went louder on Danny's machine.

'Come on Jess, dig.' She thrust the spade she was hauling, and started to scratch around, but all they found were the remains of some old farming implements. They heard Simon shouting: 'What have you found...? Anything?'

'No, just old junk.' Jess shouted back.

They worked for an hour and with each descent and ascent of the woodland they drew in closer to Simon. Then Simon's detector beeped. 'Come over, Jess. Dig here.'

Jess grunted and wondered why she had to be the one to do all the donkeywork, and she grabbed the detector from Danny and left him to dig.

Danny struggled across the deep, leafy floor of the woodland, went over to Simon, and started to rake about enthusiastically. 'Has she been asking questions then?' Simon whispered, as he stood resting his hands on his hips.

'Yep.'

'What did you tell her?'

'Nothing.' And he smiled. 'So, do you really think there'll be anything left?'

'I hope so, but there's folks who travel the country looking for wreckage but they may have been denied access because of the private land.'

Danny continued to rake and dig when his spade struck something. 'Be careful ... go easy, what is it?'

Danny fell to his knees and started to scrape with his hands and found some rusted pieces of grey fuselage.

'Bingo!'

Melanie complained at the pile of filthy junk in her kitchen. Simon's adventure was becoming all too messy.

They all stood around the table as Simon pulled a document from his folder and handed it to Jess. It read:

The Mercury Sept 1944

Last night a German plane crashed in woodland near Chardwell Grange. The plane was badly damaged and burnt. No survivors were found. It's possible the pilot perished in the fire, but the police and the RAF are asking the public to be vigilant.

CHAPTER 21

Danny was wearing his best baggie jeans, with the crutch and pockets slung low. He thought his grey marl hoodie would look threatening and his black Nike beanie was pulled low over his forehead; he was roasting and he was anxious; it was the first time in his life that he'd been in a pub alone. He stood at the bar of The Three Feathers and ordered a John Smith's, but they'd run out. He didn't know what else to order as Simon had told him the Extra Smooth was the best. 'Er.. What else have you got?' Danny glanced nervously along the bar as the barmaid impatiently suggested five others. He chose one and hoped his choice didn't make him look stupid.

As he leant on the bar with his pint in hand, he glanced around but didn't recognise a soul. It was late evening on a Friday. The bar appeared to be packed with girls all having their last few drinks before the nightclubs opened. Danny decided to stand with his back to most of them and watched the barmaid at work. He was playfully nudged several times but didn't respond. He just smiled at a cute blonde who was the first to purposely apologise to him. His pulse was racing and he wished he'd brought a mate with him. Danny slowly sipped his beer, and hoped he could make it last because he needed to have his wits about him. It took two pints of uncomfortable purgatory before Graham Langhorne finally came to talk to him.

'How's the investigation going then, lad?'

'Well enough.'

'Have they got any more clues?'

'Ask your brother.'

'Oh, he's not in on this one.'

'No, I guess not.'

'So are they any nearer then?'

'Oh yes, they've a good idea what it's all about.'

'Found any more bodies?' Graham Langhorne laughed loudly and everyone looked at Danny. But Danny was purposely animated and looked around to see who was listening as he moved in closer. He cleared his throat to deepen his voice. 'Are you interested in a bit of White Horse memorabilia then, Graham?'

'I've got enough mugs.' Then he rubbed his belly, 'and I'm not built for t-shirts.'

'No, no. I mean other stuff. Stuff the police *don't* know about.'

'What've you got then?'

Danny quickly finished the second pint of beer that was now affecting his judgement and hoped he could keep his senses. 'Come out back and I'll show you. It's in my pocket. It will cost you, mind.'

Graham Langhorne now looked over his shoulder. 'Car park ... fifteen minutes.'

Danny went to the men's toilets, locked himself in the cubicle and fell back on the door. He threw his head back and took a deep breath. His stomach churned and he was compelled to use the toilet. He sat there and looked at his watch, felt in his pocket, then flushed.

He heard footsteps so he unlocked the door, and was surprised to see PC Alec Langhorne, in uniform, waiting.

'Hi ya.' Danny just said and attempted to pass him, but the policeman blocked his way. 'Hope you're not driving home, young Danny.'

'Nope.' He was wise to that one.

'Hope you're not carrying any weed.'

And Danny tried again to push his way forcefully by the policeman but he saw the landlord, Graham Langhorne, at the door.

'What have you got then?' PC Langhorne muttered.

'Nothing for *you*.' Danny was looking at Graham standing at the door and hoping he would intervene.

'Come on, son.... Show us what you've got. We'll keep it between the three of us. What I know, Graham knows. I didn't think you had it in you, Danny, to double-cross Simon Naylor, but maybe you have.'

'I need the cash, PC Langhorne. Anyway if you insist, I'll have to show you what I've got, won't I.'

'Oh, I do insist.' The policeman took another step closer.

Danny thrust his hand down deep into his pocket. 'If you can guess what it is I'll let you have it, for a price, remember.'

'Come on, Dan.... Stop fooling around. Show me what you've got or I'll do you for withholding police evidence.' The policeman grabbed Danny by the front of his hoodie.

'Ah yeh ... right. I can believe that.' Danny gasped as he felt the pain through his hoodie as the policeman grabbed the skin on his chest. 'Well, I've got this and that.'

The policeman shoved Danny against the back of the toilet and he nearly slipped into the urinals and had to put his hand on the cold enamel to stop himself from falling.

'Don't mess with me, kid.'

'I'm not messing.' Danny pulled his beanie straight, and pulled something out of his pocket and held it out concealed in a closed fist. 'How much are you interested?'

Graham Langhorne moved in closer. 'Let's see what the lad's got, Alec.'

Danny saw a space between the two of them and knew he could run, but he resisted. 'So, how much are you interested?'

'You're playing silly games now.'

'No, no. I'm not. I think it's you two that's been playing games. You see I know you used to live up there at The Grange, didn't you.'

'Clever boy.'

'What I have could spoil your reputation if it got into the wrong hands.'

'You're lying.'

'Well, I think you have to trust me. You see there wasn't much left up there. It was all, well, burnt. But metal doesn't burn does it.'

Graham went to grab the boy's hand but Danny again was too quick for the older man. And he clenched his fist tighter.

'I don't know much about the war, but I know what this is. You see I was first in the pit. They couldn't get in there. Simon Naylor's too big. I took this out and didn't tell them. I thought it might be worth something. How much is it worth?'

'You little scum bag.... You're not in a position to barter.' The older man brushed his reddened face with his hands and pushed back a few stray strands on his balding head.

'Oh, and you are? It's like this, you see ...' Danny was getting confident. 'I reckon this is the only bit of evidence the police need to know who was buried on that hillside. How he got there and *why* he got there. I'll give you a clue if you like. It's bronze and it's shiny ... I've polished it up. It's yours if you want it but it doesn't come cheap. I sweat a lot up on that bank, helping Jonathan, and he's lucky to be alive. I like to relax at the weekend with my girl. She has expensive taste; she likes to get "labelled" up, if you know what I mean. I have a few other habits that don't come cheap.'

Graham went to grab Danny's arm and knocked him. Danny dropped a bronze belt buckle from his hand, and as it went clinking on the floor, it skidded off into one of the cubicles; all three men lunged at it like addicts, longing for a pill. But again, Danny was quick. And he dived on the floor before them. But then he felt the pain as he was kicked in the stomach. He curled his knees under him as he felt more pain. He released his grip on the buckle, and he heard a great noise as someone else rushed in, shouting. Police swept in from all angles.

Danny heard them arrest both Graham and Alec Langhorne for assault.

It was Simon that pulled Danny up and squatted beside him. 'Are you okay, Dan?'

'Oh man, that hurt.' And Danny held his stomach as he sat up. 'Did you hear everything?' And he put his hand on a small microphone concealed in his hoodie.

Katie was constantly worried about Jonathan. He'd been up and walking - slowly -painfully. He was told he would have to lie on his back for three more weeks; the prognosis was good if he did what he was told. But Katie was still concerned for Jonathan's mental health. He was strangely distant from her. She guessed he was feeling sorry for himself or perhaps punishing her for the way she'd treated him. It still hurt that he spoke more to the nurses than her. And often as they sat together in the small room with the television on, he lay back with just a soft pillow under his head, she would glance at him and notice he was staring at the wall; in fact, if Katie all but knew, it was a small tear in the wallpaper that he was staring at; it looked like the shape of a yacht.

Jonathan would cheer a little if Simon or Danny called in, but then as soon as they left he would go back into a reverie. So she tackled him about it.

'Jon.... When you come home. I will be there you know.'

He didn't respond.

'Jonathan?'

This time his brown eyes rolled as he looked across at her.

'Did you hear what I said?'

'You'll be there when I come home.' He said and held up his hand for her to take. She rested her hand in his, and he pulled it to his mouth and kissed it.

'Will things be as we were before?' He spoke in low tones.

'No. Things will be better, Jon.'

His body tingled at her response, as Jonathan had thought long and hard about his relationship with Katie. He was ecstatic she would be returning and, in reality, he couldn't wait till they were home together.

'Are you worried, about how you'll be?'

'I'm not going to be useless.... I'll get over this, Katie. I'll be fine. Everything's working properly, I know that.' Yet he also knew that his back felt like it had a vice clamped around his ribcage. He was sick of having indigestion from lying on his back, and heartburn creeping up his gullet. He was tired of hospital food and of being plied with painkillers that upset his system. He'd had a scare this week as he'd passed more blood in his urine. Jonathan really just wanted them to patch him up and send him home; he'd had enough. He wasn't certain if he'd ever work again or even run again. No one had said and he hadn't dared to ask, so how did she expect him to feel? His mother was now in negotiation as to which nursing home she would go to, so that meant he had two properties to maintain; one cleverly signed over to him years ago and the other mortgaged up to the hilt.

It was late in the evening when Simon called to see Jonathan. Katie was ready to go home; she too was desperately tired of the place; visiting Alice and keeping her happy and then sitting with Jonathan night after night. When Simon called, it gave her the excuse to leave a bit earlier.

Simon had a small package in his hand and an envelope. He gave Jonathan the package and he rested it on his chest as he opened it. The silver i.pod was already downloaded with what Danny had said was Jonathan's favourite music.

Jonathan thanked Simon; he knew these things were expensive.

'I've got something else to show you, Jon.... If you're ready.' Jonathan thought that anything was better than staring at the wallpaper yacht or the television screen.

'This is what you're father died for. What all the trouble's been about.' Simon pulled out of his pocket the small belt buckle. Jonathan lifted it to his head, to slowly peer. He saw German writing; he saw an eagle's crest and a swastika.

'What is it...? What does it mean? Was it in the pit?' Jonathan brought it closer examining it in his hands and tried to read the inscription.'

'Yes, it was, along with other things. It says ... Gott Mit Uns.... It means God is with us.... Well, that's what the German's thought. But that's not all we found, Jon. We found Nazi documents, signalling equipment, maps.... All burnt but still recognisable. You can't light a fire up there for long without someone noticing.'

'Man alive.'

'The other guy was an airman - German. We found the wreckage of the plane in the oak plantation. Andrea had done the research – she found old newspaper cuttings about it dating back to the 40's. The pilot must have parachuted out as the plane lost control. He may have fallen heavy on the bank or have been sheltered at The Grange. His plane was probably guided in by the equipment. Its destination, the airfield down the valley only three miles away. If it hadn't have crashed, he would have bombed it. That's why the horse was covered up in the first place during the war so enemy planes wouldn't know their bearings. That pit was purpose built in the cave by someone to guide in the planes.'

'So how did the airman get in the pit with Sam's brother?'

'Oh, he's been in the pit a lot longer than Sam's brother. The airman must have climbed or parachuted from the wreckage and been shielded by someone. He must have later died of his injuries and the sympathizers couldn't call in the local undertaker could they. The pilot had to be buried somehow. Sam's brother was put in much later, probably the same night your father died.'

'Do we know who did this?'

'Right ... well, that's the bad news. That's why I'm here. Er, Danny's in A and E. He's done a good job for the police tonight. He tried to sell the buckle to tempt a confession. But I'm afraid he got beaten up in the process.'

Jonathan inwardly moaned.

'The police have arrested Graham and Alec Langhorne for assault, and hopefully, once their computers have been checked, an awful lot more.'

'Oh man.... How's Danny?'

'Well enough. He'll go home later. I wanted to stay with him.'

'How did you know it was the Langhornes?'

'The Langhornes' father owned The Grange during the Second World War. I always had my suspects; too many if the truth be known. And Sam saw Alec close by that day you fell. It was probably him who slit your ropes and weakened them, and your poor old father's, just because you were all close to the bunker.' Then Simon pulled from his pocket a small bundle of photographs.

'These are from Sam.'

Jonathan, still lying on his back, flicked through the photographs, one after another, and recognised his father with groups of men, happy, smiling. He recognised his uncle, Jack Albright. He didn't know the other man.

Simon pointed. 'That was Tom, Sam's brother, with your father.'

Jonathan felt his throat constrict and he set the photographs down on his chest. Then he broke down; his shoulders shuddered, as he couldn't suppress the tears. Simon was still standing over him, uncomfortable, unsure of what to say, so he rested his hand on Jonathan's bare shoulder. 'I'm sorry, Jon ... I thought ...'

Jonathan muttered. 'No, you did right....Tell Sam, thank you.'

'Look, I'll leave you alone if you like.' Simon walked slowly backwards to the door.

'No, stay, please.... I need to talk to someone.' Jonathan wiped his brow with his hand and desperately wished he could sit up straight. 'I've seen these photos before. At home.... At my mother's. She's never shown me a thing. I didn't know why. I've only ever seen their wedding photograph on the mantelpiece at home. As a boy, sometimes, I'd sit and look at it if she was out and wonder what he was like. I'd take the photo frame up to my bedroom and look at it secretly. If I asked her for more photographs, she just told me to be quiet. I think it upset her too much. I asked Jack about my dad and he told me a little bit of his character. He said he was always larking about; he said he was a postman and that was all I knew. But I didn't know the truth.' And Jonathan broke down.

Simon fidgeted as he hovered over him and looked for some tissues. He pulled out a handful and, touched by the moment, had to resist from using one himself.

Jonathan blew his nose then continued. 'I went to stay at my mother's house when Katie left me.' He sniffed and paused and continued to breathe heavily. 'I'd been working up at your place. I'd already agreed to work on the horse. I was behind with everything as usual and our solicitor was pushing me to get Power of Attorney for my mother, so I had to scour the house for her documents. I found stuff I shouldn't have. Stuff she must have had hidden for thirty-odd years. When I saw these photos of my father, I cried like I did just then.' Jonathan actually cried more, but he couldn't tell Simon that. 'But that wasn't all I found. If you go to her house, take Katie, you'll find more evidence for the police. Letters - blackmail - Oh man, how she could have kept them and not thrown them away, I'll never know.' He stopped and grunted back the tears. 'No wonder she had a stroke, Simon.'

'I'll go to the police now, Jon, if you like.'

'No ... don't, Simon. I'd rather you read what was in those letters first. But I also know that whoever wrote those letters and cut my ropes didn't kill my father.'

Simon's brain was working overtime and not getting anywhere. 'How.... How do you know?'

'When I first came in hospital and came out of surgery, I felt as sick as a pig. I couldn't speak, I couldn't open my eyes. I was afraid to try. When

Jack came to see me and told me about my father dying on the bank. He thought I was dying and that I should know … a kind of confession. I didn't tell you everything. Family ties and all.'

Where had Simon heard all this before?

'It was Jack.... It was an accident, a dreadful accident. Jack let my father fall, he wasn't watching what he was doing and he's lived with the guilt and the secret all these years.'

'But the ropes had been cut, Jon.'

'Well, yes and no. He said my dad was mucking about - always mucking about. They'd had trouble with the horse as we had. Opposition and all. Jack felt so bad about him falling, but he couldn't admit it, so he cut the ropes afterward to make it look like sabotage, to distract the attention away from himself. He wanted it to look like the opposers had done it. He didn't know poor Sam's brother would take the rap. But he couldn't face up to the truth. He did it to take the blame away from himself.'

CHAPTER 22

As usual, Andrea Briscoe didn't go straight to bed. She'd no husband to worry about, the overtime and the booze had seen to that. She had a smile on her face thinking of what she could write about the Langhornes' arrest. So, as soon as she got home she booted up her laptop and went straight to work.

As she drank a whisky and soda and waited, she cringed as she recalled Danny Wytherstone's moans transmitting live over the radio in the police car she'd been waiting in. Danny had been a brave lad, but Andrea knew the good hiding wasn't totally unexpected. Danny was naïve.

Before The Three Feathers was closed early for the evening and the landlord unexpectedly arrested, Andrea managed to wander to the bar and the corridors, reading and collating the names and dates under each photograph on the wall that Simon had prepped her about; a huge list. It would take all night to find the information about these people. She would do it now; there was no point in waiting until morning; no point in her trying to sleep. She guessed by now Simon would be home from the hospital and Danny discharged, with nothing more than bruising and a very sore stomach.

Andrea opened the files and waited; she was putting together the bones of a huge story that could be written but not published for some time. She searched most of the night and called Simon at eight in the morning.

'Did Danny get home okay?'

'Yes, his mother was upset. I had to pacify her somewhat.' Simon was just buttoning up his shirt.

'The Langhornes didn't give too much away, did they?'

'No, but the police are sure it's them. Did you find anything else?'

'Yes, are you ready?'

'Fire away.'

'Some of the guys in the photographs were businessmen - German. The Langhornes had investments in Germany and Europe. The war brought an unhealthy end to their business ventures and they went bankrupt. It would have suited their interests for Germany to have won.'

'That figures.'

'Graham and Alec would have been too young during the war to have anything to do with the pilot and the equipment up there. But they were old enough back in the 70's to protect their father's reputation. They must have known about the pilot. I feel both of them by the way they treated Danny were capable of murdering Tom and Abraham, and cutting Jonathan's rope. Did you see Jonathan last night?'

'Er, yes,'

'Was he surprised about the Langhornes' arrest?'

'Yes, he was, but ... I'll have to go now... I'm sorry. I'll speak to you soon.' And Andrea heard the abrupt click as the handset was set down; the nervous tone to his voice told her he knew more than he was letting on.

Simon finished dressing and kissed Melanie. 'I might be a while.'

'Have your breakfast first, Simon.'

'I will. . . I will.'

But she knew he wouldn't.

Simon met Katie at Alice's house. He quietly tapped the front door and as he entered, he carefully negotiated the clutter of china in the hallway. A large porcelain jug and bowl displayed precariously on a low table. He could almost hear his mother telling him as a boy to be careful not to break anything. Katie led him to a dining room, full of mahogany furniture and silver. She unlocked a bureau.

The untidy state of the room was visible evidence of Jonathan's asylum.

'I think I've got everything, Simon.'

'Are you sure about this?'

'Jonathan said we had to read everything; he insisted.' She handed him some letters. 'You read them first.'

Simon took the wad of letters wrapped in string and went to sit on a plush Draylon dining chair. As he unfolded each one out on the table, he was mindful not to mark the beautiful furniture.

He could see the letters were done on the same old typewriter, but some were new and done on a laser printer. They were just like the ones posted to Sam and The Mercury but there was a difference in their content. The abuse was still as strong; some written to Alice and some addressed to her late husband, Abraham.

In part, they said: '*You're a thief Abraham Miller. I'll stay quiet, but if you don't keep away from Chardwell Bank, I'll expose you.*'

'*I've got secrets ... you've got secrets.*'

'You'll end up in prison - what will that wife and boy of yours do then?'

'You've robbed every house in Chardwell. I can prove it - keep away.'

'You have stuff from The Grange. It's mine. Keep away or I'll ask for it back. Think of the shame.'

'You're a small time crook, Abraham Miller.'

And to Alice they read: 'Don't pursue this or I'll expose that bent husband of yours.'

'Do you want to see his name in the papers?'

'What will that little lad think of his daddy?'

Katie heard Simon sigh and watched him rub beads of perspiration from his brow. 'Katie, I don't know if you want to read this.'

She looked at him forlorn. 'Jonathan wanted me to read them.'

'Yes, yes I suppose he would. He's as honest as they come.'

Simon reluctantly handed her the letters and went and stood by the patio doors and he looked out into Alice's garden. The grass badly needed cutting and the roses were neglected. He would encourage Danny to do it - when he was fit.

He wandered around the room and looked at all the silver now bronzed through neglect. He picked up a candlestick and twisted it in his hand, wondering if it had been stolen from The Grange or whether that stuff had been sold on to buy this fine house. He thought about his own father, an honest but ruthless businessman and he'd disliked him for his cutthroat dealings, legal as they were. He pitied Jonathan Miller because the memories he had longed for, had a cruel and bitter taste and Simon

271

continued to rue the day he'd begun his self-seeking project to restore Chardwell's White Mare.

Katie couldn't stop crying, but she couldn't let Jonathan see her like this. Simon had dropped her home; she had run straight upstairs and had fallen on her bed. Moses was purring around her face. She knew Jonathan would be waiting for her; he would be sullen. The letters were now strung up in a carrier bag on the floor, and Katie wondered if she should just throw them in the fire.

She glanced at her watch; it was time to go.

This was the second time that Sam Parkinson had visited Jonathan, but the first time Jonathan couldn't recall. He was standing, slumped over his crutches by the window, desperate for some fresh air. He was dressed in a blue and yellow Leeds United shorts and shirt, he was bare legged and bare footed. Katie was clinging to his arm, for her reassurance more than his support. Sam could see some colour had returned to Jonathan's skin, the bruising to his face now clearing and there was re-growth on the side of his head where his hair was shaved. He had grown a short beard and was no longer covered in white paint.

When Jonathan saw Sam he hobbled back to his bed, eased himself down, and threw his crutches in the corner.

'Do you want me to go?' Katie said, straightening the crutches.

'No, stay... please.... Is that okay, Sam?'

Sam shrugged his shoulders because he didn't know what to expect.

'Give him the letters, Katie.' Jonathan beckoned.

Katie handed Sam the carrier bag and he briefly looked inside and recognised by the paper what they were.

'I wanted to see you anyway, Jonathan.'

'I know that, Sam. And I appreciate that; there'll be plenty of time for visiting. But I needed to get things straight in my head - sorted out - if you can understand. You see everything depends on you now.' Jonathan shifted uncomfortably on the dry cotton hospital sheets that were burning his backside.

Sam took in a sharp breath. He guessed things had always depended on him. He had played a hard game with Simon and was glad to discover the truth. He was sorry Jonathan was hurt, but relieved his injuries were healing; he never expected this.

'I've got what I wanted, Jonathan.'

'Yes, I guess you have. Simon doesn't know what to do now.'

'No, I can understand that. Will the letters give the police the evidence?'

'They may.... They may implicate whoever tried to kill me, but I doubt they can ever prove it, or who killed your brother,' and he hesitated, 'and my father.' Jonathan would never tell a soul about Jack Albright's secret deception.

Sam sat in the chair and read only two, and then put them away.

'Does it surprise you?' Jonathan said.

'I'm sorry to say, Jon, it doesn't.'

'I did wonder. The problem is, it doesn't sit right for me now. My poor mother, I know why she couldn't tell me. Oh yes, Dad was happy and smiling

273

but he was a thief wasn't he - a common thief. And the threats and the blackmail said as much. I wondered at first whether to believe it, but it's true, isn't it Sam?'

'I'm sorry, Jon. I'm sorry. I did tell Simon this horse would be trouble.'

'Well, at least I know the truth. Streuth, he was a postman - a postman! I always wondered how she managed to have that nice house, and she signed it to me. So now I'm Jonathan Miller - charity mugger - son of a thief. Jonathan Miller - Superman – Superstupid.' Jonathan's voice broke and Katie squeezed his hand.

Sam pulled up the chair and came closer, and wanted to weep with him. He waited before he next spoke. 'Answer me this, Jon. Why did you stay with Simon when you knew the truth about your father?'

'I was doing nothing, Sam. My mother was dying – Katie well,' and he just looked at her. 'I'd nothing to lose. And I thought it would be one last challenge to see if all this was true and to see why.'

The fire in Sam's cottage was blazing. He'd had his eyes shut sometime, but didn't think he'd slept. He had really, but these days there was little definition between the two. Sam noticed Emmerdale had been and gone and he wasn't interested in what was now showing. He clicked the television off. The Border Terrier that was sprawled across Sam's feet, grunted as it slept. Sam had grief in him that he would have to bear alone. He had lived with the thought that his younger brother was alive and well and living a good life, in exile, away from Chardwell, with a wife and a family perhaps, but that wasn't the case. And it

274

saddened Sam to think Tom's life was cut short so young. He thought of Jonathan, Katie, and poor Alice. What they would tell Alice, he didn't know. He was glad Jonathan had Katie. He recalled Abraham Miller and the memory of him always brought a wry smile to Sam's face; Abraham had a compelling personality that was echoed in Jonathan. And yes, of course, he knew he was a thief, none of that was news to him. Most folks in Chardwell knew Abraham was a rogue, but he couldn't tell Jonathan that. When Jonathan had run his guts out for charity, it somehow compensated for Abraham's mis-deeds. People trusted Jonathan and didn't judge him, in fact, if they felt the same as Sam, every penny given to some worthy cause was like Jonathan, innocently and silently, paying back for what his father had stolen.

Sam bent low over the fire and one by one threw the letters away, watching them burn, not needing justice anymore because he had vindication; he was now the better of all of them. The Langhornes, whatever they admitted and revealed, would still be exposed as being Nazi sympathisers and for Sam that was justice in itself. For Jonathan, the beloved memories of his father were now tainted; Sam wouldn't do him anymore harm. And that made him feel good.

CHAPTER 23

The police had left a gaping hole in the horse's head after they'd emptied the contents of the pit. Simon arranged to have the pit filled in with rubble and cover it over with top-soil. It was right on the eye of the horse.

Before his fall, Jonathan had already ordered the turf to cover the eye. He wouldn't be able to do the job himself, but was certain he could get to the top of the bank on his crutches and sit on the bench with Sam to shout instructions.

Danny took on the temporary role of project manager while Jonathan was convalescing. He was running the garden business almost single-handed, with Jack Albright being, un-characteristically, cooperative. It was mostly grass cutting and tidying gardens ready for the winter, but that was okay because Danny was being paid; yet, a pile of work was still accumulating because Jonathan Miller had made a name for himself.

Simon didn't think the day would ever come that his horse would be completed, and it took the energy of eleven young farmers to finish her; all carefully watched, tackled with rope and guided.

Jack Albright was forthcoming in his time and promised to build, free of charge, a small stone memorial in aid of the three men that died. Tom Parkinson, Rudolf Messmer and Abraham Miller. It would say no more.

Jack still believed his secret was safe. And although he'd unburdened himself on what he thought was a dying Jonathan, he continued to carry his guilt as a just punishment.

Jonathan would keep quiet, so would Simon. The horse was used to keeping secrets.

Village life for Simon became pleasurable. He was finally respected and admired. The White Horse Committee would remain and meet bi-annually to discuss further maintenance and funding. The local tea-shop continued to sell postcards, pens, tea-towels, t-shirts, all sorts of memorabilia to help build up funds. The patron asked if she could change the name to The White Horse Tea Shop. Simon had a fear that things could become out of control if he let her, he didn't want to spoil Chardwell and yet it was hard for him to refuse. Although he had no real say in what she called her shop he made his objection known, and the patron complied.

One Sunday afternoon after lunch, Simon, Melanie and Lucy sat in the conservatory drinking coffee. Simon told Lucy how he'd jumped to conclusions, and that he now believed his father's death was just a tragic consequence. Whether his father had worried over the horse or not, no one knew. Lucy left most of her coffee as she always did; she needed a nap. She kissed Simon on the cheek and just as she was leaving said: 'Simon, do you think there's any chance you could look at the wall in the kitchen. There seems to be a damp patch.'

Simon knew he would have a lipstick smear on his face.

Jonathan Miller sat up in bed wearing his Superman t-shirt. His wife was in his arms. Katie was wearing a pink, satin top with fluffy straps, and she looked like a fairy. Jonathan had his eyes closed. He was exhausted and his hands were cold. He'd run the Brooklyn Bridge with Katie in New York's cold November air, using as a goal the majestic buildings on the skyline that were framed by deep blue sky. With each painful step, they came in closer. They'd watched the marathon, and it wasn't until Jonathan saw the runners head for the finishing line did he miss it all. Well, there was always next year.

Tomorrow they would run through Central Park.

Simon sat in bed with Melanie in his arms; he could hear Boris barking outside.

From his bedroom, in the darkness, he could see hazy outlines of the white horse; it still took a good moon to see her clearly from his bedroom at night, and tonight broken clouds covered the moor and drifted by. Simon waited and peered hoping the light would improve. Then he saw the clouds and mist dissolve and a cool blue light emerge. He saw his horse come out through the haze; a beautiful shape, a real thoroughbred, and for one brief moment, he could swear that she winked at him.

THE END

We hope you enjoyed reading To Paint a White Horse.

Why not try another novel by Lindsey?

NORTHERN SPIRIT

How would you feel if your family name was splashed over the front of the tabloids because of the sins of your father? David Keldas is trying to live down the shame. It's 1973 and in the heart of the hills and mountains of the English Lakes, David is trying to run the family farm and care for his mother and younger brother and sisters. He's striving to right the wrong his father caused, when he makes a dangerous liaison with a young woman and finds he's walking exactly in his father's footsteps.

Can friendship and love survive in even the most extraordinary circumstances?

Read a free sample on Amazon UK
Also in that series
The Last Boat to Nowhere
Keld Head: The Keeper of the House

The World of Jamie Keldas series
Jamie: Through Monochrome Eyes
Jamie: Raining Kats and Dogs
Jamie: Between a Rock and a Hard Face

Keldas Chronicles

Printed in Great Britain
by Amazon